"If I thought going to bed with you would get you out of my system I'd say yes."

"You know better," Ryan growled, unable to stay silent.

Lifting her head, Judy gave him a troubled look. "I know. But neither am I prepared to marry you. I'm not prepared to marry anyone. It isn't personal."

"The hell it isn't. Whatever you need or want, tell me and I'll make sure you have it."

"What I want is to stay single."

"What you *want?*"

She heard the disbelief in his tone. "All right, what I *need*. If you truly feel about me the way you claim, you'll try to understand."

"I'll never understand," he stated. "And I will do everything in my power to change your mind."

Dear Reader,

The holidays are here, so why not give yourself the gift of time and books—especially this month's Intimate Moments? Top seller Linda Turner returns with the next of her TURNING POINTS miniseries. In *Beneath The Surface* she takes a boss/ employee romance, adds a twist of suspense and comes up with another irresistible read.

Linda Winstead Jones introduces you to the first of her LAST CHANCE HEROES, in *Running Scared.* Trust me, you'll want to be kidnapped right alongside heroine Olivia Larkin when bodyguard Quinn Calhoun carries her off—for her own good, of course. Award-winning Maggie Price's LINE OF DUTY miniseries has quickly won a following, so jump on the bandwagon as danger forces an estranged couple to reunite and mend their *Shattered Vows.* Then start planning your trip Down Under, because in *Deadly Intent,* Valerie Parv introduces you to another couple who live—and love—according to the CODE OF THE OUTBACK. There are *Whispers in the Night* at heroine Kayla Thorne's house, whispers that have her seeking the arms of ex-cop—and ex-*con*—Paul Fitzgerald for safety. Finally, welcome multipublished author Barbara Colley to the Intimate Moments lineup. Pregnant heroine Leah Davis has some *Dangerous Memories,* and her only chance at safety—and romance—lies with her husband, a husband she'd been told was dead!

Enjoy every single one, and come back next month (next year!) for more of the best and most exciting romance reading around—only in Silhouette Intimate Moments.

Yours,

Leslie J. Wainger
Executive Editor

Please address questions and book requests to:
Silhouette Reader Service
U.S.: 3010 Walden Ave., P.O. Box 1325, Buffalo, NY 14269
Canadian: P.O. Box 609, Fort Erie, Ont. L2A 5X3

Deadly Intent

VALERIE PARV

INTIMATE MOMENTS™

Published by Silhouette Books

America's Publisher of Contemporary Romance

ISBN 0-373-27406-8

DEADLY INTENT

This edition published by arrangement with Harlequin Books S.A.

Visit Silhouette Books at www.eHarlequin.com

Printed in U.S.A.

Books by Valerie Parv

Silhouette Intimate Moments

Interrupted Lullaby #1095
Royal Spy #1154
††*Operation: Monarch* #1268
***Heir to Danger* #1312
***Live To Tell* #1322
***Deadly Intent* #1336

Silhouette Romance

The Leopard Tree #507
The Billionaire's Baby Chase #1270
Baby Wishes and Bachelor Kisses #1313
**The Monarch's Son* #1459
**The Prince's Bride-To-Be* #1465
**The Princess's Proposal* #1471
Booties and the Beast #1501
Code Name: Prince #1516
†*Crowns and a Cradle* #1621
†*The Baron & the Bodyguard* #1627
†*The Marquis and the Mother-To-Be* #1633
††*The Viscount & the Virgin* #1691
††*The Princess & the Masked Man* #1695
††*The Prince & the Marriage Pact* #1699

*The Carramer Crown
†The Carramer Legacy
††The Carramer Trust
**Code of the Outback

VALERIE PARV

With twenty million copies of her books sold, including three Waldenbooks bestsellers, it's no wonder Valerie Parv is known as Australia's queen of romance and is the recognized media spokesperson for all things romantic. Valerie is married to her own romantic hero, Paul, a former crocodile hunter in Australia's tropical north.

These days he's a cartoonist and the two live in the country's capital city of Canberra, where both are volunteer zoo guides, sharing their love of animals with visitors from all over the world. Valerie continues to write her page-turning novels because they affirm her belief in love and happy endings. As she says, "Love gives you wings, romance helps you fly." Keep up with Valerie's latest releases at www.silromanceauthors.com.

Chapter 1

Ryan liked seeing her in a dress, Judy Logan thought as she held the garment against her and checked the bedroom mirror. He would appreciate the way the sea-foam color complemented the sky blue of her eyes and the highlights she'd had put through her ash-blond hair, newly cut in an urchin style with strands feathered around her face.

He'd approve of the way the garment's draping neckline made the most of her long neck and modest cleavage, the slinky short skirt skimming her legs. Privately, she thought they were her best feature, shapely and muscular thanks to an active lifestyle.

Seeing herself as more Australian stock horse than thoroughbred, she usually threw on whatever suited her schedule, not much caring about the result.

Realizing what she was doing, she flung the dress onto the bed, where it pooled innocently. Why did she care what Ryan thought of her appearance? He was only one of the boys her father and mother had fostered throughout most of Judy's life.

After she was born, they'd been unable to have more children although they'd desperately wanted a large family. Her father still treated her like fragile china, although these days he was the frail one with a heart that threatened to stop beating at any moment.

She frowned at her mirror image. Des Logan was the reason she was going out with Ryan tonight. Not on a date, but to decide how best they could help her father. Des wouldn't accept money, not that Ryan had much to offer. Of all the Logan foster sons, he was the least successful. He supported himself doing casual jobs on cattle stations throughout the Kimberley. Nothing wrong with that, but by Ryan's age most men had something more substantial going for them.

If Judy hadn't run across Ryan unexpectedly when she flew supplies to a remote Kimberly cattle station where he'd been working, he would still be estranged from them all. He hadn't wanted to live with the Logans in the first place, she recalled. He'd claimed he was doing fine looking after himself. According to him, losing his mother and having no idea where his father was didn't mean he needed help to run his life.

At the memory, Judy felt reluctant admiration sweep through her. As a boy he'd lived on his own for almost a year after his mother's death, convincing the authorities that a friend of hers was his caregiver when, in fact, he'd had nobody. When the truth came out, he'd been dragged literally kicking and screaming into the Logan household.

Then he and Judy had spotted each other. Like a wild buffalo transfixed by a car's headlights, he'd stopped fighting Des and stared at his new foster sister.

Just stared.

He'd looked her up and down with the insolence of a grown man. Too thin from eating whatever he could rustle up, he'd been lanky and awkward, but his eyes—how she remembered those midnight blue eyes—had been alight with masculine interest. She'd known he liked what he saw long before he'd told her he was in love with her and would marry her one day.

A shiver shook her. What had such a stripling known of love? She'd known even less. Oh, she'd been aware of the facts of life. You couldn't grow up on a million-acre cattle station and remain ignorant for long. But the chemistry between male and female had been a compelling mystery.

Nevertheless, they'd both felt its power. But with him being only fourteen then and her newly into her teens, she hadn't had a clue what her feelings signified or how to deal with them. Des Logan had solved the problem by calling Ryan into his study and ordering him to get any foolish ideas out of his head. Ryan had retorted that nobody told him how to run his life and he was going to marry Judy one day, with or without Des's approval.

Neither of them had been aware of Judy hunting for a tennis ball in the bushes under Des's office window. To her, it had seemed romantic to have a young man defy her father over her. These days, she knew Des had been right. They had been mere children, their feelings the result of overactive teenage hormones, nothing more.

Less than a year later, Ryan had run away, eluding Des's and the authorities' efforts to find him. Later Ryan told Judy that he'd lied about his age in order to get work as a jackeroo on remote cattle stations.

He hadn't stayed anywhere for long, she'd learned when they'd met again. She hadn't been able to tell if he was pleased to see her or not. His manner had been surly and distant, although he was obviously a world away from the difficult teenager she'd once known.

For one thing, he was all man. Taller, fuller in body and so broad-shouldered she'd had to look twice to assure herself he really was Ryan Smith. His red-gold hair and hair-trigger temper had convinced her. There couldn't be two men with that blend of startling good looks and fiery temperament in the Kimberley.

Since their reunion three years before, she'd persuaded him to return to Diamond Downs a number of times, although he'd never stayed as long as she'd hoped he would. She looked forward to his visits, but no more than those of her other foster brothers, she assured herself. She blamed the fact that Ryan's arrival made her heart beat faster on his dynamic personality and raw masculinity, enough to turn any woman on.

Judy wasn't immune to male appeal. She relished her physicality, whether piloting her plane, mustering cattle on horseback or enjoying a relationship to the full, provided a man accepted that she could want him without needing him. She couldn't imagine Ryan playing by this rule. He was the type to want more than she was prepared to give, so she kept a safe emotional distance.

Ryan and her father got along tolerably well these days in spite of the undercurrent simmering between them. After all this time, Judy wouldn't allow that it had anything to do with her. More likely, the mistrust mirrored two bulls in the same paddock. They were similar in temperament, neither giving an inch.

Pleasing Ryan with feminine fripperies should be the last thing on her mind. To prove it, she cast the dress a withering look and flounced out of the homestead. Passing the bunkhouse and cottages occupied by the dwindling number of staff still on the station payroll, she found him in the hard-baked earth area used for car parking.

The only sign of him was a pair of jeans-clad legs protruding from under the ancient car he'd jacked up and supported on blocks. Long, long legs betrayed his height as over six feet. His scuffed R. M. Williams boots were a size eleven at least, and she felt a blush starting as she remembered the supposed connection between men and large feet.

Automatically she frowned at the sight of tools scattered over the ground. As a bush pilot, she hated to see good tools mistreated. Evidently Ryan's drifter ways extended to the care of his equipment.

She hunkered down in time to see him lower the transmission pan in both hands and tilt it to spill the fluid into a drain tray beside him. "Need a hand?"

Without looking he said, "You can pass me the awl so I can get this grommet out."

Surveying the tangle of tools around her, she said, "What patch of dirt do you suggest I look in?"

He angled his head to stare at her and she suppressed a shiver. Fourteen years on, his eyes still had the power to mesmerize. They were so dark and deep-set that looking into them was like looking into a bottomless pool. The sun was low and shone under the car, turning his hair to flame. The devil would look like this if she caught him working on a car, she thought.

"By your left foot," he said shortly.

She blinked to banish the vision. Devil, indeed. He was nothing but a pain in the—awl. He didn't care for anyone or anything but himself. Why he was bothering to talk about Des's problems with her, she didn't know. It wasn't as if there were an inheritance at stake.

Without telling the rest of the family, her father had mortgaged Diamond Downs to a neighbor, Clive Horvath, who'd been Des's best friend for most of their lives. Clive had intended to forgive the debt but Des had insisted on proper documentation, never suspecting that Clive would be thrown from a horse and killed less than a year after they shook hands on the deal. Now his son Max, owned the neighboring property and had made it clear he intended to collect on the mortgage.

It would be bad enough if Max only wanted the money, but he had his sights set on a diamond mine Judy's great-grandfather was said to have found on Logan land. Jack Logan had disappeared before revealing the exact location of his find to anyone except the elders of the local indigenous people. Their descendants refused to talk about it, believing Jack's spirit haunted the site.

At considerable risk to themselves, her foster brothers, Tom and Blake, had recently narrowed down the location to an area of Cotton Tree Gorge. But both men had fiancées now, and lives they couldn't neglect indefinitely. So it was up to her and Ryan to finish the job before their neighbor did it for them. Some sixth sense told her they were close to finding the mine. All she had to do was persuade Ryan to help her before either Max Horvath's own financial woes spelled the end of Diamond Downs or the fast-approaching wet season made the search impossible.

Spotting the tool he needed, she handed it to him. "I've never seen a car held together by rust before."

"It goes, that's all I ask."

"Dad won't mind if you use one of the station cars while you're here."

"I'd mind."

"You would." Not sure he'd heard the sotto voce comment, she watched him work the point of the tool up inside the filter neck, pushing it against the outside of the grommet. "Want a hammer to drive that in?"

"I'll manage, thanks."

At least he'd said thanks. But did such a puny gesture merit the surge of pleasure rippling through her? This would have to stop. Ryan had barely been at Diamond Downs for two days and already she could hardly think straight around him.

She was a bush pilot, for pity's sake. She flew solo around the outback in a single-engine plane she largely maintained herself. Turning to jelly because of the way a man looked at her was for females in frilly clothes who spent hours at the hairdresser primping to impress.

She could write off the blond highlights as an aberration. But what about the slinky dress? Thank goodness she'd decided against wearing it tonight on their nondate.

Ryan walked his feet out from under the car and uncoiled disturbingly close to her. For a giddy moment, she thought he meant to touch her face till she saw the oily washer clutched in his fingers. "If you want to help, how about cleaning this?" he asked.

With an inward sigh, she accepted the magnet from the transmission pan and hunted among the tools for a scraper to clean it with. She welcomed the excuse to avoid his gaze, afraid he'd see into her soul.

What an idiot, she thought as her fingers closed around a putty knife. By the time she straightened, Ryan was sluicing the drain pan clean, careful not to spill any of the residue onto the ground. Could his preference for an old car be on environmental grounds? she wondered.

She was tempted to ask but he'd already slid back under the car and she heard the sound of a gasket being scraped off the bottom of the transmission.

Glad of something to occupy her hands, she set to work scraping the magnet clean. "I'll say this for you, you're thorough."

"Might as well do the job right," he agreed, his rich, deep voice muffled by his position. "One thing your dad taught me."

She replaced the magnet in the pan and pushed it under the car to him. "So you admit he did some things right?"

"Never said he didn't. Your folks meant well."

She couldn't resist. "Am I hearing an admission that you liked being a Logan?"

"I'm not a Logan and don't want to be."

"But you just said..."

He ducked out from under the car and swung himself upright. "You know perfectly well why I never wanted to be a Logan. That hasn't changed."

Because of her, she heard it in his voice. "Everything else has," she said, pushing away the confusing feelings the thought aroused.

"Everything but you."

She shook her head. "I've grown up."

"You think I haven't noticed?"

She knew he had. The awareness was in every look he gave her.

"I know you don't think much of me," he said. Before she could issue an empty denial, he went on, "Blake has his crocodile farm, Tom got his wish to become a shire ranger and Cade's photos are published all over the world. While I dropped out of school, drive a beat-up old car and work where and when I can."

She lifted her shoulders and let them drop. "None of that matters to me."

"It's who you are inside that counts," he quoted her father. "He also said even a saint has to be able to educate his kids and put food on his family's table."

At the thought of Ryan's children, her knees softened and she rested a palm against the sun-heated metal to steady herself. "Are you sure you've got things the right way around?"

Although she'd thought about it often enough, she hadn't meant to come out and say it. His eyes clouded as he asked, "What do you mean?"

Too late to wish she'd never opened her mouth. "Being a no-hoper is a good excuse to avoid settling down."

"You think I live the way I do to avoid taking on responsibility?"

"Don't you?"

He made a harshly dismissive sound deep in his throat. "You don't know the first thing about me."

She started to turn away. "You're right, I don't." And if she were wise, she would keep it that way.

His fingers clamped around her wrist leaving a smear of oil like a handcuff. "Such slim wrists," he said unexpectedly. "Beats me how you pack so much muscle into such a slight body."

If looks could kill, he would have been ash where he stood. "Aren't you afraid of snapping such fragile bones?"

At her sarcastic tone, his mouth tightened. "I know precisely how much pressure I'm applying."

So did she. Her whole body quivered with the awareness of his touch. Trying to shake him off would only betray his effect on her, so she schooled herself to stillness. "I prefer wiry to slight."

He eased his thumb over her pulse point, making her wish she could slow the frantic beat by willpower alone. "Wiry, then. I like a woman with good muscle tone," he said.

As if she kept herself fit to please him. "You didn't always have so much muscle of your own to throw around," she snapped.

Cruel, she told herself when she saw his dark lashes veil those memorable eyes. "Malnutrition does that to you," he said.

She placed her hand over the one holding her. "I'm sorry, that was uncalled-for. I shouldn't have reminded you."

He looked down at their joined hands and an odd light flickered over his rugged features. "You didn't have to. Some things you never forget."

Her sigh gusted between them. "Ryan, why do we strike such sparks off each other?"

"I'm not complaining, if the alternative is indifference."

He could make her mad as hell, dizzy with laughter and aching with other things she refused to name. The one thing she could never be around him was indifferent. "Are you saying you like it when we fight?"

"It's communication, isn't it?"

Her nod conceded his point. "Not very constructive communication," she observed.

He released her hand slowly, as if reluctant to do so. "I don't know. We're getting the transmission filter changed."

Other things were changing between them, too, although they were harder to pinpoint. She fell back on the superficial. "At this rate, it will be dinnertime before the job's done."

In tacit agreement, he dropped to the ground and shimmied back under the car and she heard the sound of bolts being tightened. Anticipating what he'd need next, she hunted around for a long-necked funnel and the AFT fluid. By the time he stood up again and was ready to let the car down, she had them handy.

She watched as he fed fluid into the filler tubes. His moves were sure and capable. She'd also seen him handle a horse and rope cattle with the best of them. "Why haven't you bought your own land?"

"Didn't suit me."

"To be tied down?"

Fluid slopped over the funnel, earning a muttered oath. "Have I ever questioned how you run your life?"

"Not for a long time." She placed a hand on his arm. "I wasn't criticizing. I care about what happens to you."

"I wish I could believe that."

She was glad his attention was on his task so that he didn't see her recoil in distress. "What makes you think I don't?"

He turned his head, his gaze sharpening. "If you did, you'd ask what's going on in my life instead of constantly jumping to conclusions."

"You could simply tell me."

"I could."

But he wouldn't, she heard. Annoyed at being put on the defensive, she examined her conscience. Had she jumped to conclusions about him? Perhaps he had a million dollars stashed away and chose to knock around the outback for pleasure, like the American billionaire she remembered reading about. Getty? Rockefeller? One of them, anyway.

Somehow, she doubted it. "Ryan," she said on impulse, "If you were really rich, would you use your money to help Dad save Diamond Downs?"

"He wouldn't permit it," he said, avoiding the question.

At his signal, she got into the driver's seat and cranked the engine. "But you would be willing to try?"

"Why do you think I'm here?"

She pulled the gearshift down through each gear in turn, allowing the fresh fluid to circulate through the transmission. "You do know we have less than a month to either pay off Max Horvath or find Great-grandpa's diamond mine?"

Ryan pulled out the transmission dipstick and inspected it critically. "According to Blake and Cade, Max is in financial trouble up to his neck and his creditors are pouring on the pressure. From what I've heard about Max's character, he could be even more dangerous with his back to the wall. But the wet season is going to make it hard to find anything in the area Blake and Jo mapped out."

She nodded. "Especially if the mine is where they think it is, underground near Cotton Tree Gorge." Jo Francis was a journalist who'd been working with Blake on a story when she'd tumbled into a hidden valley trying to elude one of Max Horvath's henchmen. The ancient rock paintings they'd noted were placed high above the valley floor, indicating the dangerously high levels the creek flowing through it could reach during the monsoon rains. Diamond Downs had already tasted the fury of the rains soon to come, and the wet season still hadn't started in earnest.

She could only pray the Wet would hold off long enough for her and Ryan to look for the mine. If they didn't find anything…resolutely she pushed the thought of failure out of her mind. Not only her father's life, but the only thing besides Des's family that mattered to him—his land—was at stake. They couldn't afford to fail.

Ryan swiped the dipstick with a clean rag and replaced it, then pulled it back out. "Close to full?" she asked.

"A quarter inch away from the full mark, close enough," he agreed.

She got out as he began to check the radiator hoses and clamps. For a beat-up old car, it was in surprisingly good running order, she noted. Under her hand the engine had positively purred. Why drive a car that looked as if it was about to fall apart at any moment, yet keep it practically in racing condition? Another piece of the Ryan puzzle, she decided.

She leaned on her arms on the car body, angling in under the hood to watch him work, finding more enjoyment than she wanted to in his easy movements.

The thought disturbed her enough to say, "Why don't we decide right now what we should do about finding the mine. Save us having to go out to eat later."

His wry look raked her. "Jumping to conclusions again, Judy? Don't you think I can afford to buy you dinner?"

From the look of him, a hamburger would stretch his resources. Then she considered what he'd said about asking first. "Can you?"

"I may have trouble servicing the bank loan, but I'll manage somehow."

Masking her irritation at the blatant mockery in his tone, she smiled. "Then we'd better find the diamonds soon."

He replaced the dipstick and reached to close the hood, forcing her to jump out of the way. "Not on my account."

"Won't you feel better knowing Dad's future is safe?"

"Give me some credit. Des deserves health and happiness more than most men. But not because I'm indebted to him for rescuing me. I was fine as I was."

And what was he now? "Where do you call home?" she asked on impulse.

He looked surprised at the question. "You sound as if you don't think I have one."

Something else she hadn't thought to ask. What additional surprises lay behind his inscrutable facade? "You've never mentioned one."

"Doesn't mean it doesn't exist."

Anger bubbled through her and she fisted her hands on her hips. "Is it too much to expect one straight answer out of you?"

He seemed to collapse in on himself. "You're right, there's no reason you shouldn't know. I have a home, an old pearling master's cottage in Broome."

She knew her eyebrows had risen. Such heritage properties weren't cheap to acquire or maintain. "I'd like to see it sometime."

"I don't spend very much time there."

As soon as the words left his mouth and he saw her expression become shuttered, Ryan regretted being so blunt. It wasn't her fault that she'd haunted his thoughts since his teens, making a mockery of his vow to rely only on himself and not allow anyone to get to him emotionally ever again.

In the three years since she'd shown up at a station where he was working, he'd returned to Diamond Downs only a handful of times, the last being four months ago, and he knew she was the reason. Around Judy he felt too much, wanted too much. On previous visits he'd managed to keep his feelings in check. This time, perhaps because Des's health was declining and Diamond Downs faced such an uncertain future, Ryan had felt his resistance slipping.

The solution was as obvious as it was appealing. Have a fling with Judy and get her out of his system once and for all. He'd be doing them both a favor, he reasoned. She insisted she was more interested in flying planes than in serious relationships, so easing the tension between them with a no-strings affair should suit her, too. Afterward they'd be free to get on with their separate lives.

"I didn't mean that the way it sounded. I am away a lot, but when I'm home I'll gladly show you around," he said.

"Deal," she said, and smiled at him.

The change transformed her into the woman who'd filled his dreams since he was fourteen years old. Streaked with grease and dressed in slim-legged jeans, dusty elastic-sided boots and a high-cut T-shirt that revealed an inch of golden midriff with every move, she looked sensational.

He knew only too well why every other woman who'd crossed his path on his travels around the Kimberley had left him cold. However beautiful, pliant or eager for his company they'd been, they weren't Judy Logan.

How many women would choose to spend an afternoon working on a car, as competently as Ryan himself? If she wanted him to join her hunting for a diamond mine he wasn't convinced had ever existed, he'd be with her every step of the way.

He respected Des Logan enough to want to see him restored to health. And his intended fling with Judy would go more smoothly if she had the security the diamonds would provide, so it was what Ryan wanted, as well.

"You're staring," she said softly.

He felt as if molten metal were pouring along every vein, pooling in his groin. "If you had my vantage point, you'd stare, too."

She shifted from one foot to the other as if the compliment made her uncomfortable. "Look, maybe this dinner date isn't such a good idea."

"It isn't a dinner date—it's a strategy meeting." And he was Robinson Crusoe.

"And that's all?"

He made the time-honored gesture. "Cross my heart."

"Then perhaps Cade should come with us."

Now there Ryan drew the line. "He ought to stay here in case your father needs anything."

She caught her lower lip between slightly uneven white teeth. "You're right, but—"

He couldn't help it. His hand drifted to her cheek and he brushed away a streak of dust, eliciting a shiver that told him she wasn't completely indifferent to him. "No buts. Be ready at seven."

Chapter 2

"What's going on?" Judy demanded as she followed Ryan into an old cottage a short drive from the main homestead. "I thought you wanted to come here to collect something."

He gave her a wicked grin. "I did. You."

She'd planned on spending the evening with him at a café in Halls Creek. Now she was confronted by a table set for two in the middle of what had been her grandparents' home until the present homestead was built.

The old cottage, now used as guest quarters, was presently unoccupied. She found the scarred dining table disguised by a white cloth borrowed from the main house. A utilitarian candle jutted from a glass holder. A few wildflowers drooped in a jar, making her soften inwardly at Ryan's attempt at creating an atmosphere. He had succeeded, but not in the way she suspected he'd intended. "You could have told me you planned on eating here," she said to hide her discomfiture.

"Again, you could have asked."

True. It had never occurred to her that he'd be this creative. Not wanting to give him the satisfaction of seeing how much he'd rattled her, she looped her bag over the back of a chair and sat down. "I hope you don't expect me to do the cooking," she said, her tone disabusing him of any such notion.

He went into the kitchen and she heard him moving around. "I have everything under control," he said through the open door.

Too curious to sit still, she got up and went into the kitchen. The setting wasn't the only thing he'd planned, because he pulled two thick steaks out of the refrigerator and carried them to the stove where a pan was heating. When he placed the meat in the pan, the steaks sizzled fiercely and sent up a heavenly spicy aroma. She sniffed appreciatively. The evening might not be going according to her plan—and Lord knew, she hated having her plans thwarted—but the reward might just be worth it.

"There's a tomato salad and ice water in the refrigerator. Or wine if you prefer," he said.

"Ice water's fine." She took them out and carried them to the table, then went back to enjoy the sight of the family black sheep working in a kitchen. "You never let on you could cook," she said.

He turned the steaks expertly. "If you'd known, you'd have had me pulling my weight long before this."

Thinking of the times she'd cooked for him on his visits, assuming he didn't know one end of a grill plate from another, she twisted her mouth into a sneer. "What other surprises do you have up your sleeve?"

His eyes sparkled. "If I told you, they wouldn't be surprises."

"Stop being so damned mysterious and talk. You have a house in Broome. You know your way around a kitchen. Did you win the lottery or something?"

"Or something."

He would tell her when he was good and ready and not before, she heard in his tone. Happy to watch his fluid movements, she perched on a stool. "Did you know Dad had mortgaged the land to Clive Horvath?" she asked after a while.

Without turning back, Ryan shook his head. "We only talk on birthdays and Christmas, so I'm the last to hear anything."

"He didn't tell any of us until it was almost too late. Maybe it still is. You never met Max Horvath, did you?"

Ryan slid the steaks out of the pan onto plates. "His father and mother split up and he moved with her to Perth before I was sent here."

Sent here, she noted. As if he'd been under a prison sentence. Not came to Diamond Downs, or joined the family. Typical of Ryan not to forget that the choice had been forced upon him. "Of course, you had to learn to cook while you were living alone for all those months," she said with sudden understanding. "Looks like you've added a few frills since then as well."

He picked up a plate in each hand, and nodded to indicate she was to return to the table. "Took you long enough to work it out."

She sat down at the table and he placed a plate in front of her. The aroma made her mouth water. "You're a crafty one. But when you came to us, you were so angry and introverted. And you took off before I got the chance to ask how you'd been managing your life."

He took his seat and offered her the salad bowl so she could help herself. "I probably would have told you to mind your own business."

"In words of four letters," she said, smiling to soften the reminder.

"Yeah, I knew a few of those. Still do."

But he rarely used them these days.

She sliced into the steak and took a bite, closing her eyes

in appreciation. "Who do I have to bribe to get the recipe for this marinade?"

"Just me. Do you want to know my price?"

She opened her eyes and almost recoiled at the sight of her own reflection in his dark gaze. His expression told her more surely than words that she wouldn't like his price, so she didn't ask. "There's garlic and oregano," she said, trying to keep her voice steady.

His mouth turned up at the corners as if he could read her inner turmoil and was amused by it. "What else?"

She took another bite and let it linger on her tongue. "Red wine?" He nodded. "And something spicy. Not chili. Damn it, why don't you just tell me?"

He rested an arm on the table. "Because it's fun to watch your eyes go off like firecrackers when you take my bait."

"That's exactly the sort of remark we could have avoided if we'd eaten in a public place."

"Why do you think I chose this one?"

She stared at him. "So you could provoke me?"

"Not provoke, challenge you into admitting you want me as much as I want you."

She almost choked on the mouthful of steak she was just swallowing. Suspecting how he felt and having it spelled out were very different experiences. "Now I know you've gone crazy."

"It isn't crazy for a man to be attracted to a woman, especially when she feels the same way."

"I do not."

"Do, too."

The childish exchange reminded her of all the reasons this conversation was totally inappropriate. "You can't be attracted to your foster sister."

His knife and fork clattered onto his plate and he indulged in a couple of the words they'd just discussed. "You are not and never have been my sister."

"You were fostered by my father."

"Not by choice. I lived in your house for less than a year, and I left before the relationship was made official."

She took a hasty gulp of water. "Surely Dad became your legal guardian as he did for the others?"

"He wanted to, but I didn't give him the chance. So my statement stands."

His feelings were hardly news to her, but she'd always assumed nothing could come of them as long as he was family. Or had she hidden behind the belief rather than acknowledge the power of her response to him? She'd spent most of her adult years keeping men at a distance, determined not to have a life like her mother's.

Or a death.

Judy still nursed a deep well of hurt whenever she thought of Fran Logan ignoring the pain of appendicitis and continuing to minister to her family's needs until she collapsed. By the time medical help had been obtained for her, it had been too late.

Outback women like Fran lived and breathed the belief that their families came first. No sacrifice was too much. More often then not they hid their own feelings, needs and wants, never letting on to their families and those closest to them that they might be suffering. When food was scarce, they served themselves the smallest portions or none at all. If children were sick, they were nursed day and night, sometimes through their own sickness. They set bones and mended fences with equal stoicism. Educated their children at home. Endured isolation and deprivation beyond most people's comprehension.

Satellites and cell phones might have eased the solitude, but not the need for sacrifice. Judy still encountered plenty of it on her flights to deliver supplies, medicine, news and visitors to outlying properties. The women were the ones who suffered in silence. Judy didn't intend to become one of them. She didn't have their qualifications for sainthood.

These days, there was no requirement for a woman to marry. Judy saw herself as living proof you could have a satisfying career and a social life without tying yourself down forever.

"Lots of men tell me they're attracted to me," she stated, wishing for another glass of water to ease her parched throat. "I'm not interested in anything long-term."

He reached over and poured water from his own glass into hers. "Maybe you just haven't been told by the right man."

She sipped slowly. "The right man being you, I suppose?"

He helped himself to tomato salad, but didn't eat. "We've always known what was between us. Ignoring it hasn't helped. So the logical solution is to have an affair and be done with it."

Her hands, usually so capable on the controls of her Cessna 182, fluttered helplessly. "Dad is seriously ill. We may not be able to hang on to Diamond Downs. And you want us to have an affair?"

"Blake and Tom have the same worries, but I don't see Blake living without Jo, or Tom holding off on marrying his princess. If we wait for everything to be perfect before dealing with what's between us, we can't move on."

"Blake and Tom are not..." Barely in time, she stopped herself from uttering the words long forbidden by her father. "Blood." As Des saw it, his foster sons were as much family as his biological daughter.

Ryan's expression stayed impassive, but his eyes had hardened. "You can say it. Des isn't here to jump on you. Blake, Tom, Cade and I are grace-and-favor Logans. I can't speak for them, but the situation suits me fine."

Appalled at herself, she looked down at the plate. "I guess I don't like thinking you actually prefer being an outsider."

He smiled wryly. "If I wasn't, we wouldn't be having this discussion. I know Des means well but he can't change history. All of us were born into other lives. He gave us a second chance and we respect him for it. But it doesn't make us Logans. We can't feel the same toward him and Diamond Downs as you who were born here of his flesh and blood."

"Are you sure?"

A long pause preceded his reply. "Honest answer? I don't know. When I was a teenager, I envied the other boys for belonging here when I felt as if I never would. Maybe they do feel more kinship with Des and the land than I want to think. One day, I may even ask them if we get drunk enough."

She gave a shaky smile and resumed eating. "Their answers may surprise you."

He attacked his steak as if it were his beliefs. "Wouldn't be the first time. When I got here, I was so full of my own bull, thinking nobody knew the troubles I'd seen. Then I found out Tom's dad was in jail for killing his mother in a fit of jealous rage, and Blake had been left on a doorstep when he was a baby. My problems seemed feeble by comparison."

"They were real enough to you. It wasn't fun having to fend for yourself at fourteen."

"But I'd had my mother until then, and some happy memories of my father before he vanished without trace. It's more than Blake ever had. And my dad may have run out on us, but while we lived as a family he never raised a hand to his wife."

She masked a smile, recognizing—as Ryan evidently failed to do—Des Logan's words to the boy soon after he arrived. Reminding him to count what he had, rather than what he lacked. Her father had been more of an influence over Ryan than he knew.

Finishing the steak, she pushed the plate away. "I'd like the marinade recipe one day, if the price comes down."

His expression said it wouldn't where she was concerned. Then he said, surprising her, "You can have the secret for free. It's wasabi, Japanese mustard. Just a touch makes all the difference."

She should have known. His home was in Broome, where the Japanese influence had been strong for a couple of centuries. The town even held a Japanese pearl festival each year, the *Shinju Matsuri*. "Wasabi, I'll remember," she said.

"I'll bring you some next time I visit," he promised.

She placed her knife and fork side by side on the plate. "Maybe you shouldn't."

Steel settled in his gaze. "Shouldn't bring wasabi, or shouldn't come?"

"Both. Having an affair might work for you, but it isn't what I want. I only wanted you to come back because you're part of the family."

He leaned closer. "What are you afraid of? If it's my prospects, I'm a better catch than I've let you believe."

She stood up and started to pace, her movements constrained by the small room. "Your prospects aren't the problem." It was his overwhelming effect on her.

"You can't say you don't feel anything for me."

She swung around, wrapping her arms around herself. She couldn't lie. But she didn't have to tell the whole truth. "There's a complication."

His mouth thinned. "As in another man?"

"I'm seeing Max Horvath."

Ryan looked thunderstruck. "You can't be serious. I know he had a thing for you a few years back, but I thought you'd made it clear you weren't interested in this or any other lifetime."

"I did. Then I—changed my mind. I shouldn't even be here with you tonight. I broke a date with Max because I wanted this chance for us to talk privately."

Looking as if he'd rather shatter them to bits, Ryan gathered the plates and glasses with exaggerated care, but stayed standing at the table. "I can't believe I'm hearing this. Max is the one with designs on your land and your legendary diamonds. Is this some kind of crazy self-sacrifice thing? Marrying him so he'll let your father keep the land? Is that your bride price, Judy?"

"No." In fact, she had started seeing Max again against her family's better judgment so she could keep an eye on his activities. They were all convinced Max was behind a string of suspicious incidents on Diamond Downs, but the police couldn't pin anything on him without proof. She was hoping if he let his guard down with her, she could obtain the proof.

The list of grievances was long and getting longer. No sooner had Tom and Shara discovered a cave of valuable rock art on the land than a crocodile attack had attracted negative publicity, threatening the income from tourism Des had hoped to bring in.

Journalist Jo Francis had arrived to write a series of stories about surviving in the outback, her editor paying well for the access. Then Blake, an expert on crocodile behavior, had caught Max's henchman Eddy Gilgai luring the crocodile dangerously close to Jo's camp.

The scheme had backfired when Eddy himself had been taken by a crocodile, but the resulting media coverage hadn't done Diamond Downs's fledgling tourism venture much good. With the wet season approaching, fewer tourists were visiting the Kimberley anyway. By the time the dry season came around again—assuming they could hang on that long—Judy hoped the fuss over the crocodile attacks would have subsided, and they could focus attention on the rock art caves again.

She couldn't tell Ryan what she hoped to achieve by dating Max, without letting him think she was available for a romantic fling with him. The very thought sent needs she didn't want to acknowledge coiling through her. Right now he looked angry enough to break something, but the fire in his expression ignited an answering one inside her. What would it be like to feel his strong arms around her and his mouth hungry on hers?

Since she couldn't find out and keep faith with herself, she tore her gaze away. "I didn't want to talk about this, Ryan. You don't control me."

"I'm not going to stand back and let you barter yourself for a creep like Max Horvarth," he said. "If finding that mine will keep you away from him, I'll find it for you."

She had hoped to convince him to help, but not like this. "Are you offering to help so I'll have an affair with you? If so, the price is too high."

"The price is the same as it's always been—your body and soul. And the chance to get this…thing…between us worked out once and for all."

"Damn you, Ryan. Don't do this to me."

"It's done. All I did was up the ante. Unless you want me to go back to Broome and forget about helping you look for the mine."

Careful to avoid touching him, she took the plates from him and carried them to the kitchen, where she started to run hot water into the sink. Mechanically, she began to wash the plates.

He came up beside her and picked up a dish towel, drying the plates as if the two of them were a couple doing their nightly chores. The image had more appeal than she wanted it to.

"What's it to be?" he asked as he put the plates away.

She lifted dripping hands out of the water to gesture futilely. "You ask the impossible. I need your help if I'm to have any chance of finding the mine before the wet season cuts off access, but I can't agree to…your terms."

He flicked the kettle on and lifted two coffee mugs down from a shelf. "What can you agree to?"

Her voice struggled to rise above a whisper. "To think about your offer?"

"Not good enough. Thinking's too intangible."

* * *

Ryan knew he'd done enough thinking about her to drive a man crazy. Already he was regretting tonight. Arranging dinner in the isolated cottage had seemed like a good idea when he'd devised it. He hadn't allowed for her effect on him. Seated across the table, knowing how easily he could carry her to the bedroom, had made this the most uncomfortable meal of his life. Before he'd known it, he'd suggested an affair in exchange for his help. Judy's presence made him forget all gentlemanly behavior—forget everything but how badly he wanted her.

"I'm sure Dad would agree to give you a share of the mine."

He slammed the coffee mugs onto the timber counter hard enough to startle them both. "I don't want a share of the bloody mine."

"Then I'll go looking alone."

"Am I so offensive to you that you'd risk your life, rather than consider a relationship with me?" he demanded.

"Oh, Ryan, no. I could make love to you far too easily if I let myself." Or fall in love with you.

His hopes, almost throttled, began to rise. "Then if I'm not the problem, what is? You can't tell me you're in love with Max Horvath."

"I have my own reasons. If you really care about me, you'll respect them and leave me alone."

He ran his hands up and down her arms, feeling the shivers of response. "What do you think I've been doing the last few years?"

Caught by surprise, she turned, right into his embrace. "Is that why you come back so seldom?"

He smoothed out the furrow in her brow with his lips. Her skin tasted of sun and heat. She rarely used perfume, but her natural scent swirled through his brain, dazzling him. He took her mouth much harder than he'd meant to, as a starving man might attack his first offering of food. The impact wound all the way to his gut and stayed there, urging him not to stop at a kiss but to plunder and take. Now. Now.

Her arms wound around his neck and she pressed against him as if she also had trouble controlling her actions. When he'd claimed her mouth, her lips had parted instinctively and he flicked his tongue against the soft corners, gratified by her small indrawn gasps of pleasure.

With his knee, he nuzzled her legs apart and pressed closer. Thinking they'd be dining in town, she'd exchanged her jeans for a long, batik-printed skirt, more like a length of cloth wound around her slender hips. The cloth parted at his probing, revealing long legs strengthened by years of outdoor work and handling heavy cargo on her own.

As his body collided with hers, she opened her mouth as if to protest, but any objection she might have made was swallowed when he deepened the kiss. He'd found her core with his thigh and now he moved gently, seductively between her legs until she released a moan against his mouth. Through her skimpy white cotton top, he felt her nipples harden and almost moaned himself. Wanting her set his belly aflame and his blood roaring. It came to him that he could take her now and end this pointless argument once and for all. She would be his, end of story.

But until he knew what kept her from giving herself to him of her own accord, he couldn't in good conscience take what was within his grasp, although, heaven knew, he wanted to. He had never wanted anything—or anyone—more.

Cursing Des Logan for instilling at least a few principles into him, he trailed kisses down her throat and stiffly, painfully lifted his head. Her eyes were cloudy with desire, her limbs shaky. He held her until he was sure she could stand on her own, then stepped back.

"Now you know why I don't return more often."

Her breathing became shallow. "I never guessed."

"You must have known I was attracted to you."

"But not—like this."

To give them both time, he finished making the coffee and carried the mugs to the living room. He was surprised nothing spilled, considering how unsteady his hands felt. She followed more slowly and sat across the table from him, her face pale.

He disliked cornering her, but he'd had to show her what was at stake. Words could never have convinced her. He realized he'd taken a risk by showing her how strongly she affected him. Sharing his feelings wasn't something he did easily, and he doubted he did it well. She might still reject him, but if she agreed to his proposition, they'd both have a chance of moving on.

She cupped her hands around the mug he placed in front of her. "I admit I feel something for you, and it's powerful. No, let me finish while I can," she said as he moved to interrupt. "If I thought going to bed with you would get you out of my system I'd say yes."

"So what's the problem?" he demanded, unable to stay silent.

Lifting her head, she gave him a troubled look. "I prefer to keep my life the way it is, free of emotional entanglements. It isn't personal."

"The hell it isn't. Whatever you need or want from me to ease your fears on that score, tell me and I'll make sure you have it."

"It isn't that simple. What I want is to stay uninvolved."

"What you want?"

She heard the disbelief in his tone. "All right, what I need. If you truly feel about me the way you claim, you'll try to understand."

"I'll never understand," he stated. "And I will do everything in my power to change your mind."

Her faint smile was his reward. "I'd be surprised if you

didn't. But I won't change my mind. And I'll find another way to go after the diamond mine."

"That won't be necessary."

Coffee sloshed over the edge of her cup. "You mean you'll help me?"

"I always intended to help you, no matter what your answer. I guess I hoped you'd fall for my bluff and give me more incentive to go looking for this blasted mine."

"Don't you believe it exists?"

"It's a beautiful legend, and as tempting as that lottery win you mentioned before. And just about as likely."

"Then why look for it?"

He couldn't hold back his smile. "Because it gives me an excuse to stay close to you for the next month. How else can I work on changing your mind?"

Chapter 3

Judy wasn't sure how she felt; everything was happening too fast. She didn't need anything else on her plate. Least of all Ryan trying to pressure her into a hot and heavy affair.

No, not an affair. She could have handled a fling. And she couldn't pretend she hadn't thought about becoming involved with him. But she doubted she could protect her heart if they took their attraction to the next level.

He wasn't the only one struggling to deal with the chemistry between them. She also remembered the awareness that had flashed between them like summer lightning when they were both too young to understand what was going on.

Every time she'd seen him since then, she'd felt the pull growing stronger, more irresistible, until she'd found herself making excuses to fly to wherever she knew he was working, usually as a stockman on some outlying property. He'd greeted her cordially enough, but she'd never been able to tell whether he was pleased to see her. Once or twice, he'd acted as if he couldn't wait for her to leave, making her wonder if there was another woman involved. Still she'd kept tabs on him. Some people never learned.

Sometimes she wished she could forget all about him, putting as much distance between them as humanly possible. Was that how he'd felt when he'd run away from Diamond Downs as a teenager? When he'd gone, she'd felt as if something precious had been taken away. She'd told herself she was worried about how he would cope on his own, although he'd been doing it long enough. The truth was she'd missed him.

Not that she'd been short of companionship. Blake, Tom and Cade were good fun when they'd been persuaded to forget that she was—shock, horror—a girl. Ryan had never needed persuading; every look and casual touch acknowledged the inescapable fact. She'd missed that, too.

Especially that.

Yet now, facing him and hearing him say point-blank that he wanted her, she wished she were anything but female. Anything but the focus of his single-minded attention. What was going on with her?

The feel of his kiss lingered on her mouth more strongly than the food they'd shared. She knew she would taste him long into this night.

Ever alert to her moods, he pushed his coffee mug to one side and rested his forearms on the table. "Where do you want to start?"

With her mind still on his kiss, she almost answered the wrong question. Then she realized he meant the diamond mine.

She marshaled her scattered wits. "You went over the map with Blake and Tom, so you know roughly where they think the mine should be found."

"The hidden valley that leads off Cotton Tree Gorge," he said, showing he'd done his homework.

She smiled. "Blake wants Dad to call it Francis Valley after Jo."

"Sounds fair. I gather she took quite a tumble falling into the place while dodging Eddy Gilgai. Then she picked herself up and went exploring. Resilient as well as smart. She did well for herself snagging Blake."

Judy made a face at him. "Couldn't he be the lucky one?"

"Ideally, the benefits are mutual."

"Big of you to admit it," she muttered under her breath.

Ryan didn't react. "They did us a favor finding the remnants of your great-grandfather's canoe in the Bowen River," he went on.

"If they're right, a branch of the river disappears underground not far from the Uru cave—where Tom and Shara found the rock paintings," she said.

"I know where it is. I haven't seen the cave yet, but the others brought me up to speed on the discovery. They were pretty excited to find evidence of a prehistoric civilization living in the area. No wonder the world's scientists are already beating a path to your door." A frown arrowed his brow. "Didn't Max Horvath find traces of diamonds somewhere near the Uru cave?"

She inclined her head in agreement. "Jo found a couple more along the creek in her hidden valley."

He drew patterns on the checkered cloth with a finger. "So the truth lies somewhere along that creek between the cave site and the floating island where Jack Logan's canoe fetched up sixty years ago."

Ryan's nails were short and blunted by hard manual work, Judy noticed, distracted. But his hands were clean and well cared for. A man's hands, she thought. Hard when touching her softness. Gentle but irresistible. How would they feel seeking greater intimacy? The thought sent streaks of flame licking through her, homing in on the places she imagined him touching.

A physical relationship with him would never be enough to satisfy her, she sensed. Against all her self-imposed rules, he would make her want more, need more, leading to the very future she was determined to avoid. So she pushed the images away although the quivers of sensation lingered, making concentration difficult.

As a pilot, she was trained to shut out extraneous images. She made herself think of the problem of Ryan as a tricky landing on a too-short outback strip littered with rocks.

In other words, a recipe for a crash landing.

"Do you know anything about a family file Blake and your dad were talking about?" Ryan asked.

She pulled out of the crash dive barely in time. "Cade's the only one who saw it. He was helping Dad by catching up on some accounts when he came across a folder of very old records that had been misfiled and forgotten. He didn't think much about them until a friend showed Blake and Jo an old photo they recognized as Great-grandpa Logan's canoe washed up on the island. According to Cade, there were more photos and paperwork from the same era, giving us more clues to the mine's location."

"And did they?"

"We never found out. When Cade went to have a more thorough look at the file later, he was attacked from behind. When he came to, he had a concussion and no memory of the attack."

Ryan steepled his hands in front of him. "Of course the file was gone."

"What do you think?"

"I think our next move should be to try and get it back."

She picked up he coffee mug and stood up. "Easier said than done. There's no proof, but we suspect that Max had something to do with the theft."

Ryan shot her a curious look. "No fingerprints or other evidence?"

"He's too smart for that. If he was involved, he would have put Eddy Gilgai up to the actual attack."

"Now that Eddy's dead, Max might have to start doing his own dirty work," Ryan mused. "Do you still think it's a good idea to be involved with him?"

She knew how reckless her insistence that she was attracted to Max made her look. But admitting the truth would only intensify Ryan's efforts to claim her. And she couldn't deal with that now. "So far Max's part in this is purely circumstantial."

"You said yourself you think he was behind the attack on Cade and the theft of the file."

She planted a palm on the table. "Look, maybe Max was behind this and maybe he wasn't. Under the law, he's innocent until proven guilty."

Ryan's chair scraped back as he stood to face her. "You know he needs the diamonds to repay his creditors before they foreclose on him. And there's a better than even chance he's behind some of the attacks on your family. Yet you insist on seeing him. I'd never have picked you for a gold digger, Judy."

He'd invaded her personal space, but she held her ground. "You'd better have a good explanation for that remark."

"Do I need one? You can't possibly be in love with the man after all he's done and is doing to your family. So you must have another reason for sticking with him. The only one I can think of is money. Did he offer you a share of the mine if you become his wife?"

Ice dripped into her tone. "You're treading on dangerous ground."

"Not really. Just stating the facts as I see them."

"You forget yourself," she raged.

Her anger washed off him. "Of course. I'm only a drifter who can't hold down a steady job for more than a few months. Max inherited a substantial chunk of land, and potentially a lot more if he gets his hands on Diamond Downs. From your point of view, he's a better bargain as a lover."

So angry she could barely stop herself from lashing out at him, she slammed the coffee cup down and spun out of the room.

Out on the veranda she dragged in a lungful of the cleansing air, hardly aware of the splendor of the night sky, like a velvet cloth strewn with the diamonds her home was named for. Did Ryan know that the sky with its myriad stars was the reason for the property's name, not the fortune in precious stones said to be located here? Did he have the foggiest idea of what this place meant to her?

The land itself was her legacy, as it had been for generations of Logans. Only her father's illness and his miscalculation in mortgaging the land to the Horvaths had changed everything. She had grown up knowing the legend of the diamonds, but never cared much about finding them until they were her only hope of holding onto the land for the next generation. The money itself was strictly a means to an end.

God, she hated to lose. And losing her heritage because she hadn't done everything in her power to retain it would be the cruelest loss of all.

Intellectually she knew why Ryan had made his vile suggestion, but in her heart she felt mortally insulted. How could he think she would sell herself to Max for money?

That wasn't the real reason she was so angry, she realized as she fought to bring her labored breathing under control. She was affronted because Ryan was the one making the accusation.

Buying and selling favors was probably second nature to him. The kind of women he was accustomed to dealing with probably wouldn't have minded, she thought. But being placed in the same category had hurt her beyond belief.

Aware that he had followed her outside, she tensed, primed for battle.

His next words came as a shock. "I apologize. I was out of line."

With the wind taken out of her sails, she didn't turn around. "Have you any idea how close you came to being smacked across your big mouth?"

"Wouldn't be the first time," he said, an infuriating note of humor in his tone. "I shouldn't have accused you of gold-digging. I know you better."

How could he know her at all? She wondered. They'd spent so little time together as adults that his memory was of her as a teenage girl, not the woman she now was. He couldn't possibly understand her fear of falling in love and losing control of her life. "Apology accepted," she said evenly. "My reasons for seeing Max are my own affair, nobody else's."

"Doesn't stop me being jealous as hell," he said.

He moved up beside her and rested his hands on the top rail. "Beautiful night, isn't it? Every time I go away from Diamond Downs I forget how magnificent this place is. Then I come back and wonder why I ever leave."

Still shaken by his admission that jealousy had caused his outspokenness, she asked, "Why do you?"

"Work mostly."

"You could work around here. Any cattle station in the region would make an opening for a man with your skills."

"And what skills would they be?"

"Working cattle, horse breaking, mending fences." She thought of the steaks he'd served tonight. "You could get a job as a cook. Not just a camp cook—in a restaurant," she added.

"I've done all that and more, but it's not the work I do," he said.

She turned to him curiously, unwillingly admiring the way the starlight turned his hair to burnished gold and made his eyes seem darker and more unreadable. "I've seen you do all those jobs," she insisted.

"What you saw was my cover story." He reached for his wallet and flipped it open to show her a card in a window-faced pocket. "This is what I do for a living."

In the pale light spilling from the house she examined the document. Credit-card-sized, it had an unflattering photo of Ryan on the left with a date beneath it. The words Security and Related Activities Control Act 1996 were printed across the top. But it was another word in large red type that jumped out at her. "Investigator? Wait a minute. This says you're a private investigator."

"Duly licensed by the Commercial Agents Squad of the Western Australian Police Service," he agreed. "Among other activities, I can run surveillance on individuals and organizations, conduct asset and liability checks, investigate insurance claims and gather information for legal proceedings."

She wondered if she looked as foolish as she felt. "I always thought you moved around so much because you couldn't hold down a job."

He made a wry face. "In the beginning you were right. Then I met an old friend from Broome who turned out to be working undercover at a cattle station where I was a jackeroo. I didn't know it when I got there, but the station was being used as a holding center for supposedly stolen cattle while their owners filed dodgy insurance claims. After I helped my mate shut the operation down, he offered me regular work. I qualified for my investigator's license. Later, when he decided to retire, I obtained my Inquiry Agent's license and bought him out."

Ryan rested a booted foot on the lower railing and his arms on the topmost one. "My home and office are in Broome and I travel around the Top End and to the Torres Strait islands, wherever the job takes me."

"My hero, the P.I.," she said on a note of wonder.

"We can skip the hero part," he growled. "This doesn't

make me some sort of glamorous secret agent. Most of the work involves tedious evidence-gathering for companies or the courts."

"With an element of risk," she pointed out.

He slanted a grin at her. "Some of the people I investigate don't take kindly to the attention."

"I can see why they wouldn't. Why didn't you tell me any of this before?"

"Being looked on as a no-hoper, even by the people closest to you, has advantages. Your attitude toward me helped convince quite a few people that I was no more than what I seemed."

She straightened. "What attitude?"

"I call it your Mother Teresa thing, trying to help the poor and oppressed."

Denial coursed through her. "I never acted like that."

"You were forever checking on my welfare, wherever I was working, and bringing me stuff you thought I needed."

He thought she'd been dispensing charity. She didn't know whether to be glad or sorry that he hadn't worked out the real reason. She'd welcomed—craved—the excuse to keep in touch with him. Now that she'd discovered the truth, what would be her excuse? "They were only books, CDs, clothing, nothing valuable. I didn't mean you to take my gestures the wrong way," was the nearest she dared come to admitting the truth.

Fortunately he didn't probe, saying, "Admit it, I was one of your good causes, like that art foundation you and Shara are so committed to."

When Shara Najran had first accompanied her father, King Awad of Q'aresh on a cattle-buying expedition to The Kimberley, the young Middle Eastern princess had been bored and lonely. Drawn together as the only teenage girls in the vicinity, she and Judy had discovered they shared a passion for ancient rock art. They'd stayed in touch for years. Then

Shara had persuaded her father to set up an exchange program for indigenous artists between their two countries. These days, Judy represented the foundation locally. She looked forward to having Shara as her sister-in-law when she married Tom.

Heat flushed through Judy, making her wish she could be more honest about her motives for checking on Ryan. On the other hand, there had been times when she had considered him in need of uplifting, so he wasn't entirely off track. "The Art Bridge Foundation is not a charity," she denied.

"But I was."

"Maybe a little."

He touched her shoulders, moving her to face him. The heat of his hands burned through her cotton T-shirt. "I didn't mind because it kept me in your thoughts," he said.

She felt her vision start to blur. "I was always thinking of you, although at times you seemed angry when I turned up and couldn't wait to get rid of me. That was when you were working on a case, wasn't it?"

"I didn't want you in any danger."

"And now?"

"Now you're mixing with Max Horvath and I can't get it through your head that the man is high-risk."

She tossed her head, wishing that her short-cropped hair didn't make the gesture so ineffectual. "All men are high risk." Another thought occurred to her. "Have you been checking Max out? If you have, I don't want to hear about whatever you turned up."

Ryan's face had turned to stone. "Because you're in love with him?"

"I'm not…" The betraying admission was out before she could stop it. "Damn you, Ryan. You know I could never love Max. I'm seeing him because it's the best way to get close to him and find out what other tricks he has up his sleeve."

Ryan extended his hand, palm upward. "I want to see it."

"See what?"

"Your private investigator's license." When she didn't move, he placed his hand against her cheek. "You're not licensed or qualified to conduct an undercover operation, yet you're prepared to put yourself on the line. For your father? For Diamond Downs? Does inheriting this place mean that much to you?"

She struggled to find the words, not least because his hold on her was clouding her thinking. "I love my dad. I'd do almost anything for him. And I love this land, but not because of any inheritance value. Andy Wandarra and the other indigenous people here would say it's my country. They'll travel thousands of miles to die in their own place, their own country. This is mine."

"So you'd never want to leave?"

The bitterness she heard in his tone had her wondering. "I didn't say that. One's country isn't necessarily where you spend your whole life. But it is the land where you're born and where you hope to return before you die, what Andy would call your dreaming place."

She saw some of the tension leave him. "I understand. I may not have a dreaming place of my own, but I understand."

"Everyone has a dreaming place."

His shoulders lifted. "I was born in Kalgoorlie and lived there until my dad disappeared. My mother came from Irish stock and had no relatives in Australia, only a pen friend in Broome. When she realized Dad was never coming back, we moved there to be closer to her friend. So is my dreaming place Kalgoorlie, Broome or where my parents originated?"

"It's wherever you feel you belong."

His bladed hand dismissed the sentiment. "When I find out, I'll let you know."

"This could be your dreaming place," she suggested quietly. "You may not have chosen to remain at Diamond Downs, but I thought you were happy here."

"I was for a time." Until Des Logan had made it clear that the destitute youth had no business making eyes at his daughter, Ryan thought. Des had been careful not to say that Ryan wasn't good enough, but what other reason could there have been? Des wasn't exactly falling over himself to come between Judy and Max Horvath, Ryan noted. He wondered if Judy had noticed that detail.

"You could be happy here again," she persisted. "The other boys will be pleased when they find out the truth about your activities."

"They won't find out because you aren't going to tell them," Ryan snapped, beyond caring that he was projecting his own past hurts into his voice. He regretted it when he saw Judy recoil. "The fewer people who know what I do, the more effectively I can do my job," he said more gently.

He saw her master her hurt with an effort. "At least I know now why you think you can get that file back from Max."

"Let's say I've had a bit of practice at this sort of work." He shifted so his face was half in shadow. "I want you to arrange a date with lover boy."

Her chin came up and her eyes glinted with shock. "You *want* me to go out with him?"

He shook his head. "Believe me, I'd rather swim with crocodiles, but I'll need you to lure him away from his house so I can go through his office."

"Don't you need warrants to do stuff like that?"

"Not if I'm there legitimately. Eddy's death left Max shorthanded. We're going to convince him to hire me, then I'll do my investigator thing while he's whispering sweet nothings in your ear."

When he saw a shudder take her, he felt gratified. He hated

throwing her to this particular wolf, but he couldn't think of a better way to keep their target out of the way while he turned over Max's place. "Just don't let him get too close."

"You will be careful, won't you? I don't want anyone else getting hurt."

He stroked her hair lightly. "Who are you worried about, Max or me?"

Before she could answer, her cell phone chimed in the background. She hurried back inside and retrieved the phone from her bag in time to take the call.

Hoping it wasn't Max, Ryan found himself following her. He should probably give her privacy but if it was the other man, Ryan knew he'd have to find a way to cut the call short. The thought of her dating that sleazy character was almost more than he could tolerate. Maybe they'd all get lucky and Max would be eaten by a crocodile before she had to see the man again.

"Is he going to be all right?" Ryan heard her say into the phone. His senses sharpened. "I'll be there as soon as I can," she said and ended the call.

"Your father?" he asked.

She nodded, so pale he ached to take her in his arms, but her body language negated the idea. "At dinner he complained of chest pains and difficulty breathing. Cade's taken him to the hospital in Halls Creek."

"I didn't think they had cardiac services in a four-bed hospital. Shouldn't he be airlifted to Perth?"

Her hand went to her hair and she pushed it back, a trick of hers when she was nervous, he'd noticed. "They're arranging for the Flying Doctor to evacuate him, but he needs to be stabilized before he goes anywhere. He'll be at Halls Creek for at least a couple more hours."

He picked up his car keys. "Let's go."

"We'll be quicker in the Cessna."

His glance inventoried her pale features and shaking hands. "You aren't in any condition to fly anywhere."

"Maybe not, but I'm going to anyway. You don't have to come."

Stopped in his tracks, he said, "Would you rather I didn't?"

Her faltering smile and slight shake of her head was the answer he needed. He swept up her bag and his jacket in one hand, and her in the other. Holding her close at his side, he walked her out to the car. "Forget the Cessna. I'll drive you there. By the time you do your preflight, take off and land, and get from the airport to the hospital, you won't get there much faster."

"How long do you plan to stick around?"

Ryan brushed her lips with his then opened the car door for her. "Consider me glued to your side from now until we find your diamond mine."

Chapter 4

The Halls Creek Hospital had been built in the 1950s as a nursing outpost before being upgraded to its present modern level. Having helped out with many medical flights, Judy knew the compact size belied the wide range of health services the facility provided to the people of the hundred and fifty thousand square mile shire.

When Ryan pulled up outside the main building on Roberts Avenue, Judy saw Cade's old Holden parked nearby. Her heart began to pound and a headache tugged at her temples. She had known this moment would come, but now it was here her hands felt clammy with fear. Her father's life was in the balance. Not even the roughest landing on the most inadequate airstrip could compare with the dread gripping her now.

Ryan cut the engine and took her hand. "He'll be okay, trust me."

Feeling his strength flowing into her, she resisted the temptation to cling. "You don't know that for sure."

"We don't know he won't."

"Mr. Sunshine," she snapped, but a little of her fear had receded in the face of his quiet confidence. "Let's get this over with."

Inside the hospital they found Cade pacing, his features taut with worry. He returned Judy's hug and nodded toward Ryan. "What's the latest news?" she asked.

"He's having some tests now. We'll know more when they're done."

Aware of Ryan shadowing her, she said, "I should have been at home."

Cade's gesture negated this. "Wouldn't have made any difference. He was fine until just before dinner. Then during the meal he complained of chest pains and had difficulty breathing. I brought him straight here."

"You did the right thing," she agreed.

"When do they plan on airlifting him to Perth?" Ryan asked from behind her.

Cade's shoulders lifted. "Not until they're sure he's strong enough to handle the transfer."

She felt Ryan's hand press on her shoulder. "You'll be able to see him before he goes anywhere."

"I'm going with him if they'll let me," she vowed, not wanting to admit to herself how much comfort she took from his touch. Cade didn't seem to find anything untoward in the gesture. Only she knew how differently Ryan viewed their relationship.

Damn him, why did he have to choose tonight to complicate everything? She wanted to keep her mind clear to focus on her father's problems, not have to agonize over where she stood with Ryan.

She didn't have to, she resolved in a snap decision. Just because he'd declared his desire for her didn't mean she had to reciprocate. She didn't have to do anything except carry on as she was. It had nothing to do with her.

Except she knew it wasn't so simple. She had feelings for him, whether she acknowledged them or not. Tonight she'd realized she was fooling herself if she thought she could remain uninvolved with him around. If she could have managed without his help, she might have had a chance to resist. As it was, she needed him.

Ryan was the original all-or-nothing man and he was in danger of sweeping her along on the tidal wave of his determination. She was going to have to tread water like crazy to keep ahead of this particular tidal wave without being dragged under.

"Have you heard from Blake and Jo?" she asked to divert her unruly thoughts.

Cade shook his head, his long raven hair falling across his piercing blue eyes. "Blake was rounding up a rogue crocodile that's taking cattle on a property near Broome. Jo went with him to write about the capture for her magazine. I couldn't reach them by phone, and they aren't expected back until tomorrow."

She touched him lightly, grateful for his steadiness. He might not be as muscular as Ryan, but his tall, thin build concealed an inner strength she appreciated. "I don't know what Dad would have done without you."

"Running Diamond Downs is good therapy," Cade said, making her wonder why he needed such a thing. "It doesn't leave much time for anything else."

Didn't she know it. Before Cade came home, her flying business had suffered as she'd tried to hold everything together in her father's stead. Her brain refused to deal with the possibility that he might not make it. Logic told her she would have to lose him someday, but not now. She wasn't prepared.

"Ryan, what are you doing here?"

Hearing the feminine voice, Judy's hackles went up instinctively. She turned to see a woman only a little younger than herself planting a kiss on Ryan's cheek. The woman's hair looked as if she'd combed it with her fingers and the skin beneath her eyes was smudged with violet, but she still managed to look glamorous. And familiar for some reason.

Before Judy could place her, Ryan took the woman's hand and tugged her into their group. "Judy Logan and Cade Thatcher, this is Heather Wilton, one of my favorite women in the world."

The woman extended her free hand and Judy shook it automatically. "Hi Judy, Cade. I've heard a lot about your family from Ryan," Heather said.

Her voice was low and sexy. Beautiful in an interesting sort of way, she had fluffy blond hair, huge blue eyes beneath winged eyebrows, and indecently full, roseate lips. Judy saw a keen intelligence in Heather's gaze and tried not to feel envious of the way she made a watermelon-colored tank and denim shorts look like high fashion.

Judy didn't recall seeing Heather around Halls Creek or on any of her regular aerial routes. "Why do I feel as if I know you from somewhere?"

"Heather used to present the weather reports on Perth television. You might have seen her there," Ryan said, sounding proud of the woman's accomplishments.

"But I live at Citronne now," Heather supplied quickly.

Judy felt her eyebrows lift. "The cattle station near the edge of Lake Argyle? That's a long way from Perth TV."

The woman rolled her eyes. "Tell me about it. Moving up there was a huge culture shock but I love it."

"Did your work bring you to the Kimberley?" Cade asked.

Heather beamed a secretive smile at Ryan. "It was nothing less than true love."

Judy felt ill. They were supposed to be worrying about her father, not rehashing Ryan's love life. It didn't seem to matter that mere moments before, she'd resolved to let him be love-struck on his own. She didn't like to think meeting one of his old flames—current flames?—had changed anything.

"Shouldn't we see how Dad's doing?" she asked pointedly.

Ryan gave her an amused look that said he knew exactly what she was thinking. But all he said was, "I'll see what I can find out." He moved purposefully toward a nurses' station.

"I gather your father is the patient," Heather said. "Is he going to be all right?"

"We hope so." Judy felt her stomach clench with nerves as she fought to stop herself imagining anything else. Briefly she explained the situation to Heather, who nodded in sympathy. "What brings you here?" Judy asked in turn.

Heather nibbled on her lower lip. "I escorted a group of children from our area to Halls Creek as a reward for doing so well at school. But my son Daniel had a bad asthma attack this morning and had to be rushed here."

"I hope your son will be all right, too," Judy said, ashamed of being tempted to jump to yet another conclusion. She'd already been wrong about Ryan on several counts. No need to add any more to the list.

Heather smiled wanly. "The doctor says he's over the worst for the moment. They're keeping him in the hospital for another day as a precaution."

"Better to be safe than sorry," Judy murmured. "Who's minding the children while you're here?"

"Luckily I'm mainly the escort. Our host is one of the former teachers from the local school, Tracey Blair. She has a house in town with plenty of spare room, so she invited the children to stay for a few days. She's well-known to their parents, and the kids jumped at the chance to stay with her. I was happy to accompany them, and enjoy a change of scene for Daniel and myself."

Judy's smile broadened. "Tracey's an old friend. You

should ask her to call my foster brother, Blake. He runs a crocodile park near Halls Creek and would love to show the children around while they're with her."

"I'll be sure to pass on the suggestion. The kids are used to seeing crocodiles in the waterways at home, so it would be good for them to learn more about them from an expert."

Judy was scribbling Blake's telephone number on a piece of paper for Heather when Ryan came back. A moment later his smile registered. "Des is fine. The heart attack was a false alarm, according to his doctor," he assured her.

She felt her knees turn to jelly. "What about the pain and shortness of breath?"

His arm came under her elbow as if he sensed her need for support. "Brought on by stress, they tell me. The tests show it wasn't a heart attack at all, so he won't need to be airlifted out."

"Thank God." Cade's heartfelt statement echoed her feelings. "When can he come home?"

"Not tonight. He's sleeping. After this, they're going to advise him to stay in town to be closer to medical help."

Judy looked at the phone number she'd just written down. "Dad could move into Blake's house at the crocodile park. Even if he's called away to take care of a problem crocodile, there's always someone at the park to keep an eye on things."

"And Blake's house is a lot closer to town than Diamond Downs," Ryan agreed, adding, "Although I don't fancy having to convince Des of the necessity."

"Blake will pen him up with the crocs if that's what it takes," she said grimly. "And we'll back him up."

Heather smiled. "Must be nice having a large family to share responsibilities at such a time."

Judy handed her the phone number and clasped her fingers around Heather's in silent support. "Don't you have family?"

"I come from Tasmania originally, so all my family is

there. Not that there were many of us to begin with. Jeff doesn't have anyone other than Daniel and me."

Judy knew her tone reflected her confusion. "Jeff?"

"My husband. He hired Ryan to help us resolve a fraud case a couple of years ago. One of our workers claimed to have been injured at work and was suing us for a fortune, when he'd actually been drunk at the time of the injury, and was nowhere near as badly hurt as he tried to claim. The case was decided in our favor, thanks to Ryan's evidence. We're in his debt."

So much for conclusions, Judy thought. Ryan was right, she would have to stop jumping to them where he was concerned.

Cade gave Ryan a curious look. "Sounds as if you get up to a lot more than jackerooing."

He made a gesture of demurral. "I was only helping out a friend."

Cade looked unconvinced, but accepted the explanation at face value. "Suit yourself." He stood up. "Since there's no point in me hanging around here any longer, I'll head to Diamond Downs and come back to see Des in the morning. Are you okay for a ride, Jude?"

She wavered. How easy it would be to return to the homestead in Cade's uncomplicated company. But she had to deal with what was between her and Ryan, and avoiding him wouldn't help. "Thanks, but I want to look in on Dad for a moment then I'll come home with Ryan. He brought me in his car."

Cade feigned amazement. "And you got here in one piece?"

Ryan punched him on the arm. "Show a little more respect, mate."

Cade grinned. "I'm showing as little as I can."

Heather gave Judy a slightly bemused glance. "Do your brothers always carry on like this?"

"Ryan isn't my brother. When we were kids he spent some time with our family, probably where he picked up so many bad habits, " she heard herself state. Why was she denying their relationship to others, while trying to act like a sister to him herself?

She ignored Cade's startled look but was well aware of Ryan's satisfied expression. All she'd done was state a fact, one he'd reminded her forcibly about earlier in the evening. It didn't mean she was interested in any other kind of relationship between them.

"Will you be all right?" she asked Heather.

The other woman pushed her hair back from her face. "I'll be fine."

"You have my cell phone number if you need anything," Ryan reminded her.

"And an open invitation to Diamond Downs anytime," Judy added. Strange how easy it was to be hospitable now she knew there was nothing between Heather and Ryan. She still had trouble understanding how Heather could give up a glamorous career in television—or any other career—to be an outback wife, but the liking was strong and, Judy suspected, mutual.

Heather gave her a tired smile. "I appreciate the offer. Don't be surprised if we accept your hospitality while we're here. I presume Tracey's whole group is included?"

Judy inclined her head. "Of course. The more, the merrier."

She and Cade walked out together leaving Judy alone with Ryan. For a normally busy facility, the hospital had gone strangely quiet. "I'm glad Des is okay," he said into the lull.

"You told me he would be."

"And I've never lied to you. Maybe not told you everything, but never deliberately lied."

"I know."

Feeling awkward now she had acknowledged the basic

truth that they weren't brother and sister and never had been, she found herself at a loss to deal with what they *were.* She took refuge in practicalities. "I'll ask if it's okay for me to see Dad now. Do you want to come?"

"I'll see him tomorrow. You go ahead. I'll wait for you at the car."

She hurried to the nurses' station, wondering what she was hurrying away from. Not the kindness she'd seen in Ryan's gaze. No, not kindness. A deeper connection she was far from ready to deal with, she admitted inwardly.

As she'd been promised, she found her father sleeping peacefully surrounded by a tangle of monitoring equipment. She took his hand and stood looking at him for a long time, willing him to improve. There wasn't much chance unless he received a heart transplant, she knew, but she could still hope.

His eyes fluttered open for a second. "Hello, Jude," he murmured. "I'm a silly old bugger, worrying you over nothing."

"Never mind about us, you rest now," she reproved gently. "We'll be back to see you in the morning. Don't give the nurses a hard time."

"Spoilsport," he said but his voice faded on the word and soon he was asleep again, the monitors bleeping with reassuring regularity.

She felt her vision blur. "You may be a silly old bugger, but I love you, Dad." Bending, she kissed him lightly, careful not to disturb him, then tiptoed out.

Ryan was leaning against the car, the shadows from the street lights giving his angular features an austere look. "Everything all right?" he asked straightening.

"For now. He stirred long enough to call himself a silly old bugger."

"Then he's definitely improving."

She shook her head. "He won't until a transplant becomes available." And we can persuade him to go to Perth to have the operation, she added to herself. That wasn't likely to happen until they'd resolved her father's concerns about Diamond Downs's future.

Too much pressure on too many fronts, she thought, feeling tiredness sweep over her. She was glad now she hadn't piloted the Cessna to Halls Creek, and could look forward to closing her eyes on the way home if she wanted to.

"This has been rough on you, hasn't it?" Ryan observed.

"Rougher on Dad. He's used to being independent and strong."

"Nobody can be strong all the time."

Not even you. She heard what he didn't say. For a fleeting moment she was tempted to lean against him and let his arms come around her. He would find her mouth with his and his fingers would thread through her hair, pressing her closer to deepen the kiss until she shivered with pleasure. With him, she would have no need of strength. He had more than enough for them both.

But there would be a price. He would insist on more, and she already knew he wasn't a man to take no for an answer. Before she knew it, she would want a ring on her finger and the course of her life would be set. A course she was determined to avoid.

She shook herself like a blue heeler cattle dog shedding water and stiffened her spine. "Time we were heading back."

"Would you like to go for a drink first?"

At the hotel they were likely to run into dozens of people she knew. She'd have to talk about her father's problem endlessly, meet their friends' concern with reassurances she barely believed herself. "I'd rather go home."

"There's still that bottle of wine in the fridge at the cottage."

She gave up trying to make sense of her feelings, knowing only that his suggestion was the best one she'd heard all evening. "Sounds good to me."

About to get into the car, she was waylaid by a man hurrying up to them. Tall and tanned, he appeared fit enough until you looked closely and saw the signs of too much good living. Unlike most bosses in the Kimberley, Max Horvath preferred to let his men do the hard work around the cattle station he'd inherited from his father. So where he might have been muscular, there was a hint of flab that was set to get worse as he got older. His charcoal hair was streaked with premature gray and his brown eyes were dulled by too many late-night drinking sessions.

"Judy, sweetie, I called at the homestead and they told me the news. Is your dad all right?" Max asked.

As he approached, her heart sank. "It was a false alarm brought on by stress, Max," she said, thinking how much of that stress could be laid squarely at their neighbor's feet.

He went on, seemingly unawares. "You should have called me. I'd have brought you to the hospital and stayed with you."

Precisely why the thought hadn't crossed her mind. "It all happened too quickly. Luckily Ryan was available to drive me to town."

Max had barely given Ryan a second glance. Now he looked at the other man with more interest. "You're new here. Do you work for Des Logan?"

"Ryan is…"

"Ryan Smith. I'm looking for work around here." He cut across her smoothly. "Judy was interviewing me for a job when Mr. Logan collapsed, and I offered to give her a ride."

"Late hour for an interview," Max said stuffily. "Still, you probably have your hands full with everything that's been going on. I didn't know you were looking to hire more people, Judy."

He didn't know she could afford to hire more people, she translated. "We're not really hiring," she said, taking her cue from Ryan. "Ryan was recommended to us by a friend, so the interview was a courtesy. Under the circumstances, we can't afford to take on anyone new. I'm sorry to be so blunt after you've been so helpful," she said with a deliberately apologetic look at Ryan.

"That's okay, something will turn up," he said. "I'm not fussy what I do."

She could hardly believe her eyes. In a few seconds Ryan had somehow transformed himself from a take-charge figure into a slump-shouldered ne'er-do-well who could barely manage to meet her eyes. It was all she could do not to laugh. How could Max possibly be taken in by such a performance?

However, it seemed he was. "Maybe we should talk. My name's Horvath. My place borders Diamond Downs to the northwest."

"That would be good, Mr. Horvath. Judy's letting me sleep at the bunkhouse tonight, so I'm not far away. "

"Come and see me tomorrow at nine. Judy can give you the directions."

With that, Max dismissed Ryan as no more than a lackey who might be useful to him, and turned his full attention to Judy. "What's happening with Des now?"

"They're keeping him in the hospital overnight as a precaution, then releasing him tomorrow. He'll be staying with Blake for a while."

Max nodded. "If there's anything I can do, let me know."

Start by tearing up the mortgage over Diamond Downs as Clive had intended to do, she wanted to scream at him, but she kept silent. Max was a different character from his father, who'd been one of the most generous people in the district. Clive would never have taken advantage of Des the way Max was doing.

"There's nothing," she said, meaning it.

"Then let me buy you a drink at the pub before you head home."

She let her shoulders drop. "Can I take a rain check? I've had a rough night."

"Sure. I should have thought of that myself. Why don't I look in on you tomorrow morning? Smith and I can talk then, if it's okay with you?"

Inviting Max home was the last thing she felt like doing, but knowing what Ryan was up to, she gave a weary nod. "You can use the office." When they attacked Cade and stole the file, Max's men had already taken what he wanted from there anyway.

She tensed as Max leaned over and kissed her on the mouth. His drink at the pub wouldn't be the first of the night, judging by his whiskey breath. She restrained a shudder as his cheek rasped against hers. "Good night, Max."

"See you tomorrow, then. You, too, Smith."

Ryan reached to tip an imaginary hat. "Good night, Mr. Horvath."

"Snake," she muttered as the other man walked back to his vehicle.

"Me or lover boy?" Ryan asked, coming around to open the door for her.

"You decide." She was capable of opening her own door, but allowed the gesture in case Max was still observing them. Or so she told herself.

"What was that all about?" she asked when they were on the road at last.

"I've seen him before," Ryan said.

In the darkened car her startled gaze went to him. "I thought you'd never met Max."

"He was involved in the insurance scam that got me into the P.I. business. We were sure he was part of the money-laundering end in Perth, but there wasn't enough evidence to lay charges against him. He went by an alias for that deal, so the name Horvath didn't mean anything to me."

"Why am I not surprised? You're lucky he didn't recognize you."

Ryan's fingers drummed a tattoo on the wheel. "People like him are users. To them, the likes of me are dirt under their feet. They don't even see us most of the time. We were never introduced, so he would only have seen me from a distance, and he was away when I lived around here. He took me completely at face value."

She would have done the same, she thought, still amazed that he could transform himself so effectively. No wonder he was good at undercover work. Uneasily she wondered how she would know when he was sincere about anything, then dismissed the thought. They weren't going to get involved, so why did it matter? "Did you notice how he reacted when you said you weren't fussy what you do?"

He nodded. "Exactly why I said it. I wanted to sound desperate enough that he'd think of me as a potential replacement for Eddy Gilgai."

Fear gripped her anew. "Most of the work Eddy did was probably shady." And had cost him his life, she couldn't help thinking.

"So Max needs someone with the same low morality to fill Gilgai's shoes. Don't be surprised if Ryan Smith acquires a police record by tomorrow."

"You're good at this," she said, not sure she meant it as a compliment.

"I'm good at a lot of things. I'm also very, very persistent," he added, his tone redolent with meaning.

"You will take care, won't you?"

"Worried about me, *sweetie?*" There was laughter in his voice as he mimicked Max, lacing the endearment with a heavy dose of saccharine.

"Only if you keep calling me that. I think I liked you better when you were acting tame and meek."

They cleared the town limits and twin beams of light leaped ahead of them as he switched the headlights to high beam. A red kangaroo trampolined across their path, disappearing into the well of darkness beyond the road. "You'd never be happy with tame and meek."

She felt as jumpy as the kangaroo. "How do you know what I'd be happy with?" Particularly when she didn't know herself.

"I know you better than you want me to. We're two of a kind."

Cleansing anger washed away some of her diffidence. "Is that supposed to be flattering?"

"It's simply fact."

"I take back what I said. You're definitely not meek or tame. You're bossy and pigheaded."

He gave a low laugh. "As I said, two of a kind."

He'd achieved one thing. No longer drained and tired, she felt charged with energy and a desire to lash out at something—or someone. She simmered for the rest of the drive home, only remembering that she'd agreed to share the bottle of wine with him when they pulled up outside the old cottage.

She stayed where she was. "I've changed my mind. I'd rather go home."

He got out. "Suit yourself. I won't be long."

Watching him go inside, she was sorely tempted to slide across and drive herself back to the homestead. But she was too well schooled in outback courtesy. If anything went wrong, he would be stranded here. She couldn't do it.

"One drink, nothing else," she muttered to herself and followed him inside.

He was already levering the cork out of the chilled Chablis with an old-fashioned opener. "Don't jackeroos just knock the top off the bottle?" she asked.

"Waste of good wine." He poured some into glasses. Two glasses, she noted. He'd been very sure she'd decide to join him.

Accepting the drink he offered, she was annoyed to find that her hand was less than steady. She raised the glass to her mouth, pleased when she didn't spill any. The icy liquid was refreshing as she waited for the alcohol to counteract the nervous strain of a hellish night.

With the white cloth and candle still on the table, the memory of his kiss clogged the air. Unfinished business. She put her glass down. "I want to make something absolutely clear. I have no interest in getting married, so I don't want any more talk of love between us."

"I can live with that," he said, putting his glass down beside hers.

She looked away, unwilling to admit to feelings of regret. How could she be disappointed when he was giving her what she'd asked for? "I'm glad that's settled," she said, not sure how convincingly.

The next thing she knew, she was in his arms. Instantly fire rocketed along her veins, the flames blazing around her heart as she was dragged against him, her softness meeting a hardness she'd suspected and now encountered in blatant arousal. Her senses ran riot, her voice almost deserting her as she demanded, "What do you think you're doing?"

"You said you wanted no more talk of love."

His mouth closed over hers, hot and heavy with demands she was far from ready to meet. So why did her body betray her by arching against him? "We can't...this isn't..." she gasped, finally managing to fling out, "I said I didn't want this."

He lifted his head, his gaze passion-fogged. "You said you wanted no more talk. This isn't talk. This is action."

Chapter 5

She might have expected such a trite response from him. Ryan Smith was a cowboy, hardly the poetic type. Just because he'd made more of himself than she'd expected, didn't mean anything else had changed.

Especially not Judy's reasons for staying uninvolved.

She should have laughed at his presumption and, if necessary, stepped on his instep with the full weight of her heeled sandal. Instead she felt as if she were balanced on the rim of a deep chasm, the strong arms around her the only thing keeping her from falling.

Clinging to a man wasn't her style. As the only, longed-for child of older parents, she'd had to fight for her independence from the day she'd struggled to her toddler feet. Having four males added to the family had been like having a team of bodyguards wished on her. Oh, she'd loved all the boys once she'd gotten to know them and her parents had smoothed out some of their rougher edges. But their protective instincts had threatened to stifle her.

Only in the air had she enjoyed true freedom. The trial flying lesson she'd begged her father to give her on her fifteenth birthday had given her a taste for soaring with the birds. She'd begun saving to buy her own plane the next day.

Now she felt trepidation at the renewed possibility of having her wings clipped, but another sensation, too. A sense of adventure almost as seductive as being at the controls of her Cessna, or having the controls of a helicopter throbbing in her hands.

In Ryan's arms, she was also flying but he was in the pilot's seat. His kiss was as enticing as an open vista of sky in front of her. The temptation to let herself soar with him was strong.

She closed her eyes, then opened them again and pulled back. His hold didn't allow her much room, but her rigidity and the resolve she put into her expression sent him a message he couldn't misread.

His hold slackened, but he didn't let her go. "What's the matter?"

Summoning her voice took surprising effort. "I don't want this."

"Okay."

He didn't argue or try to change her mind. She told herself she wasn't disappointed. "Aren't you going to try to talk me around?"

"Do you want me to?"

He could have done so with ridiculous ease, she suspected. All the more reason to step back and keep her distance. "I thought you he-men types don't take no for an answer."

His shoulders lifted fractionally. "No always means no to me. I don't play games."

"And you think I do?"

"No. You say what you mean, Judy."

What about now? She wished she knew for sure. She

hadn't wanted him to kiss her. Yet at some level she regretted pulling away. Why couldn't she make up her mind what she wanted?

Her hand went to her hair. "I can't deny I find you attractive."

His long lashes shuttered his expressive eyes. "But you don't want to."

She shook her head. "I like my life. I don't see any reason to change."

"I'm not asking you to. Only to deal with what's between us."

"You don't call that a change?"

He made a dismissive sound. "You've been reading too many romance novels. Satisfying sex is only part of a life, one of the good parts. You don't have to give up anything important, just make a little extra room."

This sounded too simplistic even for Ryan. "When did you get to be such an expert on relationships?"

"I've been around some good ones. You met an example at the hospital tonight. Heather Wilton."

Once again the thought of Ryan having an affair with the lovely former TV presenter struck uncomfortably close to Judy's heart. "Were you involved with her?"

He gave an amused snort. "Heather has eyes for only two men in her life—her husband, Jeff and their little boy, Daniel. From the moment she saw Jeff on the set of a talk show, giving an interview about cattle ranching in the Kimberley, she was smitten. The way they tell it, the attraction was powerfully mutual. They kept in touch and she vacationed up here a couple of times, then resigned her TV job and married him."

Judy walked to the open door of the small cottage, staring out into the night. The silence beckoned, making her ache with nameless longings. Over her shoulder she asked, "Why did she have to follow him? Wouldn't he move to Perth for her sake?"

"According to Jeff, he would have gone anywhere she wanted. This was her choice."

A choice Judy found hard to comprehend. She loved the outback and had never wanted to live anywhere else, but neither did she intend to give up being a person in her own right. Was there a middle course? For all her hours in the air, she had still to find one. A streak of stubbornness kept her searching.

She turned back, angling her body against the door frame and finding comfort in the creak of the old timber at her back. "Let's allow for a second that Heather and Jeff have the most perfect marriage on earth. They're good role models for anybody. What about closer to home? Your own parents were hardly examples of true love."

Seeing a shadow cross Ryan's rugged features, she felt a pang of regret. But she was only stating facts. Still, facts could hurt. "I'm sorry, I shouldn't have brought that up," she said.

"Not talking about something doesn't make it go away." He picked up his wine glass and fiddled with the stem. "I don't know what drove my dad to leave. For a time, with the conceit of a kid, I thought he'd left because of something I'd done. Later I accepted that it was his choice, nothing to do with me. He told me he'd been in a car accident that had killed his mother when he was little. He wouldn't go into details of how and why it happened, and only talked about the accident at all after a few beers, but I got the impression the experience had damaged him. He'd been raised by distant relatives who'd taken him on as a duty. As an adult, he had trouble settling down anywhere."

"Do you know where he is now?"

"Recently I talked to a man who thought he'd met him. According to his information, my dad headed back to Kalgoorlie, dying in a head-on collision on the highway outside town. I checked and the accidental death of a Nicholas Smith is on record, but it's a common name. Could have been him or a complete stranger. They're one and the same to me by now anyway. But I do know he loved my mother. They were good together while it lasted."

"I'd never have picked you for a romantic," she said.

"Or you for such a cynic," he rejoined. "Although you were putting out the No Trespassing signs for as long as we've known each other. Haven't you let anyone get close to you?"

"I'm not a hermit. I like men well enough."

"At a distance," he said.

"You make me sound like some sort of nun. I assure you I'm not."

His rugged features hardened and she saw reflected in his gaze an all-too-familiar expression. He was jealous of her unnamed lovers. She wondered what he'd say if she told him there'd only been one man other than Ryan himself, who'd made her want more than was good for her.

Neil Quinlan was a pilot who mustered cattle by plane. He was based on a large property near Derby to the north, and when they'd met at the airport over a mix-up in cargo manifests, she'd fallen hard. Divorced, he'd spoken of not wanting to be tied down again, unwittingly speaking Judy's language.

She felt her mouth curve into a smile as memories of shared enjoyment flashed through her mind. Rendezvous on remote outposts, flings in hotels in Broome or Derby. And enough flying talk to bond together like members of a rare species who couldn't believe their good luck in finding each other.

The good times had lasted for seven glorious months. Then Neil had started to talk about getting a place of their own. Moving in together. Domesticity. He'd dreamed of owning a cattle property; their time together had convinced him she was the woman who would share his dream.

She could still remember the alarm tinged with sadness she'd felt when she told him she didn't share his vision of their future. She hadn't wanted to hurt him, but she wasn't cut out for raising children and cattle in the dust and heat of the Kimberley. There wasn't enough compensation for what love demanded of an outback woman.

Ryan was watching her, she saw, pulling herself back from the memories with an effort. "Don't look so grim. I'm happy with my life," she assured him without much conviction.

"You may not be a nun, but you're not the type to give your heart lightly," he observed. "Some man must have hurt you pretty badly to put that look of sadness in your eyes."

She lifted her shoulders. "The man isn't always to blame. I was the one who hurt him."

"Yes, you would."

She waited for Ryan to elaborate. When he didn't, she went on, "Why must men always want more from me than I'm willing to give?"

He settled himself on a corner of the table, one leg swinging free. "You might equally ask yourself if what you're willing to give is enough for what you would gain?"

"I have, and my decision stands. I won't trade control over my life for love."

"So I'm hearing that sex is okay?"

Uncertainty rocked her until she pushed it away. "What you're hearing is the call of your own masculine ego."

"You think?"

The grin touching his mouth and the twinkle she saw in his gaze filled her with relief. He wasn't going to force any admissions out of her. Not tonight, anyway. Later might be a different story. Before that she'd have time to shore up her mental defenses against what he made her feel. They'd have to be strong barricades, she suspected. In a few days Ryan had unsettled her more than Neil had done in months. And she already knew Ryan was harder to get out of her system. Hadn't she been trying since the day they met?

"More wine?" he asked.

She shook her head. "I never drink much."

"Worried about losing control?"

This time there was no mistaking the teasing note. "You wouldn't want me dancing on the table."

"Might be entertaining."

"In your dreams, buster." She moved purposefully back inside. "We have more pressing concerns, like how to get you onto Max's payroll tomorrow.

As far as Ryan was concerned, he was halfway to being hired by Max already. He hadn't missed the gleam in the other man's eye when Ryan had said he was prepared to do anything for money. He'd been speaking Horvath's language. Now all Ryan had to do was let Horvath's desperation take care of the rest.

"If he's to keep your family off balance long enough to find the diamond mine, he'll need help."

"Yours," she agreed. "I'd still like to know how you did that."

He raised an eyebrow. "Did what?"

"Managed to look so shifty. When we ran into Max outside the hospital, you seemed to change before my eyes."

He let a slow grin develop. "Maybe it's the real me coming out."

"I hope not, or Diamond Downs is doomed."

"Not while I have breath in me to prevent it."

Picking up the wine bottle and glasses, she headed for the kitchen. Over her shoulder she said, "I'm glad you're on our side."

The refrigerator door swung wide as she corked the bottle and put it away. Over the top of the door, he said, "Never doubt that for a second, Judy."

Her gaze lifted. "My, you sound serious."

"I'm good at what I do. Starting tomorrow, I'm going to convince Horvath I'm his man, no questions asked. I don't want you doubting what side I'm on."

In the glow from the refrigerator light, her eyes brightened. "You are serious, aren't you?"

"Never more so. You believed I was a drifter for long enough."

When she didn't apologize, he took it as a compliment. "And now you're about to become the sort of sleazy bum Horvath would hire," she said. "What if he learns the truth? With his creditors breathing down his neck, he's desperate enough that you might be in danger."

Giving the door a gentle push, he removed the barrier between them. "Concerned about me?"

"About Diamond Downs," she insisted. "You can take care of yourself."

The next morning, as they'd agreed, Ryan had moved into the bunkhouse provided for the use of the teams of contract workers who moved from place to place doing specialized work like mustering, harvesting and fencing. A few years before, the station would have accommodated large numbers of people at different times. Today, few properties could afford the luxury of many extra hands, even without the setbacks that Diamond Downs had suffered.

Without Andy Wandarra and his loyal team, they would have had no chance of keeping the place going, Judy thought as she walked past the cluster of workers' cottages toward the bunkhouse.

All of the outbuildings were made of the same fabric, stabilized earth blocks, stone and rough-sawn timber to blend with the surrounding bush. What breezes there were flowed through louvers used in place of glass. All of the cottages boasted modern amenities, and quite a few had attractive gardens established around them.

Many of the cottages were quiet now, their occupants working out at the stock camp to complete their tasks before the wet season set in. Making the most of the cooler morning hours, a few women were working around their homes and waved a greeting as Judy passed. Some of the cottages were empty, Des having had to let many people go as he struggled to meet the payroll.

With a pang, Judy noted empty spaces where vehicles, bikes, graders and lighting plants had been sold off gradually to keep things afloat. Where once over a hundred head of horses had been kept, there were now only dozens. How long before they could no longer support those?

They would survive somehow, Judy vowed to herself, shaking off her melancholy mood. With Ryan and her foster brothers on her side, she refused to consider any other outcome.

For the moment, Ryan was the only occupant of the rambling timber building set a little away from the other houses. Built on a raised mound with concrete floor and timber framing, the bunkhouse had walls only to waist height. From there to the roof were panels of louvers that could be opened or closed to suit the weather. The inside was divided into rooms, each containing beds, lockers and chairs. A communal washroom at one end served the residents.

Judy came to the door of the washroom to find Ryan shaving. In snug-fitting jeans and his worn R.M. boots, he was bare to the waist, a towel slung around his shoulders as he leaned closer to the fly-specked mirror over a row of sinks. When her reflection loomed behind him, he nodded and finished scraping the last flecks of white from his chin.

He hadn't done a very good job, she noticed. As he swished the razor through the water in the sink, she saw his face was still shadowed by stubble. On him, it looked like a sign of dissipation. Late nights, too much drinking, maybe the jail time he'd said he might add to his background. She looked closer. His eyes actually looked bloodshot. She said so, adding, "How do you do that?"

"I have a kit of harmless but useful chemicals that can produce almost any effect," he explained.

She hated to admit it, even to herself, but the effect was powerfully sexy. He might look as if he slept on the streets, but he also looked as if he knew them. As if he cared nothing for social conventions. A man who would take anything—or anyone—he wanted without compunction.

She suppressed a shiver. "I'm glad Dad doesn't have to see you like this."

"He already knows what I do."

Her irritation flared. "You told him, but not me?"

"He helped me out once with some background information for a case. I got the impression he was highly amused."

"He'd enjoy the irony," she observed, knowing her father's nature. "I wondered why he was so sanguine about having a dropout around, and why he never lectured you on making something of yourself. How long has he known the truth?"

"A few years."

"Before or after our big reunion at Sunrise Creek?" She named the cattle station where she'd run into him again after his long absence from her life.

He lifted one end of the towel and swabbed his face, then frowned at her. "Afterward. Does it matter?"

It mattered to her. She'd been proud of being the one to bring him back into the Logan fold, as she'd believed. "Plain curiosity," she dismissed.

He touched her chin, lifting her face. His fingers felt damp and flecks of white shaving foam dotted the backs. "Or jealousy?"

She pulled away from his hand. "What do I have to be jealous about, for pity's sake?"

"Because you want me to be your special project."

He'd come so close to pinpointing the source of her resentment that she took a step back, coming up against the hard rim of the sink. "You flatter yourself. I have lots of special projects going. What you call my Mother Teresa act wasn't solely for your benefit, you know? I take stuff to people who need it all the time."

"People, as in men?" The gleam of annoyance that lit his gaze was a vindication of sorts.

"Maybe." In fact, her special projects were mostly the women of the outback. If occasionally her plane's payload was adjusted to include cosmetics, bathroom luxuries, the latest glossy magazines or a few rolls of beautiful material she'd picked up on her travels, that was her business. It wasn't that the women couldn't afford such things, but rather that they didn't choose to. Husbands and children always had more pressing needs. But they'd never refuse her gifts.

He hooked the towel over a handy rail. "Liar."

Automatically she straightened the damp towel. The masculine scent clinging to it rose to meet her, fogging her thought processes. She had the irrational urge to press the towel to her face and breathe deeply. "How do you know?"

"Part of my job is to know when someone's telling the truth. Don't worry, any admission you make won't be taken down and used in evidence against you."

She wished she could be sure. He'd already managed to twist her thoughts into knots, make her want things she had no business wanting. He moved toward her and she stiffened, but he reached past her and retrieved a T-shirt from a hook behind her.

The charcoal-colored garment was threadbare, with the fading logo of a long-forgotten heavy metal band in black on the front, she saw as he shrugged the T-shirt over his head. The cutoff sleeves hugged his upper arms and the body outlined his muscular torso. Her throat felt dry.

Producing a comb from a wet pack, he slicked his hair down. Water made the fiery red color look darker, like the embers of a fire. Even embers could burn, she reminded herself. She wished this was over, that they'd dealt with Max Horvath so Ryan could go back to his undercover investigations and leave her alone. The wish was surprisingly half-hearted.

She wanted the whole awful process to be over. To know that her father and her home were both secure. But she didn't want Ryan to leave. She didn't want to fall in love with him, but she didn't want him not to be around. What kind of stupid sense did that make?

The sound of a car pulling up outside the house saved her from the need to analyze her motives any farther. Ryan's head had come up a fraction of a second before hers. "Sounds as if Max has arrived. Showtime."

A surge of fear hit her, for him she recognized. "Are you sure we have to do it this way?"

"We have to get inside his operation, keeping one step ahead of him. We also need to find out what was in that file Cade found."

Her breath whispered out in a sigh. "I know. Be careful."

"Always." His smile was heart-stopping. When he wasn't teasing her or challenging her, he was dangerously attractive, she thought. He dropped the comb and razor into his pack, zipped it closed and took a deep breath.

Again, she was unsettled by the transformation. He let himself slouch, hooded his gaze and became, before her startled eyes, someone she'd think twice about giving the time of day to.

"Weird," she muttered.

"Something wrong, Ms. Logan?" he asked in such a weasely voice that shivers ran down her spine.

"Nothing's wrong," she assured him.

"Then let's go meet the boyfriend," he said, sounding like himself for a second, before he turned back into Mr. Down-and-out.

Max didn't seem to find anything untoward in Judy emerging from the bunkhouse. Lounging against the side of his car, he hardly spared Ryan a second glance. "How's your dad, today?"

Ryan cursed himself for not asking the question. He had been too preoccupied by the sight of Judy in the bunkhouse, he realized. This morning she wore snug-fitting jeans and a long-sleeved cotton shirt, the sunshine-yellow color making her look absurdly young and feminine despite the masculine cut.

Remembering how sexy she'd looked in a skirt last night, he found himself wishing she'd uncover those fantastic legs more often. Did she still think of herself as a stockhorse? He recalled she'd used the term self-deprecatingly, overlooking how much the men of the outback valued their horses.

Personally, he thought of her fit, muscular shape as perfect. Like the animal she claimed to resemble, she had beauty in her strength. Ryan had little time for model-thin clotheshorses. A body sculpted by hard physical activity was, to his mind, the most alluring shape in the world. Thinking of the kind of activity he'd like to explore with her made him feel hot, although the heat of the day had yet to build up.

He reined in his runaway thoughts. He needed to keep his mind on the job if he was to help her save her home.

"I called the hospital earlier," she was saying. "Dad slept reasonably well. They're keeping him under observation for a few more hours, then hoping to discharge him this afternoon."

"I'd be happy to take you to the hospital to collect him," Max offered.

"Thanks, but Cade's already taken Dad's things to the hospital. I'll stay with Dad until he's discharged, then take him to Sawtooth Park. He won't want too many people fussing over him."

Max made a move toward her that had Ryan tensing instinctively. He made an effort to relax his muscles and preserve his lackey persona. Max had barely acknowledged his presence. Now he said to Judy, "You have to let me help you. You can't fly your plane and run this place without more help."

"Cade's doing most of the work, and I still have Andy and his team."

"Too few hands to run a place the size of Diamond Downs. Maybe it would be a good thing if I take over the reins. Give you a graceful way out."

"You're assuming I want one," she said.

The other man touched her arm, making Ryan seethe inwardly. Max said, "You're a fighter, Jude. I admire that. But you can't keep up this pace. You're only..."

Max trailed off, evidently catching the warning in Judy's expression. "Only what, Max?" she asked with seeming innocence, but Ryan heard the undercurrent of steel in her voice. "Only a woman?"

"Only one person," Max shot in smoothly. Ryan guessed the other man knew he'd been inches from death by the offended female, and had decided a quick save was called for. "At least let me send some of my people over here to help out."

"We're fine as we are, thanks," Judy said tautly. "But speaking of people, do you still want to interview Mr. Smith while you're here?"

Belatedly, Max turned his attention to Ryan. "We'll talk, then I'll come in and you can give me coffee. Maybe I can persuade you to let me do more for you."

Over her dead body, Ryan read in her expression. But she smiled sweetly. "You can try."

Max brightened, hearing what he wanted to hear, Ryan assumed. "Come on, Smith, let's get this over with."

He led the way to the office, Horvath's familiarity with the setup at Diamond Downs making Ryan frown, although he schooled his expression to servility before being noticed.

Horvath sat down behind the desk and gestured for Ryan to sit opposite. "Now tell me why I should hire you."

Ready for the question, Ryan reeled off previous employers and kinds of work he could do, until the other man gestured him to silence. "Judy Logan wouldn't have bothered with you if you couldn't do all that. What I want to know is why *I* should hire you."

"I think you already know."

Max looked startled, but his voice was steady as he said, "Humor me."

"You have all the help you need running Willundina. I know because I called there before I came here." He hadn't, but Ryan doubted that Horvath paid much attention to how his property was run day-to-day. "You have no openings for stockmen."

Horvath's guarded nod rewarded the gamble. "So what else are you good for?"

"Anything you want done," Ryan said, adding, "I hear you're prospecting for diamonds."

Horvath eyed him sharply. "You know a lot for a blow-in."

"I've spent a lot of time around the area. Heard most of the stories, including the ones about Jack Logan's lost fortune."

"Then you must know the most likely site isn't on my land?"

Ryan nodded. "Don't see any problem. Word around here is that it soon will be your land anyway."

Horvath plainly liked that, and his eyes gleamed. "As you can see, Ms. Logan and her father are struggling. The way I see it, I'd be doing them a favor by taking over."

"And finding the diamonds will let you do even more for her, right?"

Horvath tilted the chair back. "I like the way you think."

Because it was the way Horvath himself thought. The man had been read like a book and didn't even know it.

"What would you have done if Judy had hired you?" Horvath asked.

"She didn't."

"You seem sure I will."

Ryan gave an ingratiating smile. "I was at Sunrise Creek Station when a mob of cattle was brought in that had been reported stolen and the insurance money claimed. The herd comprised every brand under the sun. Big operation. Cops didn't get half the people involved."

Horvath crashed the chair back onto its four legs, some of the color washing out of his face. But he held Ryan's gaze. "Why should that interest me?"

"Thought you might have heard about it."

"Everybody heard. It was big news."

"Cops hauled me in as an accessory," Ryan said.

"Were you guilty?"

"Only of turning a blind eye. They couldn't pin anything on me."

"Did you learn anything about who was behind the operation?" Horvath asked.

His casual tone didn't fool Ryan. The real question was how much Ryan knew about Horvath's part in the scam. "I got to know a few names and faces," he said lightly. "Didn't tell the cops everything I knew in case I need a favor sometime."

"Like a job?" Horvath's tone had hardened.

Ryan shrugged. "A man's got to eat."

Horvath leaned forward. "Play your cards right and you'll do a lot better than eat. Help with my diamond prospecting, and I'll see you get a cut."

Ryan nodded in apparent satisfaction. "Exactly what I was hoping you'd say, Mr. Horvath."

Horvath came around to Ryan's side of the desk. "There is one more thing."

"What's that?"

Horvath grabbed Ryan's T-shirt front and twisted hard enough to tighten the neckline around Ryan's throat. "If you ever try to blackmail me with anything you think you know, you won't live long enough to regret it."

All but lifted out of the chair, Ryan knew he could have broken Horvath's stranglehold and had the man flat on his back in the blink of an eye. But he stayed still and made choking noises. Not difficult, since the shirt was knotted against his Adam's apple.

Horvath twisted the shirt tighter. "I take it that's a yes?"

"Yes, Mr. Horvath," Ryan forced out as stars fringed his vision. He clawed air.

Making a sound of disgust, Horvath released his choke hold and Ryan slumped back into the chair, massaging his bruised throat. One more score he'd have to settle with the man very soon, he vowed inwardly.

"Get your gear together. You can come back to Willundina with me this morning," Horvath said as if nothing untoward had happened.

Ryan coughed, his abused throat protesting. "Coffee with Ms. Logan would be good."

Horvath's gaze narrowed. "I already warned you what'll happen if you get cocky, Smith. The last man who thought he could outsmart me ended up in the belly of a crocodile."

Ryan was well aware that Eddy Gilgai, the man Horvath was referring to, had been taken by a crocodile after attacking Blake's bride-to-be, Jo Francis, who had done her best to save him. Hardly the retribution Horvath was implying. "I won't forget," Ryan muttered, meaning it in ways Horvath couldn't begin to imagine.

"See that you don't."

Ryan stood up and extended his hand, but the other man ignored it. "Be at my car in half an hour," he ordered, then walked out of the office.

Untroubled by the affront, Ryan let his hand drop, allowing himself a slight smile as he massaged his aching throat. What was a little pain when he'd achieved what he wanted? He was glad Horvath had saved him the trouble of disinfecting his hand.

Chapter 6

A few days later, Horvath had forgotten or chosen to overlook that Ryan had virtually blackmailed himself into a job. With his creditors breathing down his neck, he probably couldn't afford the luxury, Ryan decided.

He'd made himself useful around the property, working his new boss's cattle when an extra hand was needed, even settling a couple of disputes among the men. Ryan hadn't been given any special status but they seemed to recognize his natural leadership, deferring to him until the head man, Mick Coghlan, had started showing signs of resentment. Ryan had pulled back at once, not wanting the added complication.

Horvath had saved him from Coghlan's attention by taking him along on what he called reconnaissance missions. To Ryan, they were trespassing on Diamond Downs land, pure and simple, but he kept this thought to himself.

"There's the entrance to Cotton Tree Gorge," Horvath pointed out on one such foray. Ryan was driving and Horvath had directed him to pull up in the shade of a huge tropical paperbark tree.

Ryan crossed his forearms over the steering wheel. "Isn't that where the rock paintings were found?"

Horvath's lip curled into a sneer. "Supposed to be the work of some long-dead race, according to the scientific types Des Logan has allowed to traipse through the caves."

"You don't think the rock art is anything special?"

"Just because the paintings look like some others found in Egypt or South America doesn't mean a forgotten race once lived here. More like the ancestors of the present mob. They don't keep any written records, so it's all speculation."

So much for art theory, Ryan thought. He'd heard Shara Najran's expert opinion about the Uru people, and she'd convinced him that an ancient race of people had once lived in the region. But he nodded as if in agreement with his new boss. "We'll never know for sure."

Horvath looked satisfied. "Right."

Ryan decided to steer the discussion in a more useful direction. "Couldn't Jack Logan's diamonds be a load of hot air, too?"

Horvath shook his head. "I found traces of gem-quality stones in Bowen Creek, close to where Jack's journal notes say his mine is located."

Ryan let his eyebrow lift. "You've read his journal?"

"Only a copy. Judy showed it to me."

Like hell she had, Ryan thought. Horvath must have seen the pages in the file he'd arranged to have stolen from Des Logan's office. Ryan's spirits rose. If the file contained copies of Jack Logan's journal entries, what else might be in there? He had to get his hands on the file soon. So far, there hadn't been an opportunity, but Horvath had boasted of having a date with Judy Logan this evening. Ryan knew he'd get his chance to snoop then.

He wasn't worried about doing the deed. If he needed to, he could turn over Horvath's entire place in a couple of hours without the other man suspecting a thing. If the file was anywhere in the house, Ryan would find it, photograph the contents with the miniature camera he had with him and report the results to Judy by the next morning.

So why did he feel a familiar ache at the back of his neck, warning him that something wasn't right?

He was confident that Horvath didn't suspect him of anything. The man had called his contact at Sunrise Creek and been told that the police *had* taken Ryan in as a suspect in the cattle-stealing scam Horvath had also been involved in. Only a few senior officers knew the arrest had been prearranged to preserve Ryan's cover story.

Judy was the problem, Ryan concluded. When he'd called to report his progress, she'd told him she planned to go out with Horvath tonight to get him out of the way.

"Won't that complicate things?" Ryan had asked, making a conscious effort to relax the hand gripping the phone. The thought of her and Horvath together on a date made him want to snap the instrument in two.

Her sigh had whispered down the line. "Perhaps, but we're running out of time. If you don't get a look at that file soon, Horvath's creditors will take us down with him."

Horvath's mortgage over the Logan land would be classed as an asset, and would be claimed by his creditors in repayment of Horvath's debts, Ryan knew. He wished most of his own money wasn't tied up in his home and business. Borrowing against them would take too long to get the Logans out of trouble. According to Jo Francis, who'd had her money market operator brother check into Horvath's financial affairs, the Logans had less than a month to find a solution.

Caught between a rock and a hard place, he'd been forced to agree to Judy's plan. Not that she'd needed his compliance.

He had a feeling he couldn't have stopped her if he'd tried. Telling himself her headstrong ways were part of her appeal didn't make him happier about the thought of her spending a minute more than strictly necessary alone with Horvath.

Ryan dragged his focus back where it belonged. "So you think the lost mine is in Cotton Tree Gorge, boss?"

"Eddy Gilgai showed me the entrance to a hidden valley opening off the escarpment not far from here. Eddy was sure the mine is located in that valley, between the entrance and the Uru cave."

"That's a big chunk of ground. Pity Eddy couldn't have been more specific."

Horvath opened the car door, letting in a blast of heat. He stepped out and stared up at the rock walls, shading his eyes. "Jack Logan's journal entry was specific enough, although it would have helped if he'd left a map."

Glad to stretch his long legs, Ryan followed suit. "I've spent some time in those hills myself. Between us, we shouldn't have much trouble locating the mine."

Horvath was practically salivating when he looked at Ryan, although his eyes narrowed with suspicion. "If you know so much, why haven't you gone looking for the diamonds on your own account?"

"Wouldn't do me any good while they're on Logan land. They'd probably pay me a reward, but the big money would belong to them."

"Whereas when I claim their land in repayment of the mortgage, I cut you in for a much bigger share," Horvath said. "Glad to see you've got your priorities right, Smith."

Ryan had, but not in the way Horvath thought. "Do you want to climb up and explore the valley today?" he asked, hoping Horvath had no such plan.

Horvath consulted his watch. "I have to get back in time for my date tonight. Can't keep a lady waiting."

Ryan's insides curled but he kept his expression impassive. "What's she going to think if you take the diamonds out from under her nose?"

"*She* is Ms. Logan to you," Horvath snapped. "Like most women, Judy doesn't always know what's best for her."

"And you do?"

"It's hardly any of your business, Smith, but yes. Once I'm in position to provide for her and her father properly, I'll marry her and merge our two operations into a cattle spread to rival the big overseas syndicates."

"You'll need good men behind you, Mr. Horvath," Ryan said in character.

Horvath relaxed visibly. "Men like you, Smith, who know when to be useful and when to keep their mouths shut. I have a feeling you and I are going to go a long way."

Horvath was going only as far as the nearest jail, Ryan thought, although he nodded. "Sure thing, boss. Whatever you say." For the moment, anyway.

Judy pulled the first dress that her fingers touched out of the closet. She'd bought the simple forest-green sheath for the funeral of a member of Andy Wandarra's clan, and the somber style seemed appropriate now. Max would probably prefer more glamour and a lot less dress, but accommodating him was well down her list of concerns.

Arranging tonight's date had seemed like a good strategy when she'd broached it with Ryan during a discreet telephone call the night before. Now, faced with the prospect of spending the evening in her neighbor's company, she wished she'd let Ryan talk her out of it. He'd tried hard enough, but she couldn't let him take all the risks. Her home and family, not his, were at stake. She wanted to do all she could to put Horvath out of business.

Resignedly, she lifted her arms and dropped the dress over

her head, settling the folds over her hips. With cap sleeves and a heart-shaped neckline, the dress should have made her look as sexy as a lamppost. Instead, the fluid lines managed to hint at curves she hadn't known she possessed.

Wonderful. Trying to look as nun-like as possible, she had only made herself more attractive to Max. Maybe there was truth in the saying that some things were better left to the imagination. Hopefully he wasn't that imaginative.

Ryan would be a different story. She had no trouble picturing his reaction to her, just as she had no difficulty remembering how he'd responded to her in a T-shirt and wraparound batik skirt.

Lost in the memory, she was running a finger over her bottom lip when she caught her reflection in the mirror. Ryan wasn't going to see her in this or any other dress. He'd made his feelings clear, as she'd explained hers. The gulf between them was too wide. However memorable his kisses, she hadn't changed her mind about staying uninvolved. Ryan might think that an affair would resolve things between them, but what if it left her wanting more? Keeping a safe distance was the best way she knew to control her emotions and her life.

Yet again, she was dressing for a date that had nothing to do with romance, she thought, thrusting a brush through her hair. The night was too hot for too much makeup, so she settled for applying waterproof mascara and a supposedly bombproof lipstick.

In theory, she had the easy task, keeping Max occupied while Ryan searched the homestead. But Max was becoming more and more pushy, determined to help her whether she wanted his assistance or not. She hoped she wouldn't end up fighting him off before the night was over.

What was Ryan doing now? she wondered as she blotted the lipstick with a tissue. Max was due to call for her at any minute, so the coast was clear at Willundina. She hoped Ryan would be careful. They might not be a good match, but she cared enough not to want anything to happen to him.

Ryan kept to the shadows as he approached Horvath's house, having no good explanation for why he was going inside while the boss was away.

The housekeeper, bless her, was a creature of habit. By now, Ryan knew from his previous observations, she would be settled in her bed-sitting room, glued to her favorite hospital drama, a generous glass of rum and cola at her elbow.

Raucous laughter came from the bunkhouse behind him where a poker game was in progress. Ryan had fended off an invitation to join them by claiming to be broke. Since he was still an unknown quantity to the men, they hadn't tried to twist his arm. He hadn't discouraged the rumor that he was an ex-con, and his efficient handling of himself and a stockwhip had added to his air of toughness. Most of the men kept a respectful distance.

All but one. The head stockman, Mick Coghlan clearly resented Ryan muscling in on his turf, and Ryan sensed the man was itching for a reason to take him on. So far he'd managed to avoid providing one.

The laughter and ribald language faded as Ryan skirted a vegetable garden and crossed a fenced-off patch of green lawn in front of the main house. In the distance, a dog barked, answered by the far-off howl of a dingo. He ignored both, focusing his attention on the job at hand.

As silent as a ghost, he glided past the housekeeper's window, smiling as he heard her talk back to the set, disputing the lead actor's medical facts, he gathered.

Then he was at the French windows leading into Horvath's office. The room beyond them was in shadow. The doors were locked, but Ryan made short work of the locks with an automated pick known only to him and the operatives of national security organizations. Slipping inside, he closed the doors without latching them, and pulled the drapes across before snapping on a light over the desk.

Horvath was neat, he'd say that for him. On the desk, a closed laptop computer was surrounded by piles of paper stacked with almost military precision. None of the papers were of any interest to him, a quick check revealed. Ryan sat down at the desk and started on the drawers, memorizing the layout of the contents in each one before working his way through them.

Cade had given Ryan a fair description of what he was looking for, but the drawers revealed no trace of the stolen file. He sat back, aware of a sensation of being watched, and looked up into the catlike eyes of a beautiful Asian woman with glossy dark hair flowing around her shoulders. She was dressed in a cerise cheongsam with an embroidered jacket draped over one shoulder.

"Miss Wong, I wonder what you can tell me," he mused out loud, and got up.

The 1950s Tretchikoff print was faded now, the timber frame cracking at the mitered corners. She'd probably hung in this room since the homestead was built, he decided. Miss Wong, as the original painting was called, had graced homes around Australia for fifty years, going in and out of fashion. Currently back in, and worth real money now, even in her tired condition, if Ryan's memory served.

Smiling a little, he went to the painting and eased it away from the wall. Right on the money. The picture concealed a wall safe.

Ryan flexed his fingers. He hadn't done any safecracking in a long time, but this model looked relatively straightforward, probably installed by Clive Horvath, rather than by Max himself.

Sure enough, when Ryan removed Miss Wong and propped

her on the floor against the wall, he faced a thirty-year-old safe finished in dull black enamel. He tut-tutted to himself about homeowners who'd had these tin boxes embedded in their walls decades before and still thought they made a safe place to keep their valuables. This one wouldn't even qualify for an insurance rating.

A crowbar or a good double-handed axe would have hacked through the thing in minutes, but Ryan didn't want to risk attracting attention. A silent drill would be better still, but the battery-powered model he owned was back at his house in Broome, so drilling was out of the question, too. That left plain old ingenuity.

Luckily, Horvath hadn't updated much else in the house after inheriting the place from his father, Ryan noticed, looking around the office. The phone on the desk was the old-fashioned kind, with a cord and a receiver that could be screwed off. The bad guys in old movies would have hidden listening devices inside phones like these, but Ryan had a better use for this one.

He carried it to the wall safe. The cord barely stretched the distance, so he dragged a chair up and set the phone down, then unscrewed the lower end of the receiver, the part you'd normally talk into. Wedging the remaining earpiece on his shoulder, he positioned the unscrewed section against the safe door. Now when he turned the combination lock, he could hear the tumblers fall into place. The only risk was that he might get the numbers in the wrong order, but there were only so many numbers he could go through, and it didn't take him long to find the right sequence.

The metal door clicked open and he was in. Child's play, he thought. In fact he'd discovered the technique as a child, when he'd experimented with his mother's telephone and discovered he could hear conversations through closed doors. He'd never learned anything interesting, but he'd impressed the heck out of a classmate, who'd thought him a genius and had allowed him to practice kissing her as a reward for giving her a turn with the device.

Ignoring a velvet jewel case, he pulled a wad of papers out of the safe and leafed through them, conscious of time passing. He wasn't sure how long Judy would be able to keep Horvath occupied. Not too long, he hoped. He grew angry thinking of her alone with that creep for a minute, far less all night.

Most of the papers in the safe concerned Willundina, and dated back to Clive Horvath's day, Ryan saw. He leafed through birth and death certificates, tax papers, Clive's probated will, only pausing when he got to the mortgage over Diamond Downs. It was only a copy, so tearing it up wouldn't help Des Logan. Not that the old man would countenance such behavior.

A couple of sepia-colored photographs fluttered to the floor and Ryan stooped to pick them up. One showed a middle-aged man standing next to a canoe beside a river. The man resembled Des sufficiently for Ryan to identify him as Jack Logan, probably taken before his last prospecting expedition. The other photo showed Jack in moleskin pants, a white shirt and bush hat. He had his arm around a much younger woman who was wearing a knee-length floral dress with wide shoulders and cinched waist, white gloves and a wide-brimmed straw hat trimmed with flowers. The little boy pressed close to her side wore a white shirt, short pants and long socks, and a cloth cap. They woman and child looked familiar, although Ryan couldn't place them off the top of his head.

Not that he wasted any time on the puzzle. He'd obviously struck pay dirt. Cade had mentioned seeing an old photo of Jack and his canoe in the file after Blake and Jo had come across similar shots planned for a historical display in Perth. They'd hoped to compare their finds, but Horvath's men had gotten to the file first. They'd evidently discarded the file itself and placed the contents in this safe.

Ryan held his breath as he opened the last bundle of papers and almost hollered with delight. The stolen pages from Jack Logan's journal were right here in his hands. Fragile and brown with age, but unmistakable even without the date written in fluid copperplate across the top of each page.

Ryan flicked a look at his watch. He'd have to read the journal entries later. The housekeeper's medical drama would have finished by now, and he didn't know if she was in the habit of doing the rounds of the house before retiring. He spread the journal pages out on the desk and took copies with his miniature camera, then replaced the originals in the safe.

Frowning, he felt his fingers touch a single sheet of paper at the back of the safe. Pulling it out, he saw it was a letter in copperplate handwriting on a solicitor's letterhead. The date was 1946, the year Jack Logan disappeared. Ryan's pulse speeded up as he realized he held some kind of deed, signed by Jack Logan himself and witnessed by the solicitor and a woman, perhaps a secretary.

Suddenly, the writing blurred before Ryan's eyes as a name leaped out at him. A name he knew well. According to this letter, Jack Logan had deeded the whole of Cotton Tree Gorge to this person.

"What the devil is going on?" he asked the faded image of Miss Wong, propped against the wall at his feet, But her inscrutable green-tinged gaze could offer no explanation for this totally unexpected development.

Judy toyed with her pistachio-crusted veal and tried not to sigh too obviously.

Max had brought her to The Blue Moon, a new establishment run by a couple in their twenties who had moved to Halls Creek only a few months before. The Chinese-Australian man cooked a fusion of international dishes while his dusky-skinned wife looked after the diners. The pair were so obviously in love with each other and their new enterprise that Judy subdued a pang of jealousy.

The café was in a former shopfront, obviously fitted out on a shoestring but with such flair that they seemed destined to succeed. Pale blue and lemon paint washed the walls. The floor was polished timber, and the furniture was black tubular metal. Overhead fans swept the air, shivering the leaves of the glossy potted plants that gave each table a suggestion of privacy. Max had chosen a table near the front window, which was festooned with ferns in hanging baskets.

Judy rested her arms on the moon-print tablecloth. "If you're so worried about me, why don't you tear up Dad's mortgage as your father intended to do?"

"My father's intentions are no longer relevant. I run Willundina now," Max said with exaggerated patience. "Frankly, tearing up the contract wouldn't be in your best interests."

Judy's fork clattered onto the plate. "How do you work that out?"

"Your father isn't up to running Diamond Downs any more, and you have enough to do operating your charter service. I know Cade's doing some of the work for the moment," he said before she could contradict. He went on, "Cade's a rolling stone. How long before he takes off again and leaves you to struggle on alone?"

She had no answer. Cade had always wanted to travel the world with his camera. As soon as he was old enough, he'd studied photography with the goal of becoming a professional. He hadn't said why he'd come home this time, and she was grateful enough for his help with Diamond Downs not to pry. She'd assumed he simply needed a change of scene. Whatever the reason, she appreciated his support.

"So you see, handing you the worry of the place would be unfair of me," Max continued.

She pushed her barely touched meal aside. "Look Max,

you should know by now that your white knight routine is wasted on me. Let's cut to the chase here. You're in as much financial trouble as we are."

Her dinner companion looked shocked at her bluntness. "Where did you hear such a thing?"

"Never mind. It's true, isn't it?"

He looked out the window at the darkened street visible through the screen of ferns. "It's true that I was left with considerable debts after Prince Jamal's visit. When I agreed to help reunite him with his fiancée, doing what I thought was a good deed, I never anticipated he'd end up in jail for treason in his own country, leaving me unable to recoup my losses."

The truth was, Max had sided with Jamal Sayed, hoping to be handsomely rewarded. Max hadn't cared that Jamal planned to force Shara Najran into an arranged marriage. The deal would have cost her father his throne, if Shara and Judy's foster brother Tom hadn't uncovered Jamal's evil scheme.

"How you ended up in this jam hardly matters," Judy said bluntly. "As long as a mortgage exists over our land, you're putting my family at risk as well as yourself. You can't tell me that's in my best interests."

Max topped up their wine glasses before answering. "I can't do what you want, Judy."

She scraped her chair back from the table. "Then there's no point continuing this farce."

His lips thinned. "I'd hoped we had more going for us than money."

"Like my great-grandfather's diamonds?" she demanded.

Max looked around uneasily, although only a few of the tables were occupied. "Lower your voice."

"Why should I? The diamonds are the real reason you want possession of Diamond Downs, aren't they?"

"I want them for both of us," he insisted in a fierce undertone. "You know I care about you, Judy. Let me do what's best for you."

She reached for her bag. "In a bizarre way, I think you mean that. What I don't understand is how you think your actions have a snowball's chance of being good for me and mine. I was a fool to try and make you see reason."

He tossed back half a glass of wine and set the glass down with a thump. "Did you really think you could sweet-talk your way around me so easily?"

Judy glared at him. "When we were younger we used to be friends. I'd hoped we could be again. Obviously not."

"We'll be more than friends when your property and the diamonds are mine. You'll have no choice but to turn to me," he warned her.

"I'll never be that desperate." Judy counted out enough cash to cover her share of the meal, and placed it on the table between them. When he stood up, she said, "Stay where you are. I'll call Blake to drive me home. As far as I'm concerned, this evening is over." So was their short-lived romance, but she had a feeling he already knew that.

Max pulled out his wallet and threw down a credit card. "You can walk home for all I care. I'm going back to Willundina to make some plans, then I intend to get seriously drunk."

"Don't do it on my account," she said with a calmness she was far from feeling. The threat in his tone shook her more than she wanted him to see.

Only as she walked out of the café did she consider that Ryan could be snooping through Max's papers at this very moment. If Max went straight home, he could catch Ryan red-handed.

Well, you handled that like a champ, she told herself, struggling to control her shakiness as she fumbled for her phone. More like a chump. Any chance of getting under Max's guard was truly blown. Worse, she had probably ruined Ryan's chance of finding the stolen file.

She called Blake at the crocodile park and explained the problem. He told her to stay where she was until he arrived, then they'd figure something out. As she waited, she hoped Ryan was doing better than she'd done.

Ryan's hand was far from steady as he stared at the letter. "What do you think of this, Miss Wong?" he addressed the print propped beneath the open safe.

The painting's Mona Lisa smile was no help.

"No comment, eh? The proper diplomatic response. No wonder they've let you hang around here for so long," he said to himself. He smiled wanly at his feeble joke, but his insides were churning. How in the name of all that was holy was he going to tell Judy what he'd found? The discovery would destroy her. All her hopes and dreams for her father and Diamond Downs would be finished as soon as she read the letter.

Unless he destroyed the document first.

An old-fashioned brass cigarette lighter in the shape of a cannon stood on the desk. When he flicked it experimentally, a tiny tongue of blue flame shot from the barrel. He held the document close to the barrel. One more flick and his dilemma would be solved. Judy's dreams would be safe.

One flick.

He couldn't make himself burn the letter.

Not now that he knew who the people in the photo with Jack had to be. No wonder they'd looked familiar. The woman was his grandmother, Lizina Smith, and the little boy was Ryan's father, Nick, at about age seven. According to the duly signed and witnessed letter, Jack Logan had deeded a thousand acres of Diamond Downs's land to Lizina Smith "as a gift and token of my love, in anticipation of our forthcoming marriage." According to the letter, the acreage included Cotton Tree Gorge, where Jack's diamond mine was said to be located. On land that belonged not to Judy and her family, but to Ryan and his.

Why hadn't Ryan's mother ever mentioned a connection between his family and the Logans? Obviously, Jack had disappeared before the marriage had taken place, but the deed contained nothing that his death would have affected. Ryan searched his memory. Perhaps because Nick had deserted his mother, she'd seldom spoken of his side of their family and may not have known about the link at all.

As far as Ryan knew, his grandmother had died when a car she'd been driving had been washed off a flooded river crossing in the Kimberley. His father, a child at the time, had managed to escape and been raised by distant relatives. Ryan hadn't known there were cars in his grandmother's day and had researched the era, surprised to learn of the variety of automobiles on the road in the 1940s.

His father had never said where exactly the accident had happened. On Diamond Downs after Lizina received the news of Jack's disappearance? Ryan wondered now. Judging by the photo, Jack had been a generation older than Lizina, so their families may not have approved. Had she been fleeing her grief, their disapproval or a combination of the two?

Speculation would get him nowhere, he decided. First, he had to put everything back and get out of here. He could agonize over details later.

Had he been thinking straight, he wouldn't have wasted this much time. He buttoned the legal letter inside his shirt pocket, gathered up the remaining bits and pieces from the safe and replaced them exactly as he'd found them.

On impulse, he lifted out the original photo of Jack Logan and his grandmother, reluctant to leave it in Horvath's hands now he knew who the subjects were. *Getting sentimental,* Smith, he told himself, as he closed the door and spun the combination lock. A patch of faded paint told him how to reposition Miss Wong. Her half smile seemed to promise discretion.

A last survey of the room revealed nothing else out of place. He adjusted the cannon cigarette lighter a fraction; then, satisfied, he pocketed the photo and his camera, and reached to turn off the desk light.

"Stop right there." The voice from the doorway froze him in mid-movement. He looked up into the barrel of a Remington .308 rifle held in Mick Coghlan's steady grip. Although half a head shorter than Ryan, the stockman had the advantage and the satisfied grin on his freckled face said he knew it. "Leave the light on and step back against the wall. The housekeeper was right when she said she'd heard a rat running around in here. Keep your hands where I can see them unless you want me to use you for target practice."

Chapter 7

Ryan started to back away as instructed, then dived sideways and caught the desk lamp a glancing blow, sweeping it onto the floor in a shower of glass and sparks. The room plunged into blackness.

A shoulder roll took him under the desk and onto Coghlan's side of the room before the other man had drawn a breath.

Obviously not combat trained—unlike Ryan, thanks to a course he'd attended given by an ex-SAS member—Coghlan made the mistake of staying where he was. By being fast and mobile, you increased the enemy's confusion and gave yourself vantage points for attack or defense, Ryan knew. In the blackness, he imagined Mick swiveling the rifle trying to draw a bead on his target.

Ryan didn't give him that chance. He kept moving until he calculated he was within striking distance of the other man. Moving swiftly, he kicked diagonally down, aiming for the side of Mick's knees. The grunt of shock and a thump as the other man was brought down told him he'd found his mark. Then Ryan was deafened as the rifle discharged.

He saw the muzzle flash and felt a rush of air past his head, followed by a sensation like a wasp sting. He cursed volubly under his breath, knowing Mick had gotten lucky. The rifle had fired as he'd gone down. The shot had only creased the side of Ryan's head, but already he felt wetness on his temple.

"I'm sure I winged you, Smith," Coghlan said, his breathing sounding labored. Ryan knew he wasn't the only injured party. "Give this up and I won't have to shoot again."

Answering such a fool challenge would only give Mick something to aim at, so Ryan bit back a retort. This wasn't a movie where the bad guy spelled out his intentions, taking enough time so the hero could win the day. Ryan had made up his mind if he ever found himself in such a position, he'd shoot first and discuss the details later. He hadn't anticipated being unarmed against a high-powered rifle.

Lights snapped on around the compound and voices shouted questions. So far, nobody had worked out that the shot had come from inside the homestead. Before they did, Ryan would have to get out of there or the evidence would speak for itself. And he didn't plan on spending a night in jail while he sorted this out.

Although his injury was minor, pain started to affect Ryan's consciousness, making him feel shaky. The other man would pay for that, but not tonight. Forcing himself to think, Ryan called up a memory of the room's layout. Then he had it. Moving silently, he came up against the leg of the desk. Above his head should be the cannon cigarette lighter. If he hadn't knocked it off the desk with the lamp.

He heard Mick moving slowly toward the door and the light switch. Grunts of pain suggested that Ryan's kick to the knees had done damage. Good. He'd hate to be the only one suffering. His groping hand closed around a heavy metal object and he grinned into the darkness. Hefting the lighter, he bowled it into the opposite corner of the room.

The crash of impact brought an instant response. The rifle fired again. This time Ryan was prepared. Using the muzzle flash to orient himself, he headed for the French doors, feeling through the drapes that the doors were still unlocked.

He rolled under the drapes and was on his feet and through the doors before the changing air current in the room told Coghlan that Ryan had escaped.

One of Horvath's men almost ran into him. "What's happening?"

Glad of the pale light concealing his injury, Ryan gestured back toward the homestead. "Mick's bailed up an intruder. He needs help."

As he'd hoped, the other man didn't stop to question why Ryan was fleeing the scene, but headed toward the house, calling to his mates as he ran. Some people didn't have the brains they were born with, Ryan thought. He melted into the shadows and groped for a handkerchief, pressing it against his throbbing temple. Feeling as if he'd touched a naked flame to his head, he bit back an oath. He'd only been grazed, and with any luck the heat from the bullet had mostly cauterized the wound, but he was going to have the granddaddy of a headache for a few days to come.

All things considered, he'd gotten off lightly, he decided. Now all he had to do was get out of here. His days as Max's right-hand man were over, but he'd achieved his aim so he wasn't about to shed any tears of regret.

Earlier in the evening, he'd left his car parked facing the main gate in case he needed a fast getaway. As he headed for it, he saw headlights sweep the driveway coming from the opposite direction, luckily without pinpointing him in their glare. He recognized the car pulling up outside the house. What the devil was Max doing back so soon?

Concern that the stakes had just been raised warred with jubilation that Judy was no longer enjoying Max's company. What was going on? Lights were springing on all around the house and Ryan imagined Coghlan giving Max a full report. Ryan swore. In a few minutes, they'd be swarming out here on his tail.

They hadn't thought of his car yet. He could see it parked where he'd left it under a tree. But before he could reach it, a pair of shapes loomed out of the darkness. His heartbeat trebled. Shock and blood loss were making him shaky. He had hoped to get away without encountering any more resistance. He pulled himself up. He could still fight if he had to.

He braced himself as the taller figure came closer. "Rye, is that you?"

The lowered voice was so unexpected that Ryan faltered. "Blake? What in the devil…"

A hearty thump on his back almost knocked him off his feet. "Not the devil, the cavalry, come to save your hide. Just in time, from the looks of things."

"Speaking of time, we should get out of here," came another low voice.

Ryan swung toward the source, his heart doing an involuntary leap. "Judy? What the hell are you doing here? Your date just came home without you."

"I didn't give him much choice, although I didn't mean to make things difficult for you."

"Let's discuss all this back at the ranch," Blake insisted. "Got your car keys, mate?"

"Yes, and my gear's in the back in case I got caught in the act." Ryan hesitated, knowing how Judy was likely to react. "The problem is, I'm not in shape to drive."

She didn't disappoint him. "You're injured? Let me see. Oh my Lord, you've been shot."

He brushed away her hand, although everything in him

wanted to let her touch him and keep on touching. And not in any medical way. This wasn't the time. "Only grazed, nothing serious. Probably looks worse than it is."

"Since I can't see how bad it looks, I'll assume the worst," she said in a taut voice. "You ride with Blake. His car's right behind yours."

He heard Blake move away. "You're going to drive mine?" Ryan asked Judy.

"No, I'm going to tow it to a hill and push it home." Her sarcasm didn't disguise the worry he heard in her tone. "What do you think?"

"I think you're amazing," he said and grabbed her. His night vision had improved to the point where the kiss landed on her open mouth. He heard her gasp in shock. "Purely medicinal," he said before she could react.

He heard her mutter an obscenity as she turned and headed for his car. Only she could make rude words sound so poetic, he decided, following Blake and holding the handkerchief to his temple.

The quiet getaway he'd planned was already shot to pieces, so there was no point trying to roll the cars without starting the engines. However they left the lights off so they were in shadow in contrast to the pools of light around the homestead. By the time Max and his people realized their quarry was getting away, Blake was speeding through the open homestead gates with Judy close behind.

"Eat our dust," Blake said with satisfaction as they accelerated away. With several back roads they could take, Max couldn't have them followed in the dark. They also had another ace in the hole—Max didn't yet know of the connection between Ryan Smith and the Logans. He had no reason to suspect that Ryan would head for Diamond Downs.

"How do you feel, mate?" Blake asked when they were far enough away to use the car's headlights.

Like he'd been kicked in the head by a buffalo. Out loud, he said, "I'll live."

"No doubt, but will the guy who shot at you?"

"Mick Coghlan is a dead man," Ryan snarled.

Blake's eyebrows arched upward. "Tell me you don't mean that literally."

For the first time in hours, Ryan felt his mouth relax into a smile. Blake had an uncanny ability to put him at ease, probably why he was so good at dealing with the public at his crocodile farm. "Despite the temptation, I didn't kill him," he said. "He got off a lucky shot, that's all."

"If he's still standing, he's luckier than he knows," Blake observed. "Pity we can't tell the cops about this."

"Not without explaining what I was up to," Ryan said. "Nothing would make me happier than seeing that bastard, Coghlan, put away. He's been itching for a chance to take me on since Horvath anointed me his favorite son."

"Then Coghlan should be pleased you disinherited yourself tonight. From the look of you, he nearly finished your relationship with Horvath permanently." As a cattle grid loomed out of the night he slowed, signaling to Judy that he was heading onto their land, then continued, "On the way here, Judy told me you were looking for the file of old family papers. Did you have any luck finding it?"

Ryan hesitated. He'd found more than he'd bargained for. "I'll explain everything back at Diamond Downs," he compromised.

Blake nodded. "Makes sense. Then you don't have to go over everything twice."

Given a choice, Ryan would rather not go over the story at all. He wondered if he could make more of his injury than was warranted to avoid telling them everything, then just as quickly dismissed the idea. First, Judy would have him at the hospital so fast his feet wouldn't touch the ground. Then she'd still want to know what he'd found. He closed his eyes, trying to shut out the pain from his temple while he considered what in blazes he was going to tell her.

By the time they reached Diamond Downs, he still had no answer. He bought himself some time while she fussed over the graze. As he'd told her, it was slight but he cursed volubly as she applied antiseptic to the wound. "I thought women were supposed to have a gentle touch."

"And men are supposed to be strong and stoic, not carry on like babies," she scolded.

But he hadn't missed the panicky look in her eyes when she'd checked him over in the light as soon as they got inside. The blood crusting the side of his face hadn't helped, but even when she'd cleaned that off, she wasn't much happier. "This ought to be treated by a doctor."

He caught her hand and pressed her palm to his lips. "I'll settle for my favorite paramedic."

She pulled her hand free. "Be sensible."

"How can I be sensible? I'm injured, probably delirious."

She frowned. "Delusional, most likely. You were in that state before Coghlan shot at you."

Was it delusional to feel as if her touch sent a thousand volts of electricity through him? Probably, he concluded. He felt stupid enough to be glad he had an excuse to have her minister to him. How crazy could a man be?

As soon as they reached the homestead, Blake had called the crocodile park to assure Cade and Des that everything was all right. At Ryan's request, he'd omitted to mention Ryan's misadventure. No sense worrying the older man unduly.

"How is Des?" Ryan asked to take his mind off Judy's touch.

Blake answered. "He's fine. Cade was having dinner with us and volunteered to stay behind, so we didn't have to leave Des on his own."

Another tendril of guilt receded. Ryan didn't like admitting even to himself how concerned he'd been about being responsible for a sick man being left alone.

"He wouldn't have been on his own in any event. His lady friend was visiting," Judy added for Ryan's benefit.

This was news. Ryan raised an eyebrow, wincing as the gesture sent a bright stab of pain through his temple. "Who is this lady friend?"

"Her name's Tracey Blair," Blake supplied.

"Why is that name familiar."

"She's a friend of Judy's. Heather Wilton brought a group of children down from Citronne Station to stay with her. Evidently, Tracey was the kids' teacher when she lived up that way," Blake said.

"Hold still, will you," Judy complained. "Tracey's a missionary. We met when she was teaching near Lake Argyle, where Heather got to know her. She moved to Halls Creek a couple of months ago for health reasons and has opened a shop selling her own hand-printed dress designs."

"A missionary dress designer? Not your usual idea of a straightlaced missionary then," Ryan mused.

Blake laughed. "Tracey's about as far from being a straightlaced missionary as you can get. She's passionate about ancient rock art as well."

Ryan tried not to flinch as Judy applied an adhesive dressing to his temple. That would be coming off as soon as her back was turned. For now, it was easier to humor her, especially as he was starting to feel decidedly unsteady. "Has Shara met Tracey? They should get along well, since they're both into that stuff."

"Like a house on fire," Blake agreed. "Tracey supplied Shara with some of her designs after Jamal shanghaied her to Australia in only the clothes she stood up in. She's a terrific woman."

"Shara or Tracey?"

Blake laughed. "Take your pick. If Tracey wasn't closer to Des's age, I could fancy her myself."

An image of Blake's beautiful fiancée, Jo Francis, sprang into Ryan's mind. "Jo might have something to say about that," he joked.

"Too late, mate, they've already bonded. Cade, Des and I could hardly get a word in edgewise during dinner. Having six kids in tow may have had a bit to do with it."

Ryan watched Judy replace her potions in the station's well-equipped medical kit. "Six, huh?"

"Seven if you count her son, Daniel," Judy put in. "I suggested they talk to you about a guided tour of the crocodile park while they're in town."

"You also gave Tracey a good excuse to call on Des," Blake said.

Judy frowned. "You're imagining things."

Blake winked at Ryan. "Your dad might have a bad heart, but everything else still works, as he's fond of reminding us. With everything Des has had to deal with lately, Tracey might be just the tonic he needs."

Judy's face was a study, as if she didn't want to accept that her father might feel more than friendship for the older woman. Ryan sympathized, knowing it was a lot to deal with. Des hadn't been involved in a relationship since Fran's death, as far as Ryan was aware. After his own father left them, his mother had dated a few times and Ryan remembered being angry at what he thought was her disloyalty to his father. He understood better now, but sometimes wondered if his mother had remained single because of his reaction. As an adult, he hoped Judy would be more understanding of Des's needs.

Judy closed her kit with a snap and Blake stood up. "What's the medical advice on giving your patient a beer?"

"Contraindicated, but if you must, make it low-alcohol," she prescribed.

Ryan nodded and wished he hadn't when shooting stars fringed his vision. "I'll need something to wash down the pain meds."

Judy made a face. "I thought you tough guys didn't need them. Don't you bite on a bullet or something?"

"Precautionary," he said and held out his hand.

With an expression that said plainly *Men!,* she dropped the aspirin he'd seen her shake out of a bottle into his palm. He swallowed the tablets dry before Blake put a can of beer into his hand. Low-alcohol, as prescribed. Well, it was better than nothing. He cracked the top and drank deeply. "Nectar," he said when he lowered the can.

"You do know it's after midnight?" Judy observed.

He shrugged. "Sun's always over the yardarm somewhere in the world."

She disposed of the debris of surgical spirit and absorbent cotton, and came back with a beer for herself. "In that case, you're not too tired to tell us what you found in your raid on Max's house."

Hoist with his own petard, he toyed with the beer can, his mind working overtime. Could he pretend that the deed didn't exist? By now, Horvath would know he had the document and might spill the beans to Judy out of pure malice. She wasn't going to take the news well, whoever it came from. Ryan decided he'd rather be the one to tell her.

So he did.

When he'd finished, she held out her hand. With no expression in her voice she said, "Can I see the letter, please?"

He fumbled unbuttoning his shirt pocket. The thumping in his head was receding with the medication, but his hands were still a touch unsteady. The photo and document he pulled out were creased but otherwise none the worse for his experience. He handed them over. "Copies of the journal pages and the other photo of Jack are in my camera," he said. "We can go over them in the morning."

She read the legal letter without comment, before passing the page to Blake who did the same. Then she fixed her gaze on the photo of Jack Logan and Lizina Smith and her child. Ryan wished the floor would swallow him up. He would have done almost anything rather than be the cause of the troubled look on her face.

Finally, she looked at him. Her eyes were misty but her tone sounded firm. "It seems we've been fighting Max Horvath for control of a piece of land we haven't owned for over sixty years."

Blake inclined his head in agreement. He also looked troubled. "Seems that way."

"A bit of paper doesn't change anything. My grandmother never married your great-grandfather," Ryan insisted. "Hell, I never knew they had anything to do with each other."

Judy smiled wanly. "I had heard tales of another woman in my great-grandfather's life but the details were glossed over, and Smith is a common name. I never thought of connecting Lizina with you. According to the little I know, Great-grandma Adelaide died from snakebite in 1940 and Jack brought Lizina to Diamond Downs around 1946. Must have been a real love match because they had to run the gauntlet of family disapproval. The few times my grandparents mentioned her, she was referred to as *that foreign woman*, as if she'd led my great-grandfather astray."

Ryan gestured at the photo lying between them on the table. "She looks to be about half his age."

Blake raised his beer can. "Way to go, Jack."

Judy frowned at him. "The age difference was scandalous enough, and she was unmarried with a child by an unknown father when they met, shocking for the time."

"Way to go, Lizina," Ryan echoed softly. He was beginning to like the grandmother he'd never known, although he wished the discovery hadn't brought such a bleak look to Judy's face. "I wonder why they didn't marry."

"He disappeared before they could do the deed," Blake suggested.

Judy smoothed out the yellowed letter. "He must have known the family would send her on her way if he wasn't around, and gave her the land so she'd be protected in case anything happened to him. Maybe he had a premonition."

Ryan finished his beer. He felt deathly tired and ached all over from his run-in with Coghlan. "We'll never know for sure."

She gestured toward the letter. "What do you want to do about this?"

He hadn't realized he'd reached a decision until he said, "Not a damned thing."

"You can't do nothing. In the absence of any other claimants from your family, you own Cotton Tree Gorge."

"And quite possibly a fortune in diamonds," Blake added quietly. "You can't pretend nothing's changed."

"I can see a lawyer and arrange to give the land back to you and Des," Ryan told Judy. "I never wanted your land, and I'm doing fine without the diamonds."

"You think Des will accept such a gift?"

Ryan stood up, gripping the edge of the table when his legs felt like jelly. "Des'll have no problem with it because neither of you are going to tell him what I found. We'll show him my photos of the journal pages and forget all about the letter."

"You're overlooking Max," she pointed out. "After tonight, he's going to do everything in his power to get his hands on the diamonds. Now he knows you have the deed, you'll be his prime target."

Ryan touched the bandage at his temple. "I became his target when I broke into his office. Before, he just wanted the diamonds. Now, it's personal between us."

* * *

Ryan hadn't said which of them would make it personal, Judy noticed. She had a feeling Ryan would make revenge as much a priority as Max would. The two were like gunslingers in the American Old West. The Kimberley wasn't big enough for both of them. Had the situation not been so serious, she might have smiled at the situation. Some women thought having men fight over them was romantic. Judy found the prospect alarming and knew it was because she didn't want Ryan getting hurt.

Her paramedic training had been useful tonight, but what if the injury had been more serious? She wasn't equipped to deal with bullet wounds. The thought of him lying in a pool of blood made her feel light-headed until she reminded herself he was here now, safe and well.

"It's late. We aren't going to settle this now. How about we sleep on it and talk some more tomorrow?" she suggested.

"Spoken like a true procrastinator," Ryan said, but his smile signaled agreement.

Blake nodded, too. "Good idea. Cade said he's happy to stay at the park overnight and help Jo keep an eye on Des, so I'll bunk down here and head back to relieve them first thing in the morning." He crushed his beer can and took it into the kitchen, then bid them goodnight and left them alone.

After tonight's adventure, Judy knew she wouldn't get much sleep even if she did go to bed. "I'm going to stay up for a while."

"Not sleepy?"

"Too keyed up."

Ryan sat down again. "Then I'll keep you company."

Her gaze went to the dressing gleaming whitely against his tanned skin. "There's no need. You should rest."

"Nah. Now the tablets have kicked in, I'm fine."

She eyed him dubiously. "Are you sure?"

"Ask me no questions, I'll tell you no lies," he recited.

"Then I won't ask. But you must promise to let me know if the pain gets worse or there's any sign of infection."

"Yes, Nurse Judy."

She swatted at his hand on the table. "A gunshot wound isn't funny."

He caught her fingers and twined them with his. "No news to me. I have the headache to prove it. But you are."

Her fingers tensed in his. "I don't like being considered funny."

"Not funny ha-ha, funny cute."

She drew herself up, unable to move away because of his grip on her hand. "The last man who called me cute is now a permanent member of a boys' choir."

"Ouch. You wouldn't take advantage of an injured man?"

"I was taught to fight by experts—you and the other boys. I'll use every advantage I can get."

"Spoken like a Logan," he said with a grin, then sobered. "What happened between you and Max on your date tonight?"

Since he still gripped her hand, she picked up the beer can with her other hand and drank before answering. "I let him rub me up the wrong way and ended up walking out in the middle of dinner. I blew it and you got hurt as a result. I'm sorry."

Not wanting to give away how delighted he was by her response, he said, "If anyone's to blame, it's me. Horvath's housekeeper heard me moving around, and called Coghlan. He got in a lucky shot. Max coming home early made no difference, although I assume you and Blake rushed over there to warn me. If you hadn't turned up when you did, I would have been in far worse straits. I don't think I could have driven home as I was."

She lowered her lashes and her fingers tightened around his. "Thanks."

"For what?" Absently he stroked the base of her thumb with his own, eliciting an indrawn breath.

She looked down at their joined hands but didn't pull away. "Letting me off the hook. I was furious with myself for letting Max needle me. He had the nerve to tell me I'd have no choice but to turn to him after he got his hands on the diamonds."

Ryan hadn't enjoyed himself so much in a long time. Had he been in the café, he'd have cheered. Right before he flattened Horvath on her behalf. "You'll never be that desperate," he assured her.

"I told him the same thing before I walked out. I was standing in the street before it dawned on me that my grandstanding had put you and our plan in jeopardy. When I realized you'd been shot..."

Her voice wobbled and he saw she was near to tears. She hadn't cried over losing ownership of Cotton Tree Gorge, despite everything the land meant to her and her father. But she was close to shedding tears over Ryan being hurt. He felt a huge lump rise in his throat. She might say otherwise but the proof of her caring was right here in front of him. He felt as if he'd been given the most valuable gift in the world.

Acting on instinct he stood, drawing her up with him by the fingers still twined in his. He tightened his grip and pulled her in closer. Her other palm came up against his chest and for a panicky moment, he thought she might push him away. But he hadn't misread her feelings. She let her hand trail down his body and slide into the small of his back, then she subsided against him with the smallest exhalation.

"I'm glad you're okay," she said in the same tremulous voice.

He kissed the top of her head. She'd never guess how okay he felt now that she was in his arms. When she lifted her head, he trailed his lips across her forehead, kissing each eyelid in turn in homage to the tears he'd seen gathered there. One droplet slid down her cheek now and he kissed it away. She tried to turn her head so he wouldn't see, but he found her mouth and stole her breath with a kiss so deep he felt as if he were drowning in her.

Everything receded in the poetry of the moment. When she opened them, her eyes shone like diamonds and he could feel her pulse racing under his fingers. The taste of her lingered on his mouth, making him hungry. After being shot, he'd felt light-headed and he did so again now, but this was pleasant, like floating. His feet felt as if they were no longer touching the floor.

She gave a shaky laugh, almost but not quite breaking the spell. "You must think I'm such a fool."

"For crying on my account? Have you any idea what that does to a man?"

Still she refused to see it his way. "I'm not normally such a—a girl."

He fluffed her hair with his free hand and lowered his voice to a murmur. "From where I stand, that's no bad thing."

"Then how come it doesn't feel good?"

"Obviously my technique needs more work."

Confusion marred her lovely features until she caught up with his logic. "I didn't mean your kiss. I meant caring so much, these blasted tears. Damn it, Ryan, you know what I meant."

He shook his head. "When the lady in my arms tells me my kiss doesn't make her feel good, honor requires that I make amends."

This time, she didn't argue. "What are you going to do?"

"What would you like?"

"We could try kissing again, to practice your technique, I mean."

Reflecting her serious look, he subdued the urge to smile. "So this is strictly for my benefit, right?"

"Right."

Her less-than-assured response made primitive needs claw at him. Breathing became difficult as the smell of her hair filled his nostrils and the curl of her lithe body against him brought dreams of discovering the wonders of her in hot, urgent togetherness. She might prefer not to need him, but it was there in the fast beating of her heart, the flutter of the pulse at her throat and the innocent way she lifted her face to him.

Spellbound, he lowered his mouth and took hers again, slowly, possessively, fighting the urge to plunder as he filled himself with the heady taste and feel of her. Her lips, were parted slightly and he probed gently. She responded by shaping her mouth to his, her tongue skimming his lips then meeting his, heating his blood to boiling point

He whispered in her ear, "Do you know how much I want to make love to you?"

Chapter 8

Judy hadn't known she could feel so needy. Even as her rational self tried to reject the feeling, her deeper yearnings refused to be denied. Not tonight, when she could so easily have lost Ryan. Another inch deeper, a slightly different trajectory and she wouldn't have the chance to lose herself in his arms ever again.

As his hands cupped her body, sculpting her against him, she decided that for once in her life she wouldn't rationalize, only feel. The longings were alarming enough to make her want to retreat into logic, but she held on to him, her anchor in terrifyingly deep waters.

Feeling herself sinking, she didn't know what answer to give him; the one her head told her was safe, or the one her heart dictated.

He solved the dilemma by answering his own question. "But not yet. The time isn't right."

Judy felt Ryan's rejection almost as a physical blow. She

knew he was right, but that didn't satisfy the hunger holding her in a relentless grip.

Her fingers lightly skimmed his temple near the dressing. "Because of this?"

"Partly. I don't want us to make love out of sympathy or reaction."

Both of those would be factors tonight, she knew. "Are you in pain?"

"Oh, yes."

She started to pull away. "I can get you more tablets."

His smile teased her as he held her in place. "As far as I know, pain meds wouldn't fix what ails me right now."

The pressure of his erection against her told its own story, and she felt the blush race up her face. Then she understood. Giving in now would be the easy thing to do.

He pushed her hair away from her face, the gesture starting her pulse thundering again. "When we make love, I want it to be for all the right reasons."

"You're right." If only intellectual knowledge were accompanied by physical compliance, she'd be fine, she told herself.

Gently, he untangled her and stepped back. "Soon."

"When?"

"When all this is sorted out."

Her breath caught. "What if it never is? Or if everything turns out wrong?"

"Not everything. We'll still have each other."

"You'd want me even without..." She couldn't bring herself to say more.

His features darkened. "I don't want you because of Diamond Downs any more than you want me because of the deed to Cotton Tree Gorge."

The denial was instant. "Oh, no. You must never think that."

"I don't. What's between us has nothing to do with land or

diamonds. It never did have." He let her go and began to pace. "To me, you were never the boss's daughter. You were the girl who made my arrival here bearable, like a promise that however badly I was hurting from being hauled through the welfare system like a piece of flotsam, my life would get better."

"You got all that from your first sight of me?" She wasn't sure she wanted so much responsibility.

"You must remember the way I looked at you?"

She nodded. "As if I was the eighth wonder of the world."

"To me, you still are. When I was fourteen, you were a lifeline. Still are."

She'd known the attraction existed, of course. But she'd never imagined he could feel so strongly toward her. Elated and a little awed by the role she'd played in her life, she pulled in a steadying breath. "Was it so bad for you back then, being forced to come here?"

She'd always believed Ryan hadn't known what was best for himself when he arrived, seeing her father as his rescuer. Now she wondered if he hadn't been better off by himself, as he'd always maintained.

"When the welfare people decided I couldn't keep living on my own, I felt insulted. I'd been doing fine, as I saw it. I didn't see the house falling apart for lack of maintenance, or my own health failing through poor nutrition. And I was scared stiff."

She thought back to the tough kid who'd acted as if he'd owned the world. "You were scared? I don't believe it."

He glanced away, then back. "Believe it. My father had left us, never to return. Then my mother had died. How could I risk getting attached to a new family when you might all disappear without warning, too?"

She'd never seen the situation through his eyes before. "So you built a wall around yourself as protection."

He nodded. "And left before I could get too attached to you

all. Or so I thought. One member of the family had gotten under my skin so completely, she never left."

For something to do, she picked up the empty beer cans and took them to the kitchen. At the door, she paused. "After you left, I never stopped wondering where you were and how you were doing. One of the reasons I loved doing the charter work was because there was a chance I'd find you again. Something told me I would."

"The same something that had me picking up the phone to call Diamond Downs practically every week."

She put the cans down in the kitchen and came back to him. This was news to her. What a difference a call would have made to her peace of mind. "Why didn't you call?"

He spread his hands wide. "What could I have said? Des, I can't come back and live with you because I'm smitten with your daughter, and nothing on Earth is going to make me settle for being a brother to her."

In spite of her tension, she chuckled. "I can see how Dad might have had a problem with that."

"I wanted to come back in my own way and time." He gave a self-deprecating smile. "I guess I dreamed of riding in on a white charger, the conquering hero returning."

"The battered jalopy wasn't what you had in mind?"

"Leave my jalopy out of this."

His comment defused some of the tension. "I'll have you know, the conquering hero of my fantasies drives a Branxton."

"You have expensive tastes."

"Not really. Your jalopy didn't let us down tonight. I got the feeling it could have gone much faster if Blake hadn't been setting the pace."

"Zero to one eighty in nine seconds," he said, pride in his tone, then grinned sheepishly. "When I built the car, I installed a Branxton engine."

She clutched a hand to her chest. "You built that thing? Be still my heart."

"Now I see the way to your heart," he said. "All I had to do was build a bigger and better engine."

Her shoulders lifted. "What can I say? Some women are turned on by sparkly things. With me, it's torque."

"As long as it's not all torque and no action," he said.

They'd come full circle to the attraction this conversation had strived to avoid. Maybe they would always return to this point.

"It's almost dawn. We should go to bed. To sleep," she said pointedly.

"For the moment." His tone was equally loaded with meaning.

"Or we could make love and get it out of our system," she suggested, aware of her heart gathering speed at the very idea.

He shook his head. "When we make love it will be a beginning, not an ending. And we will make love," he promised, as if reading her thoughts. Then he added, "Once upon a time, I thought that running away was the only solution to my problems."

Tension bristled through her. "Are you saying that's what I'm doing now?"

"Only you know the answer. I do know you're running scared about something. I hope it isn't me."

"No," she said without hesitation.

"Then it's something inside yourself. When you turn and confront it, you'll learn, as I did, that the monsters inside us are never as powerful as we make them."

"You make life sound simple."

"Mostly it is. People make everything complicated. Now go to bed. We've been through a lot tonight. You can safely postpone any life-changing decisions until you've had a few hours sleep." He rubbed his chin between thumb and forefinger. "We'll need our wits about us after this. We've both managed to pi—to aggravate Horvath tonight. He won't take that lying down."

Even without worrying about Max, Ryan was right, she knew. So she stood on tiptoe and kissed his cheek, telling herself she was content to leave things as they were for now. Knowing she was being less than honest with herself. "Good night, Ryan. Sleep well."

She hadn't expected to sleep and when she did, she was disturbed by dreams of faceless enemies shooting at Ryan and watching him fall. When she turned and tried to confront the enemy as he'd advised, the shadowy figure wore her own face.

As a result, she awoke feeling less rested than before she went to bed. When she came into the kitchen in long pajama pants and a sleeveless T-shirt top, he was already dressed in a khaki shirt and jeans and his R.M. Williams boots. The white dressing at his temple was brown-stained as if the injury had bled during the night.

She knew better than to fuss, and helped herself to coffee, shuddering when he offered her some luridly colored cereal. "How can you eat that stuff?"

"Contains all the five food groups—sugar, sugar, sugar, calcium and grain," he informed her. "Energy to burn. You look like you could use the boost."

"Thanks," she said sourly. "Toast and Vegemite will do for me."

He sat at the table and poured milk over the cereal, watching as she made toast and poured fresh juice into a glass. "Bad night?"

"Too short." She joined him at the table. "How's your head?"

"Next question?"

"That bad, huh?" She took a sip of juice. "I'd feel happier if you saw a doctor."

He shook his head and winced, then quickly covered it up with a grin. "No need, it's just a graze. I have other things to do today."

She spread the toast with a thick layer of black, yeasty spread. Foreign visitors to Diamond Downs usually shuddered at the sight, but she'd been eating Vegemite since she was two years old. When she bit into the toast, the familiar sharp taste comforted her now. "You should rest."

"Plenty of time for that when I'm dead."

She leaned across the table. "Ryan, you nearly were last night."

He concentrated on his cereal, but not before she saw pain shadow his features. He wasn't as fighting fit as he wanted her to think. She could imagine the size of the headache he must have, and winced in sympathy.

"Nearly doesn't count. I want to get up to Cotton Tree Gorge and explore Jo's hidden valley," he said.

"Your hidden valley now," Judy reminded him.

"Yes, well, that's moot."

"Not according to the deed you found."

"Right now, the ownership isn't important. What matters is finding that mine before Horvath does. After last night, he won't wait around while I put my feet up."

"Don't you see? Your ownership of the mine changes everything. Even if Max or his creditors foreclose on our land, he won't get what he's after now. You're not in debt to him. You could actually save us from him."

He'd thought of that, too, she saw from his quick nod of agreement. "Will finding the mine mean anything to you if you lose Diamond Downs?"

She looked down at her plate, letting her silence answer.

"I didn't think so." Finishing his cereal, he stood up and carried the bowl to the dishwasher. Without turning, he said, "I'd rather not have Horvath as my nearest neighbor, either.

This has been Logan land for generations. I intend to make sure it stays that way."

"But not today," she insisted. "You're in no shape to go exploring."

He dropped a kiss on the top of her head. "Yes, Nurse."

Her heart gave a lurch. "If you're admitting it..."

"I'm admitting nothing. Not even giving in. Have you seen the clouds out there? We're in for a doozy of a rainstorm."

She said a small prayer of thanks for inclement weather. "The wet season is fast approaching, in case you hadn't noticed."

"I'd noticed. I've been hoping the serious rains hold off just a little longer."

"Nothing we can do about it either way," she said with the outback person's stoicism when it came to the weather. Drought or flood, you accepted what came without complaint.

"Has Blake already gone home?" she asked now.

Ryan nodded. "He left at first light to beat the rain and get back to his crocodiles. He knew you would understand."

She cupped her hands around her coffee mug. "I do. Lately, he's given more time to Diamond Downs than we have a right to ask. You all have."

"No more than this place has given to us."

"To us all, me included." As she drank her coffee, she wondered if a sense of obligation was behind Ryan's single-minded drive to find the mine. He'd denied owing her father anything for changing the course of his life, but even Ryan had admitted he couldn't have gone on as he was. He might not have welcomed Des's intervention, but if it hadn't been her father, someone else would have stepped in.

She thought of her older foster brother Blake's experience. Abandoned as a new baby, he'd gone through a string of unloving homes before arriving at Diamond Downs with a huge chip on his shoulder. Judy's parents had gradually whittled the chip down to a splinter. More recently, Jo Francis's love had completed the process.

Tom's chip had been bigger still. Coming from a violent home, he'd seen his father kill his mother, breaking his son's arm in the process. As an adult, Tom had avoided relationships, fearing he'd inherited his father's violent streak. Meeting and falling in love with Shara Najran had finally shown him that blood didn't have to will out.

Cade's motivation was still a mystery to her. He was devoted to the family, she knew. He'd kept in touch while traveling the world with his camera. But he didn't readily share his feelings. Not surprising, since he'd been a street kid before her parents took him in, living rough in ways Judy hated to imagine. As an adult, he'd had adventures, traveling across Australia by camel train, for instance. But Cade was still an open book compared to Ryan.

There was so much she didn't know about him—what drove him, what he was passionate about. Yet last night, she'd been prepared to make love with him. Was she glad or relieved that he'd been the strong one? She wished she knew.

She carried her breakfast things to the dishwasher. Ryan took them out of her hands and placed them in the machine. The briefest meeting of hands was enough to set her heart fluttering. "We should take a look at your photos of my great-grandfather's journal," she said to cover the moment. Keeping Ryan occupied was the one sure way to get him to rest, and she was anxious to read the pages.

He nodded. "There's another photo of Jack in the camera as well. I didn't have time to examine in closely, so I'm hoping something in the photo might suggest more clues to the mine's location."

She glanced at the chaotic state of the room. Since Des's illness, she never seemed to be up-to-date with anything any more. This was one thing she could do. "Let's go to the office. If you hook your camera up to the computer, we can both see what you've got."

He was working at the computer while she studied a print-out of the journal pages, when she heard the rain start. What began as a patter of droplets on the iron roof soon became a thunderous roar as the rain sheeted down. Beyond the window, she could see the leaves of plants bounce and recoil from the impact.

"According to the forecast, this won't last beyond the morning," Ryan informed her, lifting his voice over the noise.

Even so, the downpour was the heaviest they'd seen so far this season, a foretaste of the monsoon rains that would soon set in every day until mid-March next year. Already, the red landscape was looking greener, for the early rains that had fallen after months of aridity.

Judy was surprised to hear the sound of a car engine cutting through the steady thrumming of the rain. "Expecting someone?" The questioning glance she gave Ryan earned a shake of his head.

"Could it be Horvath?" she asked, her pulse jumping.

He stood up and went to the door. "He didn't see you or Blake in the dark last night, so I don't think he'll have connected me to you as yet. Only one way we'll find out."

If Horvath had been up to no good, he was hardly likely to drive boldly up to their front door, she reminded herself. She stood at Ryan's shoulder as a mud-streaked minivan pulled up. "It's Tracey Blair."

"She should be driving a more suitable vehicle for these conditions," he said with a frown.

"The rain probably hadn't started when she set off from Halls Creek." Tracey was lucky not to have become bogged down. Sudden heavy downpours like this morning's rain could quickly make the roads muddy and impassable.

She stepped out into the rain to hug her friend and introduce Tracey to Ryan. From his expression, Judy could see that Tracey had surprised him, but then he'd probably pictured the missionary as a starch-collared, iron-haired martinet. Many people did, and were taken aback to meet the small, round woman with short, curly brown hair peppered with white. Laugh lines radiated from eyes as green as a shady creek, giving the impression of someone in love with life.

Now Tracey stepped onto the veranda and shook raindrops off her hair. "I'm sorry to land on you like this. We were on a picnic and by the time the rain set in, we were closer to you than town, so it seemed safer to come here."

"You're welcome," Judy said, "But who is we?"

Tracey opened the van's side door and Judy's jaw dropped as six brown-skinned children between the ages of six and eight tumbled out of the van. They had the bright-eyed, long-limbed look of children who spent long hours out-of-doors. Seeing Judy and Ryan, they hung back, waiting for Tracey to take the lead.

"Come on team, let's get out of this rain," Tracey ordered, gesturing toward the sheltering veranda. The children surged up the wooden steps and two of them immediately jumped onto a rocking chair, making it rock furiously and laughing in delight.

"These are some of my former pupils from Lake Argyle," Tracey explained. "I'm showing them around this area."

Judy nodded. "We met Heather Wilton when she was at the hospital with her son, Daniel. She told us what a nice thing you're doing for the kids. I suggested getting in touch with Blake to arrange a tour of the crocodile farm."

"If they don't quiet down, we'll make it sooner rather than later, say at feeding time," Tracey reproved, a smile taking any sting out of her threat.

"Heather used to help out at the school where I taught before I moved down here," she went on. "She had to take Daniel to the hospital for a checkup this morning so I decided to take the kids on a picnic, not realizing the rain would mean she couldn't follow us as we'd planned. That's Mike and Essie destroying your chair. This is Matilda, her brother John and their cousin, Lockie. What happened to Sunny? He was here a second ago."

Judy looked around. The smallest child, Sunny, had spotted Ryan. Immediately his eyes lit up and his smile broadened. He flung himself at the tall man, wrapping his arms around Ryan's long legs. "Ryan!"

For a second, Judy felt her world tilt on its axis until common sense came to her aid. The tall man and the dusky outback child were a study in contrasts. Her heart twisted as she watched him swing the little boy high into the air. He looked to be around six years old with huge dark eyes, stick-thin limbs, and hands and feet that looked as if he were still growing into them.

"Look what the cat dragged in," Ryan said as the child laughed delightedly.

From his high vantage point, the little boy giggled. "I came with Miss Tracey. She doesn't have a cat."

"Funny, I could swear I heard a cat just seconds before you arrived."

"There's no cat. You're silly," the child reproved.

Set on his feet, the child planted himself at Ryan's side, the small brown hand curled into the man's larger one. The sight caused a clutching sensation around Judy's womb. This was exactly how she could imagine Ryan behaving toward a real son. The little girl, Matilda, moved quietly to his other side and clasped his hand, completing the heartwarming picture.

Judy looked away, caught off guard by the strength of her own emotions. He'd make a good father, she realized, and found she didn't like thinking of him in a relationship that would lead to this scenario.

Dark fury rose inside her. She hadn't liked Ryan talking about a future she didn't want. Yet thinking of him with someone else set off warning flares inside her. What in blazes would satisfy her? To have him as an occasional lover, leaving her free to live her life her way? Instinctively, she knew Ryan would never settle for so little; to her surprise, the idea appealed less to her than she expected.

Tracey was watching Ryan and the children with interest. "Hello, Ryan, I didn't expect to run into you here."

"Oh, you never know where I'll turn up next," he said. To Judy, he added, "I sponsor Sunny's education through a charity group based in Broome. We don't see each other nearly often enough, do we, champ?"

The little boy giggled. "You know it's my birthday next month?"

"Have I ever forgotten?"

"Last year, I got a big truck," Sunny told Judy solemnly. "The back tipped up and you could put sand in it, like the ones at Lake Argyle."

The rain was blowing onto the veranda. "Why don't we go inside for milk and cookies," Judy suggested.

The magic words had the desired effect. The children surged into the main room, pulling Ryan with them. Judy and Tracey followed more sedately. "I'm sorry I couldn't call ahead and warn you," Tracey said. "My phone battery died right after I called Heather and explained where we were heading. But at least she knows where we are. I was afraid we'd get stuck somewhere between here and Halls Creek, so I kept driving."

"You did the right thing. If the rain doesn't let up, you can all sleep in the bunkhouse until it's safe to head back."

"Bless you. I'll telephone Heather later, and tell her we're staying the night. She's had a rough time with Daniel being ill, so she'll probably welcome a break."

"And we're happy to have you," Judy assured her. "There's

not much we can do outside in this weather anyway. Ryan and I were catching up on some work in the office."

Tracey's gaze went to the man handing out plastic tumblers of milk and cookies to the excited children. "I met Tom and Blake in town, and Cade last night over dinner at the crocodile park. I had no idea Ryan was one of your foster brothers."

"Ryan isn't related to us," Judy said, not sure why she felt the need to clarify the point. "He only stayed with us a short time, then went his own way." She was aware of Tracey giving her a measuring look, but the other woman made no comment.

"Luckily, the barbecue is under cover so we can fire that up for dinner," Judy went on in a rush.

Tracey laughed. "I don't know any child who doesn't like sausages. This will be one of the highlights of their holiday."

After Ryan organized the children's snacks, he put on the player a DVD of cartoons that Tracey had in her vehicle. They settled in a semicircle in front of the television, their laughter soon echoing around the room.

"That ought to keep them happy for a while," he said as he rejoined Judy and Tracey.

Judy put a mug of coffee in front of him and another in front of Tracey, setting milk and sugar within arm's reach. "Why do I get the feeling you're an old hand at this? And how did you meet Sunny in the first place?"

Stirring sugar into his coffee, he looked a little sheepish. "I was working at Heather and Jeff's place where Sunny's mother is the cook. He got a kick out of hanging around me, watching me work and helping with the simple jobs I gave him. When I heard about the sponsorship deal on the radio, I asked if I could sponsor him. They told me they don't normally allow you to choose where your money goes, but by then we'd bonded, so they made an exception. After I moved on from that job, I kept in touch with my little mate, although I don't get to see him as often as I'd like to."

The affection in his voice was unmistakable. "And you help out a few of his cousins, too, I'll bet," Judy guessed.

"A lot of kids need the help," he said, answering her question even as he dodged it. "Your dad sets a good example."

And his own had set the opposite, she concluded. Working out that Ryan saw a lot of himself in the needy children wasn't difficult. He seemed determined to give them a better start than he'd had. And from the closeness she'd witnessed between him and Sunny, he was doing a good job.

"You're a good man, Ryan," Tracey said. "We could use more people like you."

"What about you?" he asked, conspicuously changing the subject. "How do you like living in Halls Creek?"

"I miss the quiet and the grandeur of the bush," she admitted. "Moving wasn't my choice. But after I developed diabetes, I was advised to live closer to medical help. I daresay the reasons will be made clear to me in time."

Her simple faith touched Judy. "My father wouldn't be one of those reasons?" she asked, letting her tone show she wouldn't mind.

The older woman actually blushed and directed her gaze to her coffee cup. "Des is another good man. We got to know each other quite well while I was in and out of the hospital getting my diabetes under control and he was there having treatment for his heart. I'd like to pray that a donor heart becomes available to him soon, but…"

"But that means hoping someone else will lose their life," Ryan put in. "Exactly what Des says himself."

"I've made up my mind to let go of the question for now," Tracey explained. "He is in good hands."

Judy was sure her friend didn't mean medically and felt encouraged. With someone like Tracey praying for him, how could her father help but be all right?

With six boisterous children confined to the house by the

rain, the rest of the day provided little more time for reflection. Keeping them occupied with games and a story after lunch took the ingenuity of the three adults combined. They sighed with relief when the children settled down to watch another DVD in the afternoon.

"Typical," Judy groused, looking out the front door at the steaming landscape. "They're quiet at last, and the rain finally decides to let up."

"Perhaps we can drive back to town today after all," Tracey speculated.

The idea was vetoed by Cade, who arrived in his Jeep as they watched. The heavy vehicle was mud-caked, and he admitted to almost getting bogged down on the way back from Halls Creek. Tracey's minivan would never make it until the road dried out more, Cade assured them.

After greeting Tracey, Cade took Judy aside. "Blake told me what happened to Ryan last night. We kept it from Des," he added in response to her look of alarm. "We didn't want the two of you here alone in case Horvath decides to cause more trouble. Seeing the houseful you've got, I'm glad I took the risk."

She hugged him. "You shouldn't have worried, but I'm glad you did. Ryan is keeping his pain to himself, but he's in no shape to handle any more battles for a while."

"Let's hope it won't come to that." Cade shot a glance at the churned-up road leading to the homestead, as if expecting Horvath and his men to show up at any moment. "I don't know why, but I have a bad feeling about tonight."

She gave an involuntary shudder. "We're arranging a barbecue for Tracey and the kids, so I hope to goodness your feeling turns out to be wrong."

His mouth tightened into a grim line. "We'll soon find out, won't we?"

Chapter 9

Mountains of cumulus cloud banked up from the east and thunder rolled in the distance, but the rain didn't return that evening, although the humidity was high enough for Judy to wish the heavens would open up. The grassed area in front of the homestead quickly dried out to allow them to dine outside. Under Tracey's direction, the children pitched in and helped set up folding tables and chairs, while Judy made bowls of salad to accompany the barbecue Cade, having appointed himself chef, was getting ready.

Like all the Kimberley cattle stations, they relied on meat raised on their own land and stored in a commercial-sized freezer. Judy had been making sausages since she was old enough to operate the small machine that stuffed the bought skins with delicious mixtures of meat and herbs. Now she took strings of the homemade sausages out of the freezer ready for Cade to cook. The pantry held several weeks' supply of groceries, so there was no shortage of food.

Ryan and little Sunny, who'd barely left his mentor's side during the preparations, disappeared into the office together.

"Wonder what they're up to," Judy said as she placed a basket of bread on a serving table.

Tracey, her hands filled with jugs of ice water, smiled. "Secret men's business, no doubt. They'll let us in on the whatever it is when they're ready."

Judy unfolded an umbrella-like gauze cover and placed it over the bread to deter the flies who were already showing an interest. "Sunny follows him around like a puppy."

"I knew Ryan was involved in the sponsorship scheme. But until we came here and Sunny spotted Ryan, I had no idea he was involved with your family. Most of the people who support these schemes are women. We're grateful for their help, of course, but the program could use a lot more men like Ryan."

"As role models, you mean?"

"Yes. The kids are surrounded by males at the cattle stations, of course, but so many are hard-drinking, tough-talking stockmen that they're hardly a helpful influence."

"Ryan is a stockman," she said, mentally adding *when he isn't undercover on an assignment.* No reason for Tracey to know that he was more than he seemed. She seemed happy enough with his cover persona, Judy noted.

"What he's like among the men is his business," Tracey said. "Around Sunny and the other kids, he's a very good father figure."

The thought mirrored Judy's impression so closely that she was momentarily speechless. Then Sunny came running out of the office, his eyes shining. "Wait till you see what we made."

A slightly sheepish-looking Ryan followed carrying a large poster made from several sheets of paper taped together. On it he had drawn and colored a large kangaroo. Judy had to look at it for a moment to realize that it was missing a tail. The oddly-shaped paper streamer Sunny carried suddenly made sense.

"Looks to me like Pin the Tail on the Kangaroo," she said with a laugh. Why hadn't she thought of party games?

He held the poster at arm's length. "It's a bit crude. Never was much of an artist."

She raised herself on tiptoe and kissed his cheek. "It's Skippy the Bush Kangaroo to the life. The kids will love it. It was kind of you to think of it."

"There's no kindness involved," he dismissed gruffly. "I thought if they were occupied, they'd keep out of mischief at least until bedtime."

"Spoken like a true parent," Tracey said approvingly. She took the poster and, under the children's direction, taped it to a tree to await the fun later. Small strips of tape were also added to the tail.

With the onset of rain, Andy Wandarra had returned from the muster camp, and Judy had invited him and the other workers' families to the barbecue. Andy's wife was too shy to join them, but some of the other staff had accepted, and it was obvious the children from Lake Argyle were having the time of their lives meeting the people they immediately dubbed aunties and uncles.

"How does your head feel?" Judy asked Ryan a little later, after everyone was settled with plates of blackened sausages, bread and salad. The appetizing smell of barbecue lingered on the night air. Cade and Tracey were deep in conversation, giving Judy the chance to have Ryan to herself at last.

He rolled a piece of bread around a sausage and bit into it. "Can't feel a thing."

"Because of the aspirin I saw you downing when you didn't think I was looking?"

"Didn't know they were rationed."

She curbed her impatience. "They're not. But your endurance is. You've run yourself ragged helping with the children today. I'd hoped you'd take time off to rest."

He touched the tip of her nose with his finger. "When a woman worries this much about me, it has to be love."

She swatted his finger away but not before a shiver threaded through her. If they hadn't been surrounded by people, she would have been tempted to kiss him. He'd shown himself in a completely new light today, a most attractive light. "I'd never have picked you for a father figure," she said, using Tracey's term.

He dumped a daunting amount of tomato sauce onto a second sausage, then ate with gusto, not meeting Judy's eyes. "I warned you there's a lot you don't know about me."

"You weren't kidding," she said, wondering what other surprises lay in store. To disguise a sudden rush of feeling for him, she made her tone deliberately flippant. "Let me guess. You just dumped your third wife, and you have a dozen children scattered around the outback."

"That I know about," he conceded with a crooked grin. "My nickname's not Stud Smith for nothing."

The name was news to her, and she suspected had been made up for her benefit, but a fresh wave of desire rolled through her anyway. "I wouldn't know, would I?"

"There's one way to find out."

The teasing had gone from his voice, and she realized he was serious. She was too, she acknowledged. Seeing him with the children, acting as a family man, had increased her desire for him rather than dampening it. Confusing, considering how much she resisted the family role on her own account. She gestured around them. "Is this what you want for yourself?"

"Eventually. Don't you?"

"It's easy for a man." She couldn't suppress a touch of bitterness. "You get the best of all worlds—a wife, children, the life you choose. You don't have to give up a thing."

"And you think a woman does?"

"Of course she does. Next time you're at an outback cattle station, open your eyes. At the end of the day, while you and the men are sprawled in the shade, drinking beer and yarning, take a look at what the women are doing. They're the ones supplying you with drinks, putting laundry on the line and keeping the children out of your hair."

"Does the idea bother you because of what happened to your mother?"

She felt her gaze narrow. "You believe in cutting to the chase, don't you?"

"Then I'm right?"

Judy's voice became vibrant. "She didn't want to worry anyone, so she delayed getting the treatment that could have saved her life."

"And it might not have worked. You'll never know for sure."

"You don't know either. You weren't here."

He put his plate down on a table and asked quietly, "Are you holding that against me?"

"Yes. No. I don't know. All I know is I don't want a life like hers. All sacrifice and nothing left for me."

He chuckled softly, earning a savage look. "What?" she demanded.

"I love your idea of self-centered."

"Explain."

He ran a hand lightly down her arm. "You're determined not to become an outback wife. Yet you're running your father's household and a good slice of Diamond Downs, taking care of him in his illness, catering to stranded travelers, and worrying about my health. Yep. A charter member of the Me Generation."

She hadn't considered any of that. "I'm only doing what's right."

"Don't you think Fran Logan felt the same? Doing things for others when it's what you want to do can be the most selfish indulgence of all, because it makes you feel good." His gaze sought out Sunny, kicking a ball across the grass with another child.

"Is that how you feel about Sunny?"

Ryan nodded. "Everybody thinks I'm Mr. Generosity, sponsoring kids like him. The truth is I'm selfish. They give me back far more than the time and dollars I donate."

He watched as Tracey cleared away the debris of the meal. Andy got out his didgeridoo, marked with traditional designs, and began to play a throbbing melody on the hollowed-out log instrument, while some of the other guests joined in, clicking pairs of rhythm sticks together.

To the children's delight, Andy produced a variety of animal sounds, then the sound of a road train roaring down the highway and finally a kookaburra's laugh. All her life, Judy had been entranced by the sounds Andy could produce from the traditional instrument, and got a fresh kick out of watching the wide-eyed response of the new arrivals.

When the impromptu concert ended and Tracey announced it was time for a game, the children cheered. While Cade located a bandanna to act as a blindfold, Ryan helped Judy carry the remains of the food back to the kitchen. "A plague of locusts couldn't have done a better job," he said, surveying the cleaned plates.

"Leftovers won't be a problem," she agreed. His earlier comment about altruism sometimes having selfish benefits had struck home. It was hard to believe her mother's sacrifices had made her happy, but Judy began to wonder if she'd seen the full picture.

Ryan finished loading the dishwasher and straightened. "Car's coming."

"You can hear an engine over all that racket?"

He nodded. Then she heard it, too, and the children's squeals quieted as Cade greeted whoever had come to call.

Given the muddy conditions after the rain, Judy couldn't think who would have risked the treacherous roads. Perhaps someone was in trouble. She wiped her hands on a cloth and hurried outside.

Judy came up short at the sight of Max Horvath getting out of a Land Cruiser. Of all things, he had a bunch of flowers in his hand. To Cade, she said quickly, "Tell Ryan to keep out of sight."

Her foster brother nodded and went to the kitchen door in time to stop Ryan from being spotted by their neighbor. Max didn't know of Ryan's connection with the family and after last night's incident, Judy wanted to keep it that way.

"Hello, Max, I didn't expect to see you here after yesterday," she said, referring to their argument in the café.

He held out the flowers. "I came to apologize."

His threats had gone way beyond anything an apology could fix. She made no move to take the flowers. "As you can see, we're busy. What do you really want?"

He placed the flowers on a table. "Only to make things up with you. Can I come in and talk?"

She didn't want to cause a scene in front of Tracey and her young charges, but neither did she want him seeing Ryan. "We have nothing to say to each other."

"I have something you might want to hear about Ryan Smith."

Out of the corner of her eye, she saw Cade nod to indicate that Ryan was safely out of sight. "Very well, but only for a couple of minutes. You know Andy and my foster brother, Cade? And this is Tracey Blair and her charges from Lake Argyle. Max Horvath from Willundina," she said by way of general introduction.

He acknowledged the others with a few words, but his body language telegraphed impatience. She couldn't see Max readily sponsoring a needy child or going out of his way to provide them with a role model. In fact, she couldn't see Max in any meaningful role in her life after he'd revealed how he really felt about her last night. She hoped Ryan would have the sense to keep out of his way.

"A beer would be nice, thanks," Max said, although she had pointedly not offered him anything as he took a seat at the kitchen table. In the outback, this was tantamount to heresy, but she wasn't interested in making Max comfortable any more than she would have welcomed a venomous snake into the house.

Rather than get into an argument, she cracked open a beer and placed the can in front of him. "We said everything we needed to say yesterday."

He took a drink and wiped his mouth with the back of his hand. "Yes, well, I'd had a glass or two of wine and I was hurt that you seemed to be rejecting me."

"I *was* rejecting you." Her tone said nothing had changed. "Any chance we had as a couple withered and died years ago."

"You must have thought we had something going when you agreed to go out with me."

"I was wrong, wasn't I?"

"I didn't mean to hurt you," he said, not giving up. "That's why I came with a peace offering."

"I appreciate the thought, but flowers won't…"

He didn't let her finish. "Not the flowers, a friendly warning about Smith. After all, he came to you first before you referred him to me."

"What about him?" she asked guardedly.

"While we were out last night, he broke into my safe and stole some documents and valuables. Mick Coghlan caught him red-handed, then took a shot at him when he refused to surrender. He winged the man, and I thought he might turn to you for help."

"Because I'm a soft touch?"

Annoyance darkened Max's expression. "Damn it, I'm trying to help you, Judy. Heaven knows why, when you keep throwing my efforts back in my face. You refuse to let me step in and take the worry of Diamond Downs off your shoulders. Now you won't listen to a friendly warning. Smith had accomplices who helped him escape. We didn't get a look at them in the dark, but they might be part of a gang working their way around the district."

"Was very much taken?" she asked, curious to hear Max's response.

Her interest mollified him a little. "He got away with some valuable heirloom jewelry and sets of coins my dad had collected. And a few old photos and letters of mainly sentimental value."

I'll bet they are, Judy though, keeping her face impassive with an effort. Max probably intended to solve a few of his immediate money worries by blaming Ryan for stealing valuables he hadn't touched, if they'd existed at all. Max must know the real haul lay in the journal entries Ryan had photographed and the deed to Cotton Tree Gorge, but Max wasn't about to admit any such thing to Judy. "I appreciate the warning," she said noncommittally. "But it really wasn't necessary."

"Always so independent," he said, standing up. "I won't interrupt your party any longer. Can I use your bathroom before I go?"

Anything to get him off the premises as quickly as possible. "Sure. You know the way."

He headed toward the bedroom wing where the main bathroom was located. She almost jumped out of her skin as Ryan sneaked up behind her. "Don't do that," she hissed.

"It's what we jewel thieves do," he said.

"You heard what he said?"

"I had the pantry door open a crack. Taking that man down is going to give me great satisfaction."

She touched a hand to the side of his face. "Don't underestimate him."

He nibbled the tips of her fingers. "I'm the one you shouldn't underestimate."

"Never," she confessed as gusts of heat swirled through her. His slightest touch made her a quivering mess. She masked her response with a frown. "You'd better get out of sight. He'll be back in a couple of minutes."

He caught her hand and kissed her sensitive palm. "If you need me, I'm not far away."

He disappeared into the pantry and Max came back shortly afterward. Something had changed about him, she thought. His movements seemed more predatory, and she shivered at the cold look in his eyes. Then she saw the photo he held in his hand. *Stay calm,* she instructed herself. "The bathroom came before my bedroom last time I looked."

"True, but your room is far more revealing. My eye was caught by this photo lying on your dresser. I couldn't help taking a closer look."

Her dresser wasn't visible from the hallway, so he must have gone in expressly to snoop. The thought of him pawing through her possessions made bile rise in her throat. She swallowed hard. "What could possibly interest you about an old photo of my great-grandfather?"

"Who's the young woman with him?"

"I don't know, a family friend, I suppose. The photo came to light after a clear-out of the office, so I'll have to ask my father about it if the name matters to you."

"Don't bother," Max said nastily. "We both know the photo came from my safe."

She dropped all pretense. "Where you put it after stealing the file containing it from us."

His eyes slitted. "Be careful with your accusations. The papers were among Eddy Gilgai's possessions found after his death and placed in my safe until the owners could be identified. If anyone stole your property, it must have been him."

Trust Max to blame an employee who could no longer defend himself, she thought. Eddy hadn't been an angel, but his gruesome death in the jaws of a crocodile, had surely absolved his sins. "The photo belongs to us. Along with any other papers of ours you found—among Eddy's possessions," she added pointedly.

Max sidled closer, letting the photo drift onto the table between them. The shrill sounds of children playing outside was in eerie counterpoint to the chill silence in the room. "Why don't we stop fencing around, Judy? Was Ryan Smith your plant to get access to those documents?"

"I don't know what you're..." She stifled a cry as he grabbed her arm and twisted it cruelly behind her back. "You're hurting me. Let me go."

"When you answer my question."

"I'm the one you should ask, Horvath," Ryan said, stepping into the room.

Max's hold tightened, making her bite her lip as pain radiated along her tortured arm and shoulder. "So the pair of you are in this together. Is he the reason you lost interest in me, Judy?"

Her eyes watered, but she kept her head high. "I never had any interest to lose. It was a ruse to find out what you were up to. Ryan was only acting on my instructions."

"Are you going to let her suffer to protect you, Smith?" Max demanded.

"Let her go, then we can talk."

Max shook his head. "The only thing I'm interested in is what you took from my safe. Is a bit of paper worth a broken arm, Judy?"

"We both know the paper is the key to Jack Logan's diamond mine. If I give it to you, will you let her go unharmed?"

"It's a deal."

"Ryan, no," she said, biting back a scream as Max jerked her arm upward.

But Ryan pulled a rolled-up yellowing sheet out of his shirt pocket and placed it on the table. "Now let her go."

"My pleasure." Max spun her hard across the room so she fell against Ryan. His arms came around her to steady her. By the time she recovered, Max was pocketing the paper. "Don't do anything foolish. There are all those children outside and I have a gun," he said, the implication frighteningly clear.

Ryan kept his arm around Judy. "You and your men like playing with firearms, don't you Horvath?"

Max's gaze went to the dressing on Ryan's temple. "Let's say they speak louder than words. It's a pity Coghlan's aim wasn't better. Even so, that must hurt like the devil."

"No need to sound so pleased about it," Ryan said in a matching conversational tone. "You did say you were leaving?"

Max turned, then spun back. "Smith? You wouldn't be related to the Smith on the title deed to Cotton Tree Gorge."

"The world is full of Smiths."

"But not here in this place, at this time." His finger stabbed the photo lying on the table. "Let's see, she'd be your grandmother? No wonder you're taking such a keen interest in this business. And no wonder you've gained Judy's affections so easily. You have what she wants."

Judy spat out an oath, earning a look of astonishment from Ryan. "Not everybody has the same motives as you, Max," she said.

"Don't bet on it. When did she start taking an interest in you, Smith? Before or after she found out you're the heir to the diamond country?"

Judy wondered if Ryan was remembering that they'd almost made love only a short time after he broke the news.

Coldness washed through her. Surely he couldn't think she was only interested in him for that?

"It doesn't matter anyway," Horvath went on. "Without the deed, you have no chance of claiming the land. We're back to square one, with me holding a mortgage over the lot."

"Get out," Judy snarled. Ryan's hold on her was all that held her back from clawing Horvath's eyes out. Bad enough that he'd taken back the hard-won document. He had no right to suggest her motives were in any way similar to his.

"Keep the flowers to remind you of me," Max said and walked out. Soon afterward, they heard the sound of his Land Cruiser start up and drive away.

Judy sagged against the table. "How could you hand over the deed to him after all you went through to get it?"

"Who says I did?"

"But I saw..."

"What you saw was one of your mother's old recipes I found at the back of a shelf while I was listening from the pantry. Hopefully Horvath won't look at it until he gets home, then he'll find he has everything he needs to make a nice batch of pickled mutton."

The stress of the moment gave way to the urge to laugh hysterically. "Good grief, Ryan. If he'd checked the paper while he was here, he might have killed you."

"He wouldn't have pulled anything with so many witnesses around," he said with a confidence she didn't share. "He's been too careful to distance himself from everything that's happened. He isn't about to dirty his hands now, when what he wants is within his grasp, or so he thinks."

She thought of the coldness she'd seen in Max's eyes when he'd showed her the photo. "Max may not have wanted to be implicated up to now, but he's getting desperate. Filing a false insurance claim for the burglary may buy him a little time with his creditors, but there's a limit to how much he can pretend to have lost. These days, insurance companies generally prefer to replace goods rather than hand over large amounts of cash, so he may not come out of it as well as he hopes."

Cade came in carrying the barbecue grill. "I saw Horvath hightailing it out of here. What did he want?"

When Ryan explained, Cade gave a low whistle. "He'll be on the warpath after this. You sure you want to stick around, Ryan? You've set yourself up as his prime target."

Ryan's hand went to the dressing at his temple. "The feeling's mutual. I'm not leaving until this is finished, one way or another."

Judy struggled to keep her expression from betraying how much his promise meant to her. She told herself it was for the sake of her father and Diamond Downs, and the people depending on them, but in her heart she knew the truth. She wanted Ryan to stay while she explored her feelings toward him.

Having him stay was dangerous, she recognized. And not only because Max would have him in his sights. The longer she and Ryan were together, the more she risked falling for him. Needing him when she didn't want to need any man.

She looked up to find his gaze on her, the fire in his eyes telling her she'd been read like a book. Could he possibly be aware of the physical needs clamoring inside her whenever he was within touching distance? Or the confusing yearnings he sparked in her for home, family, a future she'd sworn to avoid? If she had half an ounce of sense, she would send him packing now, for his safety as well as her sanity.

She was glad Cade was in the room, stopping her from falling into Ryan's arms and making a complete fool of herself. How could she, when her feelings were in such turmoil? Sleeping with him for mutual pleasure wasn't the issue. But she doubted Ryan would be content with casual sex. And with everything he made her feel, could she be sure it was enough for her any more?

Chapter 10

The next morning, Judy and Tracey were organizing breakfast for the children at the barbecue tables they'd left set up when another car pulled up. A woman and a small boy got out. Tracey's face lit up with pleasure. "Heather and Daniel made it through after all."

Judy was happy to see the glamorous woman she'd met at the hospital the night Des had suffered a suspected heart attack. From the way the little boy raced toward his companions, Judy gathered he was fully recovered from the bout of asthma that had put him in the hospital for a time.

Heather approached the table where Judy was pouring orange juice into glasses. "I hope everything's all right. I would have come sooner, but I was told the road wasn't safe in the heavy rain."

"There was no need to risk it, everybody's fine here," Judy said. "How is the road this morning?"

"Churned up in parts but dried out now, and my car has

four-wheel drive, so we had no trouble. After the sun bakes the mud for a few more hours, Tracey's minibus shouldn't have a problem getting through."

"Have you and Daniel had breakfast?"

Heather glanced toward her little boy. "We ate before we left Halls Creek, but Daniel's probably ready for another round and I'd kill for a cup of coffee."

"No need to go that far. There's plenty," Judy said with a laugh. "My day doesn't get going till I've had my caffeine fix."

With Heather's help, the children were soon settled with bowls of cereal, thick slabs of toast and Vegemite or the bush honey known locally as sugarbag. Judy poured coffee for the adults and carried it to the table.

"Where are Cade and Ryan?" Tracey asked when Judy joined her and Heather.

"Dodging this lot, I suspect. They drove out to the muster camp. Andy had a few questions about some cattle they rounded up yesterday, and one of the muster vehicles was acting up. That's Ryan's specialty."

Judy suspected that her foster brothers mainly wanted to make sure Horvath and his men weren't hanging around to cause trouble but she didn't say so, not wanting to alarm the visitors.

"So his injury isn't giving him any trouble?" Tracey asked.

Heather's eyebrows lifted. "He was injured? What happened?"

"Only a graze, nothing serious," Judy said without further explanation. How did she explain Ryan's close call with a bullet while indulging in a little breaking and entering? Before he left this morning, he'd discarded the dressing, revealing a livid mark on his temple that would settle into an interesting scar, she thought. He'd refused her offer to redress the injury, insisting he was fine.

She wished she could say the same for herself. Half the

night had been spent tossing and turning, worrying about what Max Horvath might do. After discovering Ryan had foiled his plan to steal back the deed to Cotton Tree Gorge, Max wasn't likely to rest until he'd exacted revenge. Thinking of Ryan, vulnerable out at the muster camp, made her uneasy until she reminded herself that he wasn't alone. Cade was with him, and Andy and the men would provide backup if Max tried anything.

The heat of the coffee penetrated her fingers and she put the cup down hastily, spilling a few drops onto the checked tablecloth. "You're distracted this morning," Tracey observed, watching her. "Worried about your father?"

Guiltily, Judy lowered her gaze. She should have been worrying about Des; instead, her thoughts were divided between him and Ryan, and her longing to be with him. "I spoke to Dad this morning at the crocodile farm," she said. "He relaxed once I assured him everything's under control here. He's been helping out with a few light chores and showing visitors around. I got the impression he's enjoying the break."

"Tracey arranged with Blake to take the kids to Sawtooth Park the day after tomorrow," Heather put in. "Thank you for suggesting the idea."

Judy sipped her coffee. "What else do you have planned for this week, Tracey?"

"Weather permitting, we're going to Windjana Gorge and Tunnel Creek," Tracey said, naming two local landmarks. She added, "The kids are keen to see Wolf Creek crater, so we're going there tomorrow. I told them it's a huge hole in the ground made by a meteor millions of years ago, but I think they expect signs of alien life-forms."

Heather spread Vegemite on a piece of toast. "TV and computer games have a lot to answer for, even in the most remote places."

The children had finished eating and were playing noisily

between the tables. "Looks like the end of peace and quiet," Tracey said and got up. "I'd hoped we could be out of your hair after breakfast but from the sound of things, the road needs more time to dry out before it's safe for my van."

"What about if we take the Bowen River Road?" Heather asked. "According to my map, that would get us back to the highway."

Judy hesitated. With Max on the warpath, she would feel happier if the other women took the children back to Halls Creek and out of danger. Last night before going to bed, she and Ryan had agreed they didn't want to alarm the visitors by telling them about the threat from Max. "Bowen Creek Road usually dries out quicker than our main access road, but it's a much longer way," she felt bound to point out.

"We're in no hurry," Tracey said. "The kids will enjoy driving back by a different route."

Judy's glance went to Heather. "You can't be ready to leave yet. You only just arrived."

"I feel we should go while Tracey's van can make it," Heather admitted. "Another time, I'd love to stay longer."

"You're welcome anytime," Judy repeated. "I don't want to rush you away." She did, but for their own protection. She hoped her anxiety didn't show too much.

Tracey gestured toward the noisy group. "They're getting restless. We should make a move before they start tearing your place apart out of boredom."

"They were great last night at the barbecue," Judy said.

Tracey smiled in agreement. "We had a wonderful time. Thanks for organizing everything. The kids thought sleeping in the bunkhouse was a treat, not that there was much actual sleeping done." She yawned as if to prove her point.

Judy's gaze went to the long, low building, with its timber sides and louvered windows. "The old place has fond memories for me, too. The boys and I used to sleep out there whenever Dad would let us. Not much sleeping got done then, either. Pillow fights were the activity of choice."

"Children never change." Tracey clapped her hands, snagging the children's attention. "We're leaving now, kids. Thank Judy for having us."

Judy struggled not to smile as the children chorused their appreciation. Sunny came up to her dragging a large piece of paper that looked the worse for wear. "Ryan said I could take home the kangaroo we made."

She hugged the child. How slight he felt, but strong, too. "You can play the game when you get home."

"Will Ryan come back and see me soon?"

"Of course he will. And you can come and visit him again, too."

His dark eyes saucered. "Can I? That'd be great. I'll be bigger then. Ryan says I can go to the muster camp with the men when I'm bigger."

Her heart went out to the little boy, so obviously longing for a father that he had cast Ryan in the role. Her admiration for his involvement in the child's life grew until she felt a painful lump in her chest. She blinked hard to clear her vision. "Ryan's right. You'll be able to do lots of things when you're bigger, but don't be in too much of a rush."

"He didn't say goodbye," Sunny complained.

"He had to leave before sunrise," she explained. "He looked in on you, but you were sleeping. He left a goodbye hug for you on your pillow." The phrase was one her mother had used many times when Des had left for work before she awoke. When she'd been tiny, she'd dragged her pillow out to her mother and demanded to be shown where her goodbye hug was.

Wiser than she, Sunny took her assurance at face value. "That's good." Then he asked, more shyly, "Can I leave you a kiss to give him?"

Warmth rushed through her. She held out her arms. "Of course."

Sunny threw himself against her and planted a wet kiss against her mouth. "You won't forget to give it to him?"

"I won't forget." Kissing Ryan wasn't exactly a hardship. The challenge would be remembering that it wasn't on her own account.

Sunny started to run off, then slowed and came back. "Thank you for having me," he said dutifully, before joining the other children getting into the minivan.

Judy touched a hand to her mouth. The child's affection had touched her in ways she didn't want to think about. The feel of his wiry body in her arms was another unwanted distraction, triggering an aching sensation in her fallow womb. What were these males doing to her?

The feeling of emptiness was strong enough to make her walk to the van and touch the small hands reaching out to her from the windows. "Watch out for the aliens when you get to Wolf Creek crater," she said on sudden impulse.

"See, I told you there'll be aliens," Matilda called out to Tracey, who was helping the last child to board.

Tracey shot Judy a wry look. "Now look what you've done."

Judy felt unrepentant. "Just because you've never seen any aliens at Wolf Creek crater doesn't mean there aren't any."

"Some things have to be taken on faith," Tracey agreed with a wink. She stretched up to hug Judy. "Like the reason we landed on your doorstep last night."

Judy didn't want to think some power had arranged the incident to show her another side of Ryan or to create this sense of aridity inside herself. How cruel would that be? But the sensation lingered as she said goodbye to Heather and Daniel and waved as the small convoy headed in the direction of Bowen Creek Road.

Slowly she turned back toward the house, where a couple

of the men who hadn't been needed at the muster camp were folding tables. No time to feel sorry for herself, she thought as she cleared away the breakfast things. There was work to be done. At an outback cattle station, there was always work to be done.

Finishing his inspection of the cattle the men had mustered, Ryan dropped the reins over his horse's head and left the animal to graze while he approached Andy Wandarra. "Everything okay here?"

Before retiring the night before, he'd told the other man about Horvath's late-night visit and his threats. They'd decided to check on the muster camp at first light to make sure Horvath hadn't been up to no good. There were many things he could have done to cause trouble, from damaging plant and equipment, to stealing horses and cattle.

Evidently nothing had been touched. "After you told me what happened, I sent a couple of the men out here last night," Andy explained. "Don't want any more trouble. Mr. Logan has got more than his share as it is."

"You said it, Andy. This place couldn't manage without you."

Wandarra looked pleased, but gestured dismissively. "That's rubbish talk, Ryan. Diamond Downs will go on long after me and my people are gone."

Ryan nodded, adding quietly, "Let's hope it's not in Horvath's hands by then."

He drank a cup of coffee out of an enamel mug with the men gathered around the campfire. Their chatter was sporadic, mostly concerning work to be done that day, peppered with the occasional ribald joke. He didn't join in, aware of a sense of unease he couldn't shake off.

Anyone connected with the land eventually developed a sixth sense for events yet to come, whether they were approaching storms or, rarely, a death. Such matters were never discussed openly, but they'd all experienced premonitions that defied explanation, like the way he felt now.

He looked around. The camp was located on an open belt of grassland a forty-minute ride from the main homestead. A creek cut a deep swath along one boundary, normally dry but now running with water after yesterday's rain. With the coming of the Wet proper, the creek, like its neighbors, would soon spill over its banks and spread across the land, creating a shallow brown sea all the way to the horizon.

The waterbirds would fly in from as far away as Russia to nest and breed. Crocodiles would migrate from their isolated waterholes to claim new territories, wildflowers would bloom and the land would complete its annual cycle of regeneration.

He looked upward. A dozen feet in the air, a battered metal kerosene can hung from a tree. Visitors always asked about the cans hanging in the trees and never believed his explanation that they marked the height the river would reach at full spate.

A movement jarred his reverie, pulling his attention away from the can. He'd seen movement in the distance. Too far away for easy identification, so he went to his horse and pulled binoculars out of the saddlebag. Training them on the source of the movement, he swore softly.

Andy came up behind him. "What is it, Ryan?"

He handed the glasses over. "Hard to tell for sure, but it looks like Mick Coghlan and a couple of his men."

After a minute Andy lowered the glasses. "That's Mick all right. What do you think they're up to?"

"They must know they're on Diamond Downs land. They could be looking for strays from Willundina." Ryan knew his tone lacked conviction. While rounding up their own straggly cleanskin cattle—cattle that had, until now, escaped mustering and branding—the men had seen no cattle carrying their neighbor's brand. The fences were regularly checked for breaks and none had been found recently.

Ryan debated following the car to investigate, then thought of Judy and Tracey and the children back at the homestead. Without consulting her, Ryan had detailed two men to stay behind, ostensibly because they had enough hands at the muster camp but really to protect Judy and the others. She'd have objected if he'd explained. Precisely why he hadn't. "Whatever they're up to, we can be sure it isn't anything good," he said.

"You want me to take some men and chase them off the land?"

"They'll be gone before you can catch up. I'm heading back to the homestead. Keep an eye on things here and call me if you see them up to anything suspicious."

Andy handed the glasses back to Ryan. "Sure thing, boss. There's more rain on the way later, so we'll be back before sunset in any case."

Ryan didn't bother asking how Andy knew what the weather would do. He and his people possessed an almost mystical rapport with the land, linked to it by millennia of living here since the Dreamtime. Ryan and his people were the latecomers, and he felt privileged to be allowed to share their land.

"You know what you're doing," he said to Andy, meaning it on every level.

He swung himself back into the saddle and turned the horse's head for home, resisting the temptation to urge the animal into a gallop. Mick Coghlan had been heading away from the homestead toward Bowen Creek. For the moment, Judy was in no danger. He thought about calling her, but decided against adding to her concerns.

Thinking of her, he felt his mouth curve into a smile. She may not be able to imagine herself as a mother, but he had no trouble visualizing her in the role. Last night with the kids from Tracey's former school, Judy had looked perfectly at home. She'd be even better with their own kids, he thought.

His mind flashed on Horvath twisting her arm behind her

back. She'd tried not to cry out, but her whimper had cut Ryan to his heart. He'd wanted to kill Max with his bare hands for hurting her.

He forced his mind to more pleasant thoughts. What was she doing now? Feeding the kids breakfast, probably sharing girl talk with Tracey? Judy was more likely to want to discuss the mechanics of Tracey's minivan than those dress designs he'd been told she did, he thought.

He swatted flies away from his face, wondering why he bothered. They only settled again as soon as he dropped his hand. He pictured Judy in her jeans and one of those skimpy T-shirts she liked. His favorite was a pale blue one that showed a band of midriff whenever she moved. He amused himself by imagining her in his arms wearing the T-shirt, how warm she'd feel as his hand slid over that enticing strip of bare flesh. A little higher and he could cup her small, firm breasts. Lower and…

He pushed the thoughts back. She'd been a part of him for as long as he could remember. He'd even dreamed they'd be together some day. Had he feared it was only a dream? Was that why he'd stayed away from her for so long? Afraid reality would bring his dreams crashing down to earth?

More than most men, he knew you didn't always get what you wanted, no matter how intensely you wished for something. As a boy, he'd wished having his father back home so hard he'd felt tears squeezing out from under his closed eyelids as he'd tried to manifest his heart's desire. Yet his father had never come back. By the time his mother died, he'd known better than to wish things could be different and had set about coping without her as best he could.

But with Judy, he couldn't stop wishing. He wanted her more than he could remember wanting anyone. Not only because she was beautiful, which she was. Her beauty stemmed from an inner glow, like a light burning inside her for everything life had to offer. She was passionate about everything she did, and her enthusiasm rubbed off on those around her.

Her intelligence was keen, too. He respected her quick mind and eagerness to learn. She'd been fourteen when he'd lived at Diamond Downs, fifteen when he'd left. Too young, according to Des, to start flying lessons. Undeterred, she'd started teaching herself flight theory ready for the moment when she was allowed to take to the skies.

But even her formidable combination of brains and beauty didn't explain how she managed to dominate Ryan's attention so completely. When he wasn't around her, she was in his thoughts or haunting his dreams. He hungered for her, only feeling complete when she was with him. The best word he could find to fit was the old chestnut, *chemistry*.

He'd tried dating other women, getting involved in relationships that might have become serious if he'd let them. The women had complained he didn't pay them enough attention. How could he, when most of his attention was already spoken for? More recently, he'd limited himself to dating women who were content to enjoy his company without demanding more. The only problem was he'd ended up dissatisfied. Coming back to Judy had been as inevitable as breathing.

Convincing her that teaming up with him would enlarge her horizons, not limit them, was going to be difficult, but he would do it because he had run out of choices. This business with Horvath had helped him to reach a decision. He was through leaving her behind. Next time, she would come with him, or he wouldn't leave. Starting again from scratch around here would be easier than giving her up.

Judy sensed, rather than heard, Ryan return. Attempting to bring some order to the house after last night's barbecue, she lifted her head like a dingo sampling the air and only then heard the whicker of his horse as he let it out into the yard.

Tempted to greet him at the door, she made herself continue wielding the vacuum cleaner.

He came up behind her and kissed her neck. "What a picture of domestic bliss."

She leaned across and hit the power button, turning the appliance off. "Domestic bliss, nothing. I'd rather assemble a Cessna from spare parts than do this stuff."

His gaze went to where the denim of her jeans was stretched over her shapely rear. "Pity. You do it so well."

"Sexist brute," she snapped, straightening.

Without a word he lifted the wand out of her hand, kick-started the cleaner and went to work on the floor, finishing where she'd left off. Welcoming the breather, she watched him, amused in spite of herself. Her father was largely responsible for all the boys being domesticated, believing they should be able to run a household when needed. When a teenage Ryan had complained about doing women's work, he'd earned himself a week of cleaning bathrooms for his pains.

She wasn't the only one with an admirable rear, she thought, as he bent to slide the nozzle under an armchair. He was dressed in khaki work shirt and moleskins, his R.M. Williams boots dusty from the trail. His sleeves were rolled back to the elbows, revealing tanned forearms dusted with fine red-gold hairs. As she watched, he crouched and pulled a pen out from under the chair, the moleskins tightening like an invitation.

A shudder traveled through her in response, firing her with defensive anger. She didn't want him here, either helping her or tantalizing her. Wanting what she wasn't prepared to give. She tried to wrest the cleaner out of his hand and a tug-of-war ensued, ending when he pushed her backward onto the sofa cushions.

He swiftly silenced the cleaner and let the wand drop to the floor before flopping down beside her. He stretched his arm along the back of the sofa behind her. "Got you where I want you at last."

She tried to match his light tone, suspecting she didn't succeed all that well. "Sitting down on the job, you mean?"

"Blame it on all that sucking, blowing and rigid steel wands putting ideas in my head."

She pretended irritation. "Only a man could link cleaning with sex."

"A man can link anything with sex, with the right woman."

Desire flared again, too strong to deny. She tried anyway. "First you need to find the right woman."

His expression became serious. "I already have."

His mouth came down on hers, so strongly possessive that her senses reeled. She didn't want to prove his point but couldn't stop her lips from parting under his, not only accepting but returning his kiss out of her own deep needs, inviting him into the barren place in her heart.

The room reeled. Logic crumbled into nonsense as emotion took over, and she poured into the kiss all the longing that had been building up since he came back. Where was the logic in the way she'd followed him around the Kimberley, telling herself she was keeping in touch for his sake? Her own was more likely. He'd been fine without her. She was the one who'd needed to see him again and again as obsessively as the need to probe a sore tooth. Being with him had hurt, but not as much as being without him.

Her hands slid up around his neck and she turned into the embrace, feeling her hard-won barriers start to crack.

Ryan felt the moment when she changed. From resisting him, she suddenly melted into him as if reaching some kind of decision. The right one, he prayed. The only one he would accept.

He tore his mouth from hers and kissed her face, her closed

eyelids, her throat, with growing urgency. The taste and feel of her filled him, making him want more, want to give her more. In his arms, her pliancy gave him hope. This time, she would let him show her what was in his heart.

"Where are Tracey and the kids?" he murmured against the satin of her throat. He didn't want to hurry his gift to Judy. For their first time together, she deserved better than a hasty, fumbling race against the clock. Still, he hadn't given their visitors a thought until this second. What was he thinking? He was shaken by how easily Judy had dominated his attention, and how completely.

Her eyes fluttered open and she seemed to have the same difficulty in focusing her thoughts. "They said to say goodbye. They're driving back to Halls Creek."

He frowned. "I didn't pass them on the way from the muster camp. And the road is still a bit of a mess."

Her hand splayed across his chest as she levered herself upright. "They didn't take the main road. Heather Wilton arrived with Daniel and stayed for breakfast, then they decided to go back by the Bowen Creek Road. It's longer but easier for Tracey's minivan to handle."

In his mind, he saw Mick Coghlan and his men driving in the same direction. He dragged his fingers through his hair. "Bloody hell."

All attention now, she stared at him. "What is it?"

He told her what he and Andy had seen earlier in the day. "I thought there was no danger because they were heading away from the homestead," he rasped.

"You think Horvath would order Mick to harass two women and a bunch of kids?" Her tone mirrored the disbelief Ryan saw on her face.

"He was willing to hurt you last night."

Instinctively Judy's hand went to her shoulder where an ache from her run-in with Max still lodged, forgotten in the throes of passion. How effortlessly Ryan could make her forget everything. She should be glad a more urgent concern had stopped them. They'd been seconds away from making love; then where would she have been? Past the point of no return and hurtling at full throttle toward a terrifying unknown.

"But surely children..." She couldn't finish.

He handed her the phone. "Call Tracey. Heather said she's staying there, too. If all went well, they should be back at Halls Creek by now."

Judy struggled to make her fingers cooperate. She compressed her lips into a tight line as the ringing tone went on and on before an answering machine clicked on. She left a message in case they'd been delayed somewhere, refusing to consider what the delay might be. Ryan watched intently. "I'll try her cell phone," she said. Seconds later, she reported the same frustrating result.

He was up and pulling her to her feet in one swift movement. "They could have stopped to sightsee along the way."

Still she clung to wishful thinking. "Even if they met up with Mick Coghlan, they couldn't be any help to him. They don't know anything."

"Horvath is desperate. He'd use any advantage he could."

"We'd better get out to Bowen Creek."

"You read my mind."

Chapter 11

Banks of clouds rolled over them from the inland as they drove in Ryan's car at breakneck speed in the wake of the little convoy. It seemed like a lifetime, instead of a few short hours, since she'd waved them away this morning.

She looked at Ryan hunched over the wheel like a racing driver. The car handled like one as well.

The road was in better shape than the one leading to the homestead, but yesterday's downpour had churned tire tracks into mud valleys that were slowly drying into corrugations. The time before the wet season was the most trying of the year. They were often threatened with clouds like the ones building up overhead; then the clouds rolled on leaving the air barely breathable, clothes clinging wetly and hair limp in the soaring humidity. The rain, when it came, was a blessed relief.

Thinking of trivial matters like the weather helped, she found. Better than imagining what could have happened to

Tracey and Heather if they'd run into Mick Coghlan and his cronies.

"I should have sent a man with them," she berated herself.

He took his eyes off the road long enough to shake his head. "Spilled milk now. No point worrying until we find out what we're dealing with."

She hugged her arms around herself. "This is too much."

"What?"

"Dad's illness, the race with Horvath to find those bloody diamonds. If I could, I'd let him have them." She didn't add that the pressure from Ryan to return his feelings wasn't helping.

He concentrated on a churned-up stretch of road before answering. "That doesn't sound like the Judy Logan I know."

"Then maybe you don't know her as well as you think," she snapped, nerves stretched to breaking point.

"I know she doesn't give in without a fight. I haven't forgotten the fencer with blood poisoning."

A chill snapped through her. "How could I forget, either?" The man had injured himself on fencing wire and been prescribed penicillin by the Flying Doctor. Believing himself healed, the man hadn't finished the course of treatment. Not surprisingly, infection had returned. Where he was located, the airstrip was only a bare patch of earth, so the Flying Doctor's plane had been unable to land. They'd chartered Judy's Cessna to fly a nurse to the delirious patient, then airlift them both to the hospital. "I don't know which was worse, landing on that apology for an airstrip, or trying to hold the plane on course while the patient thrashed and screamed," she said.

"But you did it."

She got the message. Having flown countless hair-raising missions in her charter business, she could handle one avaricious neighbor. But oh Lord, she was getting tired of the necessity.

She pulled her shoulders back and lifted her head. "Next

thing you'll be quoting the code of the outback at me." But her voice was stronger, the moment of weakness already passing.

He shifted gears. "I only heard it once, when Blake was trying to get me to shape up. I told him it was a load of cr…rubbish."

This was news to her. "You did?"

"Given my experience, I wasn't about to live by some code he'd made up, when I had no intention of joining their boys' club."

"I had to threaten to tell Dad about their hideout cave before they'd let me join," she admitted. "Ironic, isn't it? They used the hideout without knowing the Uru rock art was in the cave right next door. And you came to live by the code. Do you remember how it goes?"

He gave a rueful chuckle. "You don't back down, you don't give up and you stand by your mates."

She wasn't about to let him off so lightly. "What about the last rule?"

"No mushy stuff? I abandoned that rule long ago."

Thinking of the mushy stuff that had preceded their headlong flight, she felt herself heating. "Considering that Tom and Blake are both engaged, you're not the only one."

Suddenly, she leaned forward, knuckles whitening as she gripped the dash. "There's Tracey's minivan and Heather's car."

"Both empty," he said as he pulled alongside the other vehicles. "At least there's no sign of Mick Coghlan and his men."

He parked the car and they got out. Judy's heart was racing. Where could the others be? Surely Coghlan hadn't taken them away somewhere? Then an alien sound shattered the silence.

Relief surged through her as the sound came again. Not screams of distress. She looked at Ryan in confusion. "Can you hear children laughing?"

Ryan nodded, breaking into a smile that reflected her relief. "They must have decided to detour to the waterhole."

Setting aside the question of how Tracey and Heather had found the swimming spot, Judy scrambled through the tangled greenery until in front of her lay a sparkling expanse of water. Not really a single waterhole, the place consisted of a series of shallow billabongs or ponds flowing across wide, rocky bars linked by miniature waterfalls. To children, the resulting frothy, fast-moving playground was as entertaining as any commercial water theme park.

As children, Judy and the boys had swum there often, naming the area the Rapids, after how the watercourse had seemed to them. Now, under lowering skies, against a backdrop of towering ochre cliffs festooned with vines, the green waters looked as inviting as ever.

Unlike many waterways on Diamond Downs, this one was not concealing death beneath the surface. The dangerous saltwater crocodiles mostly preferred to live and hunt in deeper waters, although the name saltwater was a misnomer. The man-eaters could be found in brackish or freshwater, or even well out to sea. But only the freshwater or Johnstone River crocodiles lived in these pools. Growing to a dozen feet long at the most, they gave humans a wide berth unless cornered; even then, they were more interested in escape than attack.

Even the freshies, as they were known locally, wouldn't have stayed around in the face of the mayhem greeting Judy's eyes as she emerged from the bush. Slipping and sliding over rocks worn smooth by the water, the children chased one another from pool to pool, splashing and shrieking with delight. Judy saw Sunny, in the care of the motherly Matilda, throw himself into a pond, more than living up to his name.

Heather looked up and saw them, her expression reflecting surprise and pleasure. She nudged Tracey who stood up. Leaving the other woman keeping an eye on the children, she came to Ryan and Judy. "This is the most wonderful place. Have you come for a swim, too?"

A quick glance at Ryan had confirmed their silent understanding that the women and children weren't to be alarmed by needless imaginings. Nothing had happened. They would enjoy their swim in peace before continuing their journey back to town. "We wanted to make sure you didn't run into any problems with the road. We didn't bring our swimming things," Judy said.

Tracey looked over her shoulder at the children. "Neither did they. They're swimming in their clothes or underwear." Her longing look suggested she would have liked to do the same, decorum permitting.

Remembering her friend's former calling, Judy suppressed a smile. "How on Earth did you find this place?"

"When we were at dinner at the crocodile park, Blake and your father told us about the waterhole and how to find it. When we realized we'd pass so close by, we couldn't resist stopping for a break."

"We swam here often as kids. Ryan, do you remember?"

"I remember," he said before she could say more. Judy felt a tingle as he looked at her, his gaze distant as if he were seeing her as she'd looked then, on the cusp of womanhood. Dressing in a navy one-piece swimsuit, she'd thought herself scrawny and unattractive. He'd looked at her as if she were Venus rising from the water. His stay with them had been too short for many visits to the Rapids and he'd never spoken of his feelings, but she'd always been conscious of a strange electricity in the air whenever they came here together. The place had a unique magic. She felt it again now, wishing they had the pools to themselves.

She shook herself mentally. The children looked so happy and uninhibited that she had to remind herself of the lurking danger—not from crocodiles this time, but from Horvath and his men.

"I'm worried about the weather closing in. Even this

road can become difficult if we get much more rain," Ryan said, giving the most sensible excuse for why they shouldn't linger. Why hadn't she thought of anything so simple?

Tracey nodded. "We'll only stay long enough for the kids to dry off, then we'll head back to town." She gestured toward a couple of cooler bags Heather was rifling through. "We were about to pour cool drinks for everyone. Would you like to join us?"

Ryan nodded and Heather made room for them on a flat expanse of rock out of reach of the children's splashing. "Sunny will be glad to see you," she said. "He was disappointed not to have the chance to say goodbye."

On cue, the little boy hurtled out of the water and threw his wet body at Ryan. The older man didn't shy away, knowing as well as Judy did that clothes wouldn't stay damp for long in the baking heat. "Did you see me swim?" Sunny demanded.

Ryan ruffled the child's wet hair. "I sure did. You're a champ in the making."

"Matilda showed me how to do a slippery slide down the rocks."

The little boy chattered on as Tracey called the others out of the water for their snack. Dripping and happy, they scattered across the bank, plastic tumblers of juice and chunks of homemade cake in their hands.

It was a happy, domestic scene, making Judy wish Horvath to hell and gone. The looming presence of the ochre escarpment behind them made a mockery of the wish. Up there was the Uru cave with its historic rock art, and a mile or so off to the left was the way into Blake's and Jo's hidden valley, the place more than likely holding the key to finding the lost diamonds.

"After the group leaves, we'll take a look around up there," Ryan said in a low tone, as if reading her mind.

Sunny dragged him off to inspect something he'd spotted

in the water, and Heather came to sit next to Judy. "Aren't we close to the Uru cave discovered by Shara Najran?"

Judy gestured to the escarpment. "It's very close, but I wouldn't advise taking the children there. The access is difficult."

"I wasn't thinking of seeing it today. Perhaps on another visit. When I worked in television, the meteorologists were fascinated by these places. They were once part of the ancient Devonian coral reef."

Judy wrapped her arms around her bent knees. "Geology buffs have a great time around here."

"Not only geology buffs. Weather freaks like me, too. After we met at the hospital, Tracey told me about the legend of your great-grandfather and his mine. I looked up the records for when he disappeared. Around here, the Wet was particularly heavy and the creeks rose to historic heights. No wonder Jack Logan's mine was never found. It must have been a long way above the high-water mark."

"Water that would have stayed trapped in underground watercourses for far longer than on the surface," Judy said slowly. Inwardly, she felt as if she'd been struck by lightning. Jo and Max had both found traces of diamonds in the creek flowing into the hidden valley, leading them to think the mine was somewhere along the watercourse. They had never thought of looking *up* to where the creek would have flowed around the time of Jack's explorations.

Excitement made her tingle. She wished she were alone with Ryan so she could discuss the theory. But he was sitting on a rock, surrounded by children. The sight tugged at her anew.

Finishing her drink, Tracey started to collect the picnic things into a bag. "Time we headed back."

Heather stowed her cup in a bag. "Life on the land doesn't allow much vacation time, but I hope Jeff can join us next time I get down this way."

Would Judy herself still live here, or would all this beauty be in Max Horvath's hands by then? She rejected the thought instantly. She would fight for her family land as long as breath remained in her body. "We'll be here," she vowed fiercely.

She helped to carry the picnic things back to where the cars were parked. After the ritual of goodbyes and loading up the car and van had been accomplished, the group was finally on their way. She let out a huge breath. "Thank goodness. I was scared Max's men would try something while the kids were still here."

Ryan's arm came around her. "They'd have to go through me to get to them." His tone included her and she felt comforted by the assurance, although she resisted the temptation to snuggle against him. The course she'd chosen for herself didn't allow such indulgence, although the yearning was so strong it took her breath away. Why couldn't she make up her mind what she wanted?

"Feel up to some climbing?" he asked.

She threw him a scornful look. "Anything you can do, big fellow."

His interest quickened visibly. "Anything?"

Like him, she could think of lots of ways they could take advantage of the setting, but any one of them would violate her self-imposed rules. "Rock climbing," she said.

He looked disappointed, but led the way through the bush, following the course of the creek along the escarpment to where it disappeared underground. After a half hour of steady walking, he looked upward. "According to Blake, there's a curtain of vines screening the access."

She regarded the endless screen of green with a sense of futility. Could even Blake and Jo have found their way back into their underground valley when every part of the vine-covered escarpment looked identical?

Ryan skirted the seemingly impenetrable thicket. "There has to be an opening here somewhere."

"But where?"

He turned around, facing the valley. Above the calls of the wild birds, she heard the distant burble of the Rapids. He shook his head, as if at some inner thought.

"What is it?" she asked.

"According to Blake, we shouldn't be able to hear the water."

He walked on, away from the area where the Uru cave was located, the sound getting fainter. She followed. When the sound of the Rapids faded into the distance, replaced by the shrill calls of wild birds, Ryan climbed up to the green wall and began to explore.

She joined him, feeling her way along the base of the rocks, wondering if they would ever find a way in. Without warning the greenery gave way and almost pitched her into a black hole concealed by the vines. Saving herself by grabbing the edges of the rock, she called, "I found it. I've found the entrance."

He ploughed back to her side and together they pulled aside the vine curtain to reveal a tunnel-shaped hole about four feet high and three wide. Beyond was blackness. He dropped the vines and swung her into the air. "You did it."

"We did it," she said, aware of a sense of exhilaration not wholly related to the discovery.

He felt it too, and slid her down the length of his body until she was in his arms. They were both hot and sweaty, grimy from their explorations, but she had never known a more sensuous moment than when his mouth found hers.

In the steamy setting, she felt primitive and wanton, kissing him back with a hunger that made nonsense of her earlier vow. Had he wanted to make love here and now, on a bed of greenery in the shadow of the escarpment, she wouldn't have summoned a shred of resistance.

In spite of her choice to remain uninvolved, she felt slightly cheated when he set her on her feet. "We'll have to go back to the homestead for lamps, provisions and climbing gear before we can explore inside."

Had she totally misread the moment? Was she mistaking unbridled joy for something deeper? Or was he simply giving her what she'd said she wanted? Distance from him and from any relationship that demanded more from her?

Confused and irritated with herself, she helped him gather small rocks and build a discreet marker that would help them locate the spot when they returned, equipped to explore more fully. The temptation to step into the opening was almost irresistible, but she knew the danger as well as Ryan did. Blake and Jo had been trapped in the caverns overnight, finding their way out as much by good luck as good judgment. With so many people depending on her, Judy wasn't prepared to take unnecessary risks.

Ryan sensed that he'd disappointed Judy and felt his anger rise. Kissing her had been an impulsive act to celebrate their discovery. In spite of the needs clawing at him whenever she was within touching distance, he'd promised himself he wouldn't touch her again unless it was what she wanted. He hadn't meant to do so now.

If she'd been honest with him, she should have resisted him, but she hadn't. Her body had felt yielding and fluid, her mouth hot and eager. If he hadn't known better, he'd have sworn she wanted more from him. But what? Not his love, she'd made that clear.

To dissipate his frustration, he started to pile rocks together to mark the entrance of the underground complex so they could find it again when they returned with more gear.

He would need more than ropes and a lamp to work Judy out, he decided. He understood her fear of ending up like her mother. Fran Logan had been foolish to ignore the signs of appendicitis until it was too late. But she hadn't been the type to be stupidly heroic. She had probably dismissed her pain as something that would go away if she ignored it, not realizing the danger. So at worst, she'd been guilty of wishful thinking, and had paid the supreme price.

Judy seemed convinced that all outback wives had to be sacrificial lambs, but Ryan knew that such behavior wasn't exclusive to the outback. He remembered his own mother quietly choosing school shoes for him over new clothes for herself when money had been tight, and suspected mothers the world over had been making similar choices since time began.

Nor was self-sacrifice an exclusively female preserve. Thinking of his relationship with Sunny Coleman, Ryan knew he'd do almost anything for the little boy, and Sunny wasn't even his own flesh and blood. At the thought of the children he hoped to father one day, Ryan's gut tightened. He'd die for them and their mother. As he added another rock to the cairn, his thoughts came full circle back to Judy. He couldn't work this one out for her. She had to solve the problem for herself.

He didn't blame her for being apprehensive. The thought of being responsible for small lives he'd helped to create awed him. Other than Des Logan, Ryan's experience of good fathering was terrifyingly limited. His birth father's example had been all too brief, but he'd had his own issues. Ryan hadn't understood when he was younger, but now he could imagine his father's terror at surviving the accident that had killed Ryan's grandmother. Ryan knew first-hand the nightmare of being left alone in the world. His father had dealt with that and the Logan family's rejection as well. Of course, they'd probably believed it was best for little Nicholas Smith to live with his distant relatives. And since Jack Logan hadn't survived to marry Lizina, the law wouldn't have allowed the Logans to keep Nicholas with them anyway.

Full circle indeed, Ryan told himself, placing a final rock

on the knee-high pile. First, his grandmother and her child had been rejected by the Logans; now, Judy was doing it to him. Well, to the devil with needing anyone. He had come this far on his own, he could go right on the same way.

The thought didn't cheer him as much as it should have.

Ryan's silence began to unnerve Judy. He was giving her the distance she wanted, so why was she so unhappy? The lowering clouds reflected her gray mood as she helped him build the cairn. After a time, she straightened and arched her back. "I wish it would rain. This period just before the Wet is the worst time of the year."

"It is oppressive," he agreed, looking at the leaden sky. Apart from the soaking shower two days before, the mountainous clouds had built up every morning only to roll away around midday, leaving clear blue skies. Today, the clouds had lingered longer and seemed lower and heavier, making rain seem more likely. "We could use a downpour just to wash away this blasted humidity," he observed.

She swiped her sleeve across her forehead. "I'm beginning to wish I'd gone into the water with the kids."

"It wouldn't have helped for long. Fifteen minutes later, you'd be sweating again." He looked around. "We've done all we can for now. Time we headed back."

She thought of the walk back to where they'd left his vehicle. "If it does decide to rain, I'd rather not get caught out here."

He offered her his hand to climb down to the road. After the slightest hesitation she was sure he'd noticed, she let him help her down the incline. He was as sure-footed as a rock wallaby. But no wallaby ever made her heart beat so fast at the slightest contact. Or made her wish she wasn't so resolute in her determination to remain a solo act.

Reaching the road, she stopped and lifted her head.

"What is it?" Ryan asked, watching her.

"I don't know. Something's not right."

"The stormy atmosphere?"

"Probably." She looked around, trying to pinpoint the source of her unease. Then suddenly she stiffened, her fingers tightening in Ryan's. "Is that smoke?"

He looked in the direction she indicated, and she felt his reaction through her arm. "It's coming from the homestead."

"Oh, my God. Do you think Horvath…"

His arm around her, he began to urge her in the direction of the car. "There's no time to think. Let's go."

They made the car at a run, reaching it streaming with perspiration and on legs that felt like jelly. Judy didn't care. Her home was in danger and she had to get there. If she could have made it faster on foot, she'd have run all the way.

She threw herself into the passenger seat as Ryan got behind the wheel and gunned the motor in a series of fluid movements. She was still fastening her seat belt as he spun the car around, the tires spitting gravel.

Smoke mingled with cloud on the horizon so Judy couldn't tell how bad the fire was from this distance. She resisted blaming herself for leaving the homestead protected only by a couple of the stockmen. Making sure the children were okay had been more important. Thank goodness they were well on their way back to town by now.

"Do you think lightning struck the house and started a fire?" she asked Ryan.

Grimly focused on driving faster than conditions allowed, he didn't look at her. "Do you think so?"

She hung on to the seat as the car became airborne over a corrugation. "No."

Thick fumes from burning eucalyptus reached them before they saw the fire itself. A burned-out car sat corkscrewed near a cottage, one of the unoccupied ones, she saw in relief, but the structure already well alight. Through the acrid smoke she saw one of the stockmen aiming a hose at the flames threatening to engulf the next cottage. One of the wives was opening gates between the yards, allowing the terrified horses to plunge through. Another woman was shooing chickens out of their yard.

Ryan abandoned the car on the perimeter of the chaos. Judy threw herself out of the vehicle and into the fray. The property had its own small water tanker and she saw that it had already been pressed into use to confront the fire centered on the bunkhouse. "Have you radioed Cade and the other men?" she yelled over the fire's roaring voice.

"First thing we did," the man yelled, without turning from his task.

Her main thought was to keep the flames away from the homestead. Ryan was there ahead of her, soaking the roofline and surroundings, she saw. She grabbed a burlap bag from a pile the others had dragged out, saturated it and began to beat at the spot fires springing up all around her from the burning eucalyptus leaves falling like rain.

Although cleared areas protected the homestead, the long dry season had left plenty of fuel to feed the fire in the desiccated eucalyptus trees, savannah grasslands and accumulation of leaf litter and forest debris. The timber buildings were tinder-dry and she felt despair grip her as the bunkhouse went up with a great whooshing sound, the flames shooting high into the air and staining the sky with red.

Ryan broke away from the homestead long enough to order the stockman away from the bunkhouse. "Concentrate on protecting your own homes." The man nodded and turned his hose on the other buildings, while Ryan returned his attention to the main house.

There was a crack like a gunshot as a tree branch snapped off and connected with a power line in an explosive conflagration, showering her with sparks. She beat them off her clothes and hair, and started on the spot fires erupting around her, dodging pieces of burnt bark dropping around her like stones thrown by a malevolent sprite.

The intense heat was killing, the air barely breathable through a thick blanket of smoke. She tore a strip from the hem of her T-shirt and bound it around her mouth, filtering out the worst of the fiery particles. She could do nothing about the stinging when they landed on her skin. The pain seemed insignificant compared to the fight on their hands.

She was barely aware of other hands joining her efforts to beat out the spot fires until the roar of a bulldozer told her Cade, Andy and the other men had arrived and were clearing away all flammable material between the fire and the houses.

A gang of cockatoos flew overhead, screaming at the flames as if in protest, their white wings turning the smoke cloud ragged. The light was now an eerie reddish yellow and she couldn't see Ryan through the brown, dusty smoke.

Somewhere behind her a window shattered. She dodged flying chunks of debris and flaming branches, focusing all her attention on beating out fires as fast as they erupted around her. Her breath felt as if it were being sucked out of her lungs.

Then her exposed skin was stung by what she took to be another ember and she beat at it frantically, but her hand came away wet. It was raining. Praise be, it was actually raining. She pulled the mask off her face.

Her back muscles protested as she let the wet burlap bag fall against her side, and looked up to see the clouds finally dumping their life-saving load of water on the homestead. Moments later, water was streaming down her face, mingling with soot and tears. Slowly, the air cleared and the ground steamed as the fire met its nemesis, rain.

Ryan was still directing a stream of water under the eaves of the homestead where wisps of smoke told her how close they had come to losing everything. Too overwhelmed to move, she stood in the cleansing rain, trying to make sense of what had just happened.

Horvath had happened, of that she was sure. Ryan had seen his men in the vicinity. No doubt a lookout had made them aware of the exact moment when she and Ryan had driven away. Knowing Cade and the rest of the men were out at the muster camp, Coghlan could have taken his time setting the fire. When she investigated, she'd probably find it had started in the bunkhouse, the most flammable structure, now reduced to a smoldering pile of rubble.

Automatically, she took stock. Besides the bunkhouse, one unoccupied cottage had gone, as well as several smaller outbuildings and most of the fencing closest to the house. The horses were safe, having instinctively sought safer ground as soon as they were let out. She could see them huddled together on a low hillside, nervously sniffing the air. The people around her were soot-blackened and looked as exhausted as she felt. But they were all safe, she found, when Cade ordered a head count. Not even one of the working dogs had been lost.

Glad of the rain camouflaging her tears, she let her knees soften and the sack drop to the ground. How much more of this was she going to have to take? The urge to throw herself down and howl was strong, but she couldn't. She needed to provide leadership for the remaining staff.

For one second, she buried her face in her hands, then resolutely lifted her head and walked back to the waiting crew.

An hour later, as much order as possible had been restored, although the acrid smell lingered. The horses were secure in a makeshift paddock and Cade was already overseeing the clearing of the bunkhouse, the women supplying a steady stream of tea and helping hands where needed.

Ryan came up behind her in the rain and began to massage her knotted neck muscles. His touch felt wonderful, but she didn't melt against him in spite of the temptation. "Is the house okay?"

"No serious damage. None of the burning embers managed to get in."

"We have you and Cade to thank for saving the house. In his condition, Des couldn't have handled losing the place."

"What about you?" Ryan asked.

The gentleness in his voice was her undoing. All at once, her control evaporated. She turned away. If he said one more word, she would bury her face against his shoulder and let the tears come.

Chapter 12

She was aware of Ryan leading her inside the homestead but didn't resist, not wanting the others to see her break down. She fought the demeaning tears. She couldn't come apart. Too many people needed her.

He steered her to a chair but stayed close. "It's okay to let go. The worst is over now."

Her head came up. "Is it?" she demanded. "What comes next? You, Cade or one of the others gets killed?" The very thought was enough to threaten her fragile composure, but she dragged in a shuddering breath and scrubbed at her eyes, making them sting as soot mixed with her tears.

"We knew Horvath would raise the stakes when he learned he'd been tricked out of the deed to Cotton Tree Gorge."

"If you'd given the paper to him, this might not have happened."

She saw his body tense.

"You don't mean that. Giving in to a man like Horvath only makes him demand more and more," he said.

Her voice sounded wobbly. "You're right, I didn't mean it. But how much more is there for him to take? He already holds our mortgage. If he gets Diamond Downs, he gets everything anyway."

Ryan's hand cupped her chin, forcing her to look at him. "He isn't getting Diamond Downs."

Fresh tremors swept through her. "He nearly did today."

"Buildings can be replaced. That's all he got, Judy. Hang on to that. Don't let him win."

"It's hard."

He cupped her face. "Not impossible. Think of this. His men must have left clues when they started the fire. We may finally have the evidence to put him behind bars."

She shook her head. "You said yourself, he doesn't get his hands dirty. I bet we find evidence that the fire was deliberately lit, but nothing to connect the crime with Horvath."

His sigh ripped through her. "Yeah, I thought of that, too."

Going into the kitchen, he came back with a portable lantern and matches kept for emergencies. Soon the living room was bathed in a yellow glow. Outside, lights bobbed as Cade supervised the cleanup. The tree branch falling against the lines must have damaged the power supply. They had a generator, but it needed to be turned on. She started to get up.

Ryan came back to stand over her. "Where do you think you're going?"

"To start the generator."

He gestured toward the activity visible through the window. "Plenty of people to take care of that for now. Cade is making sure everything's under control."

She collapsed back in the chair like a rag doll, her burst of strength waning. When a glass was placed in her hand, she looked at it with mild curiosity. "What is this?"

"I opened your dad's best fifteen-year-old Scotch whiskey."

From somewhere she dredged up a laugh. "He'll kill you. He was saving this for a special occasion."

"I think saving his home counts as special, don't you?"

She raised the glass in a toast. "That definitely counts. I don't know how I would have been able to tell Dad if the homestead had gone up." Hearing her voice falter again, she drank quickly. The tawny liquid seared her smoke-ravaged throat but the heat spread quickly through her body, blunting the worst of the trauma. She swallowed the rest of the drink.

Ryan finished his and set both glasses aside. "You need to eat, then rest."

"I'm not hungry. Perhaps later."

"It's already later."

Tilting her arm to the lantern, she read her watch. During the crisis, evening had come and gone. Now it was fully dark outside and she hadn't even noticed. "We should call Dad."

"Cade said he'll do it tomorrow. Everything else will keep. There's nothing you have to do right now except go to bed."

"Not alone." She didn't know why she said it, except that it was how she felt.

His gaze bored into her, unreadable in the low light. "Are you sure, Judy?"

After the fire, the thought of being alone made her quake. She wanted Ryan to hold and comfort her. Love her? One step at a time. "I'm sure."

He adjusted the lantern to a soft glow so Cade would have light when he came in. Then Ryan all but lifted her out of the chair. When he started to scoop her into his arms, she balked. "I can walk."

"Always so independent," he murmured. However, his arm around her did a good job of holding her up. Her legs felt rubbery. Maybe she should have let him carry her. She hadn't been carried in years. But she hated feeling so weak, so—female?

In his bedroom, lit by a fat white candle, she saw herself in the mirror and winced. Streaked with soot and tears, with ashes in her hair, she looked a sight. "I should shower," she said.

"You look beautiful. We're a pair."

He meant in looking so messy, but the word disturbed her. She didn't want to be a pair like lovebirds, salt and pepper, Jack and Jill. Ryan and Judy. Lord, she must be more tired than she'd realized. The room felt as if it was spinning.

Seeing her stumble, he took her in his arms and the room steadied. "Let me."

She stood like a mannequin while he undressed her, stripping off her ruined clothes down to bra and panties. "I can manage these," she said, instinctively pulling back when he reached for her bra fastening.

"Do you want me to sleep in another room?"

She understood he was giving her a last chance to change her mind. There was only one possible answer, and they both needed to be clear about it. She wasn't only reacting to the crisis. She wanted to be with him. What would happen afterward, she didn't know. For once, she didn't feel as if she needed to know. That much *was* reaction to the fire. Forcibly reminded of life's fragility, she didn't want to risk never knowing his lovemaking.

"I want you to sleep here with me," she said clearly.

Her voice was the only decisive thing about her. Everything else was a mass of edgy nerves and nameless desires. Not hard to see why so many women fantasized about being carried off by a man. How much simpler to have the decision taken out of your hands, the pleasure unfettered by moral constraints.

Ryan wasn't the type, she knew. He would always consider her needs and wishes. But oh, how tired she was of decisions for the moment. Surrender was alien to her, but had never seemed more tempting.

He seemed to sense her mood and was galvanized to jerk her against him. "I won't ask again."

Needs slammed through her, leaving her powerless to resist the onslaught of his mouth on hers. His fingers raked through her hair, down her neck and around to the fullness of her breast. Her bra was pushed aside in his hunger to touch and hold.

As he found her sensitized nipple, she arched against him, all wanting. She started to pant, air suddenly in short supply. Her arms linked around his neck, pulling his head down until he fastened on her breast, making her head spin anew. The suckling sensation found an echo deep within her body. When he pressed her back onto the bed, she pulled him down with her, not wanting to let him go.

Her fingers tore at his buttons, opening the shirt so she could plunge her hands inside. Kneeling over her, he felt hard and hot, his chest hair teasing her palms and making her dig her splayed fingers into his unyielding flesh, kneading it like a cat clawing until his breath became as labored as hers.

Rearing back, he stripped the shirt off and flung it aside, then stood up long enough to unzip his pants and let them drop. His eyes feasting on her, he tore off his underpants and leaned over her again.

In the lantern light, she'd seen his magnificence and felt a heartbeat's pride in bringing him to that. Giddy with power, she lifted her arms in invitation.

He bent and kissed her throat, then down and down the length of her body, kissing and caressing her until she cried out with the intensity of her desire.

Her bra followed his clothes, and she raised her hips to help him pull off her panties. Reason fled with the garments. She wanted to feel him next to her and inside her. Nothing else mattered.

Ryan felt her surrender to him. For so long, he had been on edge waiting for the moment to happen, never doubting that it would. In his mind, she had always been his. This was simply confirmation.

And what glorious confirmation.

In his wildest dreams, he had never expected her to make him burn hotter than the fire they'd fought together. He inhaled the smokiness lingering on her skin and hair, tasted fine whiskey on her mouth, and gloried in all of it. With her hair unkempt, specked with ash and twigs, and her face smeared with soot like tribal markings, she looked primitive, wonderful.

She pushed him so close to the brink that he felt out of control, barely able to stop himself from plunging and taking his fill.

She deserved better, he reminded himself in the fringes of rational thought remaining to him. She deserved the very best he could give her. If that meant aching with the need to hold back, so be it.

Holding back didn't seem to be what she wanted. As he explored her, desperate to give her every bit of pleasure he could for as long as he could, she took him in her hands and gave back measure for measure, until the drumming rain outside found an answer in the throb of the blood at his temples.

Enough sense lingered to drive him to his wallet and get out a condom. He'd carried it almost as a talisman since returning to Diamond Downs. The urge to give her his child was so strong that his hand shook as he opened the packet and covered himself. She wanted him. It wouldn't always be enough, but he wouldn't think past right now.

Then he could hold back no longer. Raising her hips, he eased himself into her but she arched and took him more deeply than he'd meant to go yet. She was having none of his restraint, lifting her legs and linking her ankles behind him, astonishingly strong as she gave herself to him and took from him, moaning his name over and over.

Lightning split the darkened sky outside, reflected as jagged lights in his head. She was his storm and his shelter as he alternatively raged and quieted. She took everything and demanded more. Gave to him. Soared with him. As reckless as he was. Insatiable.

He knew the fire had kindled this response. Seen the despair that had made her turn to him. He didn't care. They would have come to this one way or another. She was his destiny as he was hers, and the knowledge sent him deeper and deeper, driving faster and faster, aware of carrying her with him until she threw her head back and cried out her release. Calling her name, he spilled himself into her and felt himself hurtle off the edge of the world.

The next morning, Judy awoke wondering if the whole world had converged on Diamond Downs. The sound of voices and machinery outside had her glancing at the clock radio. After nine. What was she thinking?

She flung away the covers and stopped as memory flooded back. She was in Ryan's room and alone, but the imprint of his body remained in the bed beside her. Sooty streaks on the wildly twisted sheets told their own story. She felt gritty, aching in every muscle, but alive in a way she hadn't felt for a long time.

His bathroom still smelled enticingly of masculine shower gel and aftershave, the scents intensified by the steam from her shower. She had to stop herself from breathing them in like a lovestruck fool, which she wasn't.

Wrapped in a towel, she padded to her own room and got dressed in jeans and a faded blue chambray western shirt. Yesterday's clothes and the sheets all needed laundering, so she left them for now. Too ravenous to go outside without eating, she sliced cold chicken into a bread roll and made coffee, downing the makeshift meal as quickly as possible. An investigation of the fire was under way outside, and she wanted to be part of it. She should really be directing the show but, looking out she saw Ryan and Cade already had this under control.

Ryan was good at taking the lead, she thought bitterly. Yet she couldn't blame him for last night. She'd asked him to stay with her, knowing what would happen. Her reaction to the fire and turning to him for comfort justified her decision, but did not explain the urgency she felt to be with him and feel him inside her. Watching him through the window, she felt the desire building again. She deliberately tried to use anger to drown out her physical needs. Allowing herself a night of passion with Ryan was acceptable, but mooning over him and imagining a life and family with Ryan was not.

By the time she emerged from the house, the old Judy was back, at least outwardly, all traces of neediness banished to the darkest reaches of her mind for now. Ryan saw her and came over accompanied by a slim, black-haired Japanese-Australian man in police uniform. "Hello, Tony," she said, recognizing him as a constable stationed in the region.

Tony Honda shook her hand. "Looks like you had quite a party here."

Her gaze went to Cade and two of the stockmen steadily quartering the burned-out rubble of the bunkhouse. "Find anything?"

The constable frowned. "Not so far. There was a lot of lightning last night. A strike could have sparked the fire."

"The lightning came later," Ryan said. "This was deliberate."

She made herself meet his gaze and shivered at the desire still there. She might have known he wouldn't let her forget so easily, as his expression made clear. Her irritation rose. Why couldn't he be happy with a one-night stand like any other normal cowboy? Because he knew she couldn't, she sensed. And he was right, damn him. Quarantining her feelings while she focused on other things would only work for a time; then they would have to face what had happened. But not now.

"The challenge is proving arson," Tony Honda went on, oblivious to the currents swirling around him. "If this was deliberate, whoever set the fire was careful and thorough."

"Not thorough enough," Ryan said. He strode to the burned-out shell of the car, the first thing to catch fire. Metal glinted in the ashes and he stirred them with his feet, then picked out a small object.

The police officer looked at it with interest. "A key tag?"

"Belonging to Mick Coghlan," Ryan explained. "I saw it on a bunch of keys hanging from his belt at Horvath's place."

"You noticed that detail while Coghlan was shooting at you?" she asked in astonishment.

Tony shot Ryan a curious look. "Do I want to know?"

Ryan rubbed the scar at his temple. "Better you don't ask. I was looking for evidence and he interrupted me."

"Your investigator's license doesn't cover housebreaking."

"I told you, you don't want to know." Ryan tapped the key tag in the officer's palm. "This proves Coghlan set the fire."

Tony closed his fingers around the tag. "It could just as easily prove you stole his keys while…ah…looking for evidence. I'll get some forensic people out here as soon as I can, but for now we don't have much to go on."

"Can't you at least interview Max Horvath?" she asked.

"I can find out what he and his men were doing when the fire started."

Ryan nodded. "I'd like to ride along."

The officer hesitated. "Normally, I wouldn't consider it, but right now everybody else is tied up looking for a couple of tourists who went missing from their accommodation last night, so your help could be useful, as long as you remember who's the law around here."

Ryan's look said he was in no doubt, and Judy guessed he'd

follow the officer's lead only as long as it suited him. She suspected Tony Honda was aware of it, too. The pair had obviously come to know and like each other through Ryan's undercover work. But Ryan wouldn't let friendship come between him and his target, in this case Max. Or her when this was resolved, she thought with an involuntary shiver. Just because they'd made love didn't mean Ryan would stop pursuing her. Or that she'd be torn between wanting him to stop, and fearing he would.

After they left, she threw herself into helping restore order. They couldn't do much about the bunkhouse without disturbing possible evidence, but she could give the men a hand. Cade was working on the fire-damaged fencing around the holding yards when she joined him.

Stripped down to a navy blue sleeveless T-shirt and low-slung jeans, with a battered Akubra hat pushed back on his head, he looked like a cover model for a romance novel, she thought. Almost thirty now, he'd come a long way from the skinny, truculent street kid who'd joined the family at fourteen. She'd been ten at the time and had been both fascinated and repelled by the life he'd led, so different from her own.

"I expected you to go with Ryan and Tony," Cade commented without looking up from the new rail he was levering into position. The pale timber stood in sharp contrast to the silvery gray of the weathered wood.

She scooped up a handful of batten screws and handed them to him. "Men's work."

Cade looked surprised. "Ryan didn't say that, did he?"

"Not if he wanted to live. I got the impression he and Tony were mates from a previous life, so I didn't want to play fifth wheel."

"It makes sense he and Tony would get along if they've worked on the same cases. I got a surprise this morning when Rye told me what he does for a living. I thought jackeroo was pretty much it. But I knew a jackeroo wouldn't have been as skilled at investigating this fire, so he had to come clean about his real occupation."

She felt gratified that Cade hadn't known about Ryan's undercover work either. "Dad was the only one who knew. I used to wonder why he didn't get on Ryan's case about living up to his potential, when he came home."

Cade strained to slide the old cap rail back into place. The timber was scorched but still sound. Just as well. They could make a claim on their insurance, but replacing everything they'd lost would still stretch the budget. She appreciated Cade trying to salvage as much of the original material as he could.

"I half expected him to be on mine this time," he said as he worked.

Her hand stilled on the other end of the cap rail. "You're entitled to a vacation, aren't you?"

"I'm not on vacation. I'm back for good."

"I thought you didn't want to be a cattleman? You always said you loved being a free agent, roving the world with your camera."

He stared off into the distance. "Yeah, well, after a few years being free isn't all it's cracked up to be."

"Is anything wrong, Cade?"

He brushed sawdust off his hands. "Can't a man decide to come home without something being wrong?"

"I guess not." Despite his assurance, she felt uneasy. Cade had always been proud of living his life his way. He'd been her role model when she decided to start her air charter business. Whenever she'd wondered if she was missing anything by not getting married and starting a family, she would think of him. Happily self-employed, a high achiever, free of permanent ties. If he hadn't exactly had a girl in every port, he'd never lacked for female companionship, although none of his relationships had lasted for long. "Cade, are you gay?" she blurted out.

His startled look raked her, then he laughed. "That's quite a stretch, isn't it? For the record, no I'm not."

"Not that I'd care either way," she hastened to add. "You'll always be my foster brother and part of my family, no matter what."

An unreadable expression flitted across his features, then was gone. "That means a lot to me, more than you can guess." He began to gather the tools into a box. "What does a man have to do to get lunch around here?"

Knowing a change of subject when she heard one, she said, "Make it."

"I'll mess up your nice, clean kitchen. And use up all the good stuff before Ryan gets back."

"It isn't my nice clean anything. I just happen to use the kitchen more than the rest of you. I sure clean it more often."

He grinned. "You know what they say? Practice makes perfect."

"Explains why you're so good at putting your foot in your mouth."

He threw a cracked leather glove at her and missed. "Snippy today, aren't we? Probably didn't get enough sleep." A theatrical wink followed.

Heat rolled over her. Cade couldn't have missed seeing Ryan take her inside after the fire, and her unused bedroom would have confirmed his suspicions. "If I agree to make lunch for you, can we not go there?" she demanded.

"It's okay to discuss my sexuality, but not…all right, you made your point, I'll behave." She thwacked at him with the glove, and he recoiled in mock alarm. "Can I help it if I touched a nerve?"

"You did not touch a nerve."

"And there's absolutely nothing going on between you and Ryan?"

"I said I don't want to go there."

He held up his hands. "No call for you to be bashful. Anybody with eyes can see the two of you have been smitten for years. I'm glad you're finally doing something about it."

She rolled her eyes. "What's the point of arguing with you?"

His expression sobered. "One thing I learned on my travels is that you never know what lies ahead. If you love Ryan, don't waste time fighting your feelings. Grab your chance with both hands and hang on. Doing anything else leaves too much room for regrets."

Was there was something he wasn't telling her? "Do you have regrets?" she asked.

Cade gave her a long, measured look. "More than I should have, little sister. Now how about that lunch? I'm starving."

Ryan came into the kitchen while she was carving cold roast lamb to go with the salad she'd made. "How did you get on?" she asked, batting away his hand as he reached for a piece of lamb.

He feinted with his other hand and grabbed the lamb while she was distracted, stuffing the meat into his mouth before she could protest. "We didn't see hide nor hair of Horvath or Coghlan, and—surprise, surprise—none of the staff could tell Tony where they were or when they might be back."

"Surprise, surprise," she echoed, wishing he would give her some space. Standing this close, the musky scent of him, a mixture of trail dust and perspiration, was a potent reminder of how much closer they'd been last night. She pushed the memory away. "Where's Tony?"

"Gone back to his headquarters to help with the hunt for the tourists," he said. "Andy and some of his people asked if they could use their tracking skills to help. Since there's not much more we can do here till the police finish their investigation, I told them to go ahead."

"And Cade?"

"He's eating with the men before they go. Said something

about not being a fifth wheel. Do you know what that's about?"

"No idea." Inwardly she cursed Cade for his clumsy attempt to maneuver her and Ryan into spending time alone. Getting them together seemed important to Cade, and his reason baffled her as much as her own reluctance. She carried the plates to the table and sat down while Ryan washed his hands then joined her. "Cade said he's home to stay."

"So he tells me."

"You don't find that unusual?"

Ryan cut into the tender lamb and ate before answering. "None of my business."

"You don't care if something's wrong in his life?"

"If there is, he'll tell us when he's ready."

"Men," she said in exasperation, forking her salad and eating it angrily.

"Last night you didn't have a problem with my being a man," he pointed out, further fueling her annoyance. "I got the impression you found our differences stimulating."

Her heightened color betrayed just how stimulating. "Last night, I was overwrought because of the fire. It doesn't count."

His interest sharpened visibly. "So we have to make love again when it does count?"

"That's not what I mean." She put her knife and fork down. "I don't want us to make love again at all."

"I know I didn't disappoint you."

"Far from it," she said before realizing that the admission was unlikely to strengthen her case. "That isn't the point. Cade's already planning our trip down the aisle. How many others are thinking the same?"

"I don't care what they think," Ryan said.

"Then you're the only one," she denied, wishing she felt more sure of her ground. "Being good in bed doesn't mean our next words have to be, 'I do.'"

"This isn't over, Judy."

Why did he have to make such an issue out of last night? Her body tingled whenever she thought of their lovemaking. Spectacular didn't begin to cover the roller-coaster ride she'd taken with him. But there had to be more to a relationship than good sex. Such as wanting the same things from life.

Ryan was unlikely to be happy having her wheel around the sky and return for nights of glorious lovemaking when her charter business allowed, although the prospect made her heart pound. No matter what he said now, if they got involved and even tried to build a future together, he'd eventually start thinking in terms of children, then she'd be trapped.

It wasn't that she disliked the idea of children, only that she wished she could have them on her own terms. Biology was hell sometimes.

Her train of thought was derailed when the phone rang. Ryan picked it up, his light greeting quickly changing to concern. "Where are you? How long has he been missing? Have you informed the police?"

Judy's heart jumped. When Ryan put the phone down, she looked at him in dread. "What's happened?"

"Tracey and Heather took the kids out to Wolf Creek crater as planned. One of the kids was stung by a wasp. While they were attending to her, Sunny wandered off. He's missing."

She clutched a hand to her throat, well aware of how much Sunny meant to Ryan. "Oh no. How long ago?"

"Best part of an hour. They started a search on their own, thinking he wouldn't have gone far. Then they called the police."

"But they're all out searching for those tourists."

"They're going to split the team into two," he said.

She was all business now. "Can they get a helicopter or a plane up?"

"The police are diverting a chopper to Wolf Creek from the other search, but the pilot needs to refuel first."

She pushed her chair away from the table and stood up. "They're not the only pilots in the area. The Cessna's ready to fly. I can be in the air over the crater before the helicopter pilot has finished fueling up."

"We," he amended quickly. "I'm coming with you."

"Don't you trust my piloting skills, Smith?" she snapped.

"You're going to need a spotter. I have good eyes."

Accepting his argument, she nodded. "Finding one little boy in country that rugged will take more than good eyes. Better start praying for a miracle."

Chapter 13

"I didn't mean for you to start praying until we reach the crater," she said as she settled into what she did best, getting the Cessna into the air. In the seat beside her, he was gripping the seat belt as if it were a lifeline.

"A few extra prayers can't hurt," he said, sounding as if his nerves were wire-tight. She might have blamed his tension on Sunny's disappearance but had flown with enough nervous passengers to recognize the symptoms.

Confirming her suspicion, he sucked in a breath as the small plane rattled and shook, gaining height. "Could this be why you haven't flown with me before?" she asked.

He kept his gaze fixed on the horizon. "Could what be why?"

She glanced at his hands. "White knuckles."

He made an obvious effort to relax. "Imagination. I never had the need to go up with you, that's all."

She gestured out the window. "See those pink creatures flapping past the plane? They're pigs."

At least he could still raise a laugh. "Okay, so I'm not the world's most comfortable flier when it comes to small planes. Satisfied?"

She banked smoothly before answering. "I've seen you go into a corral with a kicking, screaming stallion and gentle it using nothing but a length of rope and a piece of cotton cloth. Everybody has their own idea of a nightmare. That would be mine."

His breathing eased. "Thank you."

"You're welcome. I only wish I'd had time to replace the brake disks on my baby before we needed to do this."

She heard him gulp. "Brake disks?"

"They're supposed to be micrometer-checked at each annual service and replaced when they get to minimum thickness. Mine were due to be miked this month."

"Did you have to mention that now?"

"Oh, sorry. Look, they're fine, really. I always err on the side of caution."

He shot her a wry glance. "You've no idea how that reassures me."

She checked gauges. "Relax. We're in good shape, and we will find Sunny."

He nodded tautly. "Do you carry parachutes."

"One," she responded.

He grabbed a handhold. "One?"

"For the pilot, in case something goes wrong and I have to go for help."

It was an old flier's joke but produced the intended effect. He leaned closer to the window, forgetting to be nervous as he concentrated on the landscape below.

After they'd flown straight and level for a while, he turned to her. "We should be over Wolf Creek soon. Tracey said when they last saw Sunny, they were in the crater not far from where the road ends at the base of the western wall."

Judy nodded, bringing them lower until details of the landscape became more distinct. What looked like a low, unimpressive range of hills from a distance soon resolved themselves into the shattered quartzite walls of Wolf Creek crater. From the air, the crater looked like a giant thumbprint on the edge of the Great Sandy Desert. Most of the landmark was buried under windblown sand, but enough remained above ground to create a moonlike landscape.

More than a million years before, according to her reading, a meteor weighing thousands of tons had hurtled to Earth from the northeast, spreading most of the material ejected from the crater to the southwest. This had resulted in steeply sloping sides on the northeast side and gentler slopes to the southwest.

Aboriginal mythology told of two rainbow snakes whose paths across the desert had formed two nearby creeks. The crater they called Kandimalal was where one of the snakes had emerged from the ground. Whether made by mythical snakes or a meteor, the result was spectacular, she thought.

"This place always reminds me of a giant campfire site," Ryan commented.

In the center of the raised rim was a darker smudge that did look like the remains of a campfire. It was an illusion, she knew. The flat floor of the crater was dotted with rugged spinifex grassland and sinkholes containing mineral-laden water. In the center, the trees were closer together with denser canopies, creating the appearance of a dark patch from above.

When Judy had last walked the crater, she'd seen brown ring-tail dragons stalking insects on the flowering shrubs along the rock wall. Red kangaroos lived in the area, but she'd seen none during the heat of the day. However, she had watched the spectacular pink Major Mitchell cockatoos feeding on seed from the wattle and paperbark trees on the crater floor. It wasn't hard to imagine how any of these creatures might have distracted Sunny so he lost sight of the others.

A banking turn put them over where the road ended at the base. "There's Heather's car and Tracey's minivan," she said.

Ryan was scanning through binoculars. "I see them. Looks like Tracey and Heather did as I suggested and got the rest of the group together near the information shelter. One lost child is enough to deal with."

Below them, the adults waved in recognition. Judy waggled the wings and then began to circle the crater, looking for any sign of the little boy. In her phone call, Tracey had told Ryan that Sunny was wearing a yellow T-shirt and jeans and a red baseball cap. The bright colors would hopefully make him easy to spot from the air.

"Anything?" she asked Ryan as he peered through the glasses.

"A flash of red near the rim on the western side," he said.

She nosed downward as low as she dared, leveling off almost at treetop height. Ryan didn't enjoy the experience, she saw as he white-knuckled the glasses again. But he focused on his task, swearing under his breath. "Nothing but some flowering bushes," he said.

The plane disturbed a mob of red kangaroos who leaped away as the plane roared over their heads. No sign of a little boy. "When did the police say they'd have people on the ground?" she asked, her eyes scanning steadily.

"An hour," he reminded her. "They should be here anytime."

She completed a few more circuits with no sign of anything red or yellow. Pointedly she avoided thinking of the water-filled sinkholes Sunny could have stumbled into. Last time she was here, she'd seen enough bones scattered around the waterholes to warn her what could happen if you drank the stuff, much less fell in.

Ryan lowered the glasses. "What if we're looking in the wrong place?"

She shot him a puzzled glance. "This is where he wandered off."

"Or was taken."

A cold sensation prickled the back of her neck. "What are you getting at?"

"Horvath wasn't at home when Tony Honda and I called there this morning. What if Horvath was tracking Sunny, waiting for an opportunity to grab him?"

The sensation of cold intensified. "Because he found out that you had a relationship?"

"He could have some crazy idea of using Sunny to pressure me into handing over the genuine deed to Cotton Tree Gorge."

She nodded slowly, taking this in. "The fire didn't burn us out and you tricked him out of the paperwork. But would he be desperate enough to resort to kidnapping?" Her heart ached at the thought of the little boy in Max's clutches.

"I think he's at the point where he'd try anything."

She chewed her lip. "Wouldn't he get in touch, make demands?"

"He can't while we're up here."

"Then we'd better set down so he can contact us." If Ryan was right and Max was behind this, she added mentally. There were a lot of ifs.

Ryan touched her arm. "Not here."

"A hunch?"

He inclined his head. "Cotton Tree Gorge."

It made a crazy kind of sense, she thought. Max wanted to explore the gorge. He would know they'd be searching Wolf Creek crater, so if he had taken Sunny, why not hide the child in the last place anyone would think to look? Anyone but Ryan.

A distant plume of dust along the rugged approach road caught her attention. "Looks like the cavalry's arrived."

The radio crackled into life as the police searchers made contact. Unhooking the mike, Judy reported what they'd seen and learned. She was about to explain Ryan's suspicion when he shook his head in negation. "Why not tell them what you suspect?" she asked after she clicked the transmitter off.

"In the first place, I could be wrong. I'd rather they made a thorough search of the crater to eliminate any chance that Sunny is lost down there."

She arched an eyebrow. "And if you're right?"

"The fewer people who converge on Cotton Tree Gorge, the more chance of Sunny staying unharmed."

She heard what Ryan wasn't saying. At least until they gave Horvath what he wanted.

Activating the mike again, she reported their disappointing search results in full, then said she was returning home because of a technical glitch. Knowing the brakes hadn't been properly checked, she wasn't straying far from the truth, but she still felt uneasy leaving the area.

"If we don't find any trace of Horvath at the gorge, we're coming straight back here," she stated.

"You'll get no argument from me."

"How did you and Sunny get together?" she asked to fill the time as she steered the plane into a turn and headed back.

"His mother and I worked for the same boss. Marion Coleman was raising Sunny on her own after her husband was killed taking part in a rodeo. She was still grieving when we met, and didn't have the resources to give Sunny what he needed. Having me as his mentor gave her the space to come to terms with her own loss, so she could get back to being a good mother again. I was never involved with her," Ryan said, as if reading Judy's mind.

"Wouldn't matter to me," she said with less than complete frankness. "We're both free agents."

"I haven't been free since the day I set eyes on you," he growled. "Last night…

"Last night we needed each other. It wasn't a marriage proposal," she said, forestalling him.

He shrugged. "Suit yourself."

She didn't bother dignifying that with a response. "Pity Max Horvath," she said instead. "He has no idea what he's taken on."

A cleared area near Cotton Tree Gorge provided a place to set down. The landing was bumpy, and she was aware of Ryan hanging on like grim death as they slewed to a halt within a hundred feet of a rock wall, but he kept his eyes open.

"You're getting better at this," she said in admiration.

"If I'm going to die, I prefer to meet it with my eyes open."

She shut down the engines, the sudden quiet deafening. "Oh ye of little faith." Unstrapping herself, she turned to him. "We're here. What now?"

He pulled his cell phone out of the pack he'd thrown into the plane on departure. "I call Horvath."

"You expect him to answer, just like that?"

He punched in numbers and waited, then his face became set. "Horvath," he said grimly. "I believe you and I have some unfinished business."

Just like that.

Climbing the eroded walls of Cotton Tree Gorge was arduous at the best of times, but killing in the high humidity of the approaching wet season. Judy was drenched by the time they reached a shelf on the sheer rock where a small boab tree clung to the valley wall. The sight was unusual because boab seeds and fruit were too heavy to be carried on the wind. Rock wallabies were the answer, scattering a number of different seeds in their droppings. The seed of this particular tree would have come to rest on the ledge until the first rain germinated it.

Ryan braced his hands on his hips and looked around. "This is the meeting place Horvath specified."

She had already recognized where they were. A few hundred yards to the west was the vine-screened wall concealing the access to the underground cavern, and probably also to Jack Logan's diamond mine. "Max must have found the way into the hidden valley," she said, heart sinking. If he knew how to get into the cavern, they were probably too late already. Only Ryan's ownership of the land was keeping Max from claiming his prize.

Ryan's look hardened. "I believe Horvath is holding Sunny in the cavern."

"And he's all right?" She had heard Ryan insist on speaking to Sunny before making any deals.

"So far, Sunny thinks they're playing a game, but he sounded tired and fractious," Ryan said.

Horror coiled through her. "You don't think Horvath would renege on the deal and leave Sunny in the cave?"

"He isn't the type to have much patience with a crying six-year-old."

Ryan sounded as if he were running out of patience himself, she noted. "Surely Max won't leave the little boy alone while he keeps the rendezvous with you?"

"He's sending Mick Coghlan to meet us."

"But you don't have the deed with you." They had never planned for this eventuality.

"As it happens, I do. After last night, I wasn't letting it out of my possession."

She plucked at a stalk of wiry grass growing out of the rock, made uncomfortably aware of how much the document meant to him. "I doubt whether Horvath or Coghlan would fall for another substitution. If Coghlan suspects any tricks, he'll contact Horvath." She didn't need to spell out the risk to the little boy.

Ryan was well aware of what was at stake, she saw, when his eyes darkened. "We'll have to make sure Coghlan doesn't get a chance to contact his master."

She unsheathed her cell phone but was stopped when his hand closed over the instrument. "We have to involve the police. You're an investigator, not a secret agent," she said.

His hand stayed in place. "And they'll do what? Send the search party here?"

She knew her expression betrayed her. "It makes sense. The chopper will be over Wolf Creek by now. We can save them and the people on the ground wasting time, and Tracey and Heather from worrying themselves sick. Now we know Sunny is safe..."

He didn't let her finish. "We don't know anything of the kind. We believe Horvath has him, but not where. The gorge is my call. I don't have any evidence to back it up. Do you want the search stopped on the strength of my gut feeling?"

"You're right. Until we know more, we should let them do their job in case Horvath is keeping Sunny hidden in the vicinity of the crater." She pocketed her phone. "How do you suggest we handle this?"

In words of one syllable, he told her.

Could anything be crazier than this? she asked herself as Ryan tore at her shirt buttons, shredding the fabric and making her look thoroughly disheveled. They'd already gone through the motions of a noisy argument. Now he tangled his fingers in her hair, surreptitiously rubbing bark and sand through the strands. She dropped her head back as if he was pulling her hair.

"How am I doing?" she asked, looking up at him as if begging him to stop. In truth, she didn't want him to stop. Surely she wasn't turned on by the game? Knowing she was safe in his hands made the play-acting surprisingly arousing.

"You could look more distressed, as if I was really attacking you," Ryan suggested, taking her by the shoulders.

She let her head rock back and forth, as if he were shaking

her instead of pretending. "I'd better focus on Coghlan then, since this is for his benefit." They'd agreed that Horvath's head man was likely to be watching them from a distance.

Ryan's expression softened momentarily. "Do you find it so hard to imagine me taking you by force?"

"Try impossible," she said, although a shiver she refused to connect with desire rippled through her. She dismissed the possibility out of hand. Apart from Ryan's own moral code ruling out any such thing, why would such an attractive man need to resort to violence? All he had to do was smile at a woman the right way and she melted. Wasn't Judy herself proof? "You're not the type," she denied, throwing the words at him like an accusation for the benefit of their watcher.

"You have to make Coghlan think I am," Ryan said, going through the motions of shaking her again. "We need the element of surprise."

Yelling meaningless accusations at him, she pretended to scramble out of his reach, only to be dragged back, her heart speeding up of its own accord as she was hauled against his rock-hard chest. "Let's hope he's buying this," she said, finding her voice hard to summon. "He'll be surprised, all right."

And Coghlan was.

When the freckle-faced man climbed up to the ledge, a gun tucked in his belt, he stopped short at the sight of Judy apparently alone, slumped on a rock, gulping back tears and holding her clothes together with a shaking hand. "What happened to you? And where's Smith?"

She forced a sob into her voice. "He attacked me, then took off."

The head stockman's pale blue eyes narrowed. "You're supposed to be on the same side. Why would he attack you?"

"He persuaded me to fly him here by lying that he'd discovered the way to my great-grandfather's mine. When I found out he intended to give Max the deed to the gorge, I tried to grab it from him. This is my family's land. He has no right to give it away. I tried to fight, but he was stronger. He took the deed and ran, leaving me like this."

Coghlan looked more appreciative than affronted at her sorry state. "Didn't Smith tell you his kid's life depends on him handing over that deed?"

So they thought Sunny was Ryan's son? She wiped her mouth with a dirt-streaked hand. "What do I care about his bastard?"

Coghlan leered. "What is this? Jealous because he didn't give you one of your own? What you need is a real man to take your mind off things. I'd oblige, but Mr. Horvath is waiting for the deed. He won't like hearing that Smith didn't keep his end of the bargain."

She sniffled. "Max won't harm the boy, will he?"

"I thought you didn't care? It's a female thing, I suppose. Women worry about kids. My boss will keep him hidden until I report success. That's what we agreed."

"But Wolf Creek crater is crawling with police and searchers," she said, making her voice a pitiful wail.

"Then it's just as well they're looking in the wrong place, isn't it?"

She didn't let a flicker of an eyelash betray her response to this news, but exhilaration pumped through her. They were on the right track. "There's still the problem that Smith took the deed. How will you get it back?"

"I know a thing or two about tracking. No ham-fisted cow cocky is going to get away from me in the bush."

She let her face fall. "Then you'll give the deed to Max, and I'll be back where I started."

Mick looked interested. "Do you have a better idea?"

"Why make your boss rich? We can tip the police off where

to find Max and the boy. Get the title deed back for me and I'll share the diamonds with you—as a reward, I mean. And you can show me what a real man can do."

"This land means that much to you?"

"More than you can imagine. I'll do anything to keep it," she said.

Mick frowned, torn between liking her offer and worrying about his boss, she could see. The worry won. "Max won't like me muscling in on his territory," he said.

"He'll be too busy defending himself on charges of kidnapping. With me as your alibi, he'll be on his own."

"I like the way you think." His tone said he liked a lot more as well as he advanced on her, flicking aside the torn front of her shirt. She heard his breath catch as her fuchsia lace bra was revealed, and he actually licked his lips. Then screamed as he bit his own tongue at the shock of being lifted from behind and flung bodily against the rock wall.

Winded, he staggered to his feet and pulled out the gun, but Judy aimed a kick at his wrist that sent the weapon flying. She heard it clatter somewhere down among the rocks.

He touched a finger to his tongue. The finger came away red. "What the hell is this?" he demanded thickly.

"It's called a setup," Ryan said pleasantly, closing on the man. He motioned Judy back. "Let's see if you're as cocky without a gun as you were aiming one at me."

"Pity I only winged you," Coghlan spat at him. "And didn't get a chance to show Miss Smart-Ass here what a real man can do."

The ledge didn't allow much room for sparring, and by dropping down from above, Ryan had made the most of the element of surprise. But as soon as he got close to Coghlan, the other man braced his torso against an outcrop of rock and swung his feet up, planting them viciously in Ryan's midriff. The sound of Ryan's breath rushing out as he shot backward set Judy's internal alarms screaming. She hadn't allowed for Ryan losing this fight.

Neither had he, it seemed. Clawing at bushes and rocks to arrest his slide perilously close to the edge, he bounded to his feet and threw himself at Coghlan before the other man could repeat his maneuver. He had his hands around Coghlan's throat when the other man forced his arms up and between Ryan's, breaking the hold. Inches from their feet, shale rattled over the edge and careened down the canyon.

A swift uppercut from Ryan threw the other man to his knees but she saw what Ryan could not—Coghlan's hand closing around a large rock. "Ryan, look out," she screamed as Coghlan swung the rock in a wide arc.

Her warning allowed Ryan to duck, so he caught only a glancing blow from the rock. He took advantage of Coghlan's momentum to ram him headfirst against the rock wall. The man went down as if poleaxed.

She came away from the corner, where she'd tried to stay out of Ryan's way, and looked at the man slumped between them. "I hope you haven't killed him."

Ryan check for a pulse, then straightened. "He's alive. Not feeling sorry for him, are you?"

She didn't bother to hide her revulsion. "I was hoping for the chance to finish him off myself."

Ryan licked blood from a scraped knuckle. "You'll get your chance in court."

She lifted his hand and inspected the graze, wanting to rub her cheek against it. Instead she brushed her fingers over the back of his skull where the rock had caught him. "You'll have a nice lump there tomorrow."

He caught her hand and brought it to his mouth, kissing her knuckles. "Thanks to your timely warning, that's all I'll have. You okay?"

"Fine, considering I was cheated of the chance to know a

real man," she simpered. She had to restrain herself from kicking the inert figure at her feet.

Ryan's head came up. "If he'd have touched you, you wouldn't have to ask if he was alive."

She suppressed a shudder. "When he reached for me, I was itching to damage his real manhood."

His hands dropped to her shoulders. "You did well enough disarming him. Self-defense lessons?"

"Soccer practice," she said with some satisfaction.

He grinned. "You'd do well in my line of work."

"Not if it involves dealing with lowlifes like him."

"Not always. And it has its rewards."

He looked as if he was about to kiss her and she braced for the contact, but instead he began slowly and carefully to remove the debris tangled in her hair. With no comb or brush on hand, he could only do the job with his fingers, but the massaging touch against her scalp made her want to purr.

She closed her eyes, savoring the sensation. When he finished, she wanted to grab his hand and make him continue. But a little boy's life was still at risk. And the fact that Max thought he was Ryan's son made the situation even worse. She pulled the front of her shirt together, fastened the one button still attached, and knotted the ends under her breasts.

Ryan's appreciative look brought a warmth to her cheeks, telling her he also regretted the lack of time for them. Later for us, his expression seemed to promise.

"At least he confirmed your suspicion that Max is holding Sunny nearby," she said.

Worry darkened his gaze. "I heard. My guess would be Horvath found a way into the hidden valley and took Sunny in there."

She shook out her hair, her scalp still tingling from his touch. "That's what I thought. It's an hour's hike to where we found the entrance, and there's nowhere to set the plane down closer than this."

"Maybe we're already close enough. Jo Francis discovered her valley when she fell down a crevice beneath an overhang not far from this ledge."

"You're suggesting we fall down a hole?"

He shook his head. "If Horvath took Sunny down there, he must have improved the access. Where he can go, we can follow."

Tucked at the far end of the ledge was the backpack he'd stowed behind a bush before they staged their mock fight. He went to it and pulled out his cell phone. She heard him contact Tracey at Wolf Creek and relay details of their location and what they'd learned, and ask her to pass the information to the searchers.

Pulling out a water bottle, he handed it to Judy. She drank thirstily and handed it back so he could do the same. "You don't want to wait for the police, do you?" she asked, aware of his tension.

"It'll take them time to get here. Horvath could smell a rat long before and take it out on Sunny."

"Then what are we waiting for?"

His hand on her arm stopped her. "I was thinking of going in alone."

She looked down at his hand. "Then think again."

He didn't release her. "I heard you tell Coghlan you'd do anything to keep this land."

Incensed that he'd think this was her reason for wanting to come with him, she snarled, "I also suggested I was part of the package. Did you believe that, too?"

He jerked his hand away. "No."

"You can apologize later. Right now, finding Sunny is our priority."

"As soon as we get Coghlan trussed up. He'll be in a nasty mood when he wakes up."

He wouldn't be the only one, she thought. However quickly

withdrawn, Ryan's suggestion that she might be sticking with him for personal gain had hurt.

Why did she care what he thought? she asked herself as she watched him tie Coghlan's hands and feet with lengths of the pliant vine cascading from the top of the escarpment. She didn't want Ryan to care, did she? He was right about her putting her family's needs above everything else. Not for selfish reasons, admittedly, but did motives matter when the outcome was the same? She *was* in this to find the diamonds that would save her father and her home. Maybe she was the one who should be apologizing to Ryan.

The sobering notion kept her mind busy as she followed him down to the valley floor, where he quartered around like a hound on a scent. In the end, she was the one who spotted the cavern tucked beneath a vine-strewn overhang a dozen yards to the right of the ledge where they'd left Coghlan unconscious and tied up.

Climbing up, she caught her breath at the sight of the rock paintings covering the walls and ceiling. Ryan joined her, motioning for silence and gesturing toward a line of footprints in the sand. Two sets, one large, one small, she saw. Her heart gave a jagged leap. "What now?" she mouthed.

He pointed at a clump of bushes growing around the edge of the overhang and into a corner where the footprints ended abruptly, pantomiming climbing. She nodded. Silently he slid his arms out of his pack and set it down, tucking something into the belt of his moleskins. A gun, she saw. His search of the area must have turned up Coghlan's weapon. Wanting to feel reassured, she felt her edginess increase. He knew what he was doing, she reminded herself. She had to trust him.

She did more than trust him, she suddenly realized. The emotions ripping through her were as powerful as they were unwelcome. Sometime during this adventure, she'd fallen in love with him. The thought of him walking into danger filled her with dread. She wanted to claw him back from the shadowed recess, insist they wait for the law.

Skywriting wouldn't be any more revealing, she thought, imagining herself writing Judy Loves Ryan in the smoke as she barreled the Cessna through loop the loops. She blinked the image away. Love was only another word for wife, the one thing she never wanted to be. She was secure only as long as he didn't know how she felt. Then he'd never take no for an answer.

So she'd have to make sure he never found out.

Rattled but resolute, she followed him to where he'd parted the greenery to reveal the steep, moss-covered walls of a hidden crevice. He reached over and pulled something closer. A rope ladder, she saw, understanding how Max had managed to take Sunny into the hidden valley. The little boy would have considered the climb down an adventure.

Ryan went over the edge, climbing with commando-like stealth, reminding her of the training he must have done as part of his covert career. Emulating him, she was glad he waited for her at the bottom, steadying the ladder. She found herself in a long, sinuous cavern with sheer rock walls towering above a fern-shaded pool. Moss underfoot made the going slippery. The far end of the pool was blocked by a fallen log forming a bridge to a wider, fern-filled amphitheater.

From a distance came the unmistakable sound of a child crying.

Chapter 14

Judy's body jerked in reaction. When she would have surged in the direction of the cry, Ryan held her back, indicating the fern-shrouded pool at their feet. Slick with moss, the log bridge between them and the main cavern was going to require caution to cross safely. Judy nodded to show she understood and wondered how Sunny had managed the feat.

Never having liked dark, enclosed spaces, she shivered slightly in the moist air as she followed Ryan across the log bridge. It gave slightly as her weight settled on it and she stifled a cry, but the log didn't move again as she inched across.

On the far side, she almost fell into Ryan's waiting arms and let him hold her for a second or two, then pushed away although every instinct urged her to stay. She looked around.

Above their heads a frieze of Aboriginal rock art adorned every surface. The paintings ran the full length of the valley, disappearing into the gloom. The only light filtered through a ceiling of ferns thatching the space where the towering rock walls leaned close together, creating a mystical twilight that she suspected was as much light as ever entered this place.

Abruptly Ryan pulled her back against the rock wall. As she flattened herself, she saw what he'd seen. Fifty feet ahead of them, Max stood at the foot of a steep rock incline. Above him, Sunny was climbing steadily toward a small outcrop. Her heart leaped into her mouth.

"You get back down here kid, or else," Max growled.

Sunny's determined pace slowed. "No. You said I'd get a surprise if I came with you, but I don't like it in here. I want to go back."

Max's expression became wheedling. "You haven't seen the surprise yet."

"I don't care. You're a bad man. I want my mommy."

The little boy stretched out the last syllable into a tragic wail that Judy felt through her whole body. She longed to hold him and assure him everything would be all right. As he continued his upward climb, she began to pray. He looked so tiny and vulnerable.

"Your daddy's coming for you soon," Max said. "If I were really a bad man, I wouldn't have told him where we are, would I?"

Sunny sniffled loudly. "Where is he?"

"On his way. Climb down and we'll wait for him together, all right?"

Reaching his goal, Sunny clambered onto the outcrop and sat down, his chubby legs dangling over the edge. He folded his arms across his small chest, a picture of defiance. "No."

Max ducked as sand and stones showered over him. "Cut that out, kid. If you don't come down, I'll come and get you."

Sunny seemed to sense that Max couldn't manage the climb, despite his threat. "I want to go home," he wailed again.

"Why you little…" Judy gasped as she saw the gun appear in Max's hand, the muzzle lifting in the child's direction.

Ryan stepped away from the wall. "Leave him alone, Horvath. It's me you want. I've brought what you asked for."

Horvath spun around, bringing the gun to bear on Ryan. "Just in time, too. Get over here."

Motioning Judy to stay in the shadows out of sight, Ryan slid his gun into her hand. Her heart pumped as she closed her fingers around cold, heavy metal. Then Ryan lifted his palms to shoulder height and moved toward the other man.

On the outcrop, Sunny's legs pumped in excitement. "Ryan, you came."

"Stay where you are till I tell you to come down," Ryan cautioned, his gaze on Horvath. "You're right. He is a bad man."

"Am I in trouble for coming with him?"

"You're not in trouble, but I need you to stay where you are, okay?"

"'Kay, Ryan."

Horvath's eyes narrowed. "How come he calls you Ryan?"

"Because I'm not his father. You got it wrong."

The gun never wavered. "But he does mean something to you. That's all I need."

Ryan patted his shirt pocket, ignoring the gun's sudden jump. "What you need is right here. There's no need to threaten an innocent child."

"Who's threatening? I found him wandering in here lost. The kid's word against mine."

"You won't wriggle off the hook this time. Half the region is out looking for Sunny. I've already called the police. They know you took him."

Horvath gestured again with the gun. "I have a helicopter hidden in the bushes on top of this ridge. By the time anyone else gets here, I'll be gone. Put the deed down between us. No sudden moves."

Moving slowly, Ryan complied, placing the fragile document on a rock between them. "The deed to this gorge won't be much use to a wanted man."

Max fumbled for the paper, glancing at it long enough to ensure it was genuine this time, before tucking it inside his shirt. The gun stayed steady on Ryan. "I'll get someone to mine the diamonds for me. They'll give me a new start somewhere else."

"There is nowhere else you won't be hunted down and caught. Give it up, Horvath. You've lost."

"You're the loser, Smith. Not that you'll have much time to worry." Aiming at Ryan's heart, Horvath's finger began to tighten on the trigger. A deafening report was followed by a shot ricocheting around the rock walls, sending chips flying. When the dust cleared, Horvath was cradling his hand and cursing.

Ryan launched himself into a flat dive, but pain made Horvath desperate. He scrabbled away, slamming Judy against the rock wall as she tried to intercept him. Recovering, she swung the gun around, but Horvath had already been swallowed by the gloom.

Ryan rushed to her side. "Let the police take care of him. Are you okay?"

"Grazed and winded. I'll live."

"Good shooting," he said.

"Lots of practice on feral pigs. Like this one," she added.

"Can I come down now?" came a plaintive cry.

Ryan turned back, holding out his arms. "Come on, son. Take it nice and slow. The bad man can't hurt you now."

Moments later, he held a sobbing little boy in his arms. He lifted a tear-stained face to Judy. "Did you shoot the bad man?"

She brushed the damp hair away from his forehead. "No, I only shot his gun out of his hand."

"Wow, like on TV?"

Holding the child tightly against him, Ryan caressed her with an admiring look. "Just like on TV."

Outside there was no sign of Horvath. Banks of thick, dark cloud hung low overhead, threatening an imminent deluge. When Tony Honda arrived with a group of the searchers, Ryan gave up Sunny to Tracey and reported Horvath's admission about having a helicopter on standby.

Tony palmed his radio. "I'll get some people up on the escarpment to look for him. At least you got Coghlan. And Horvath is injured so he won't get far, thanks to you and Annie Oakley here."

"Annie's the sharpshooter," Ryan said. "How's Coghlan?"

The trussed-up head stockman had recovered consciousness and was now in the custody of a police officer. "As an accessory to kidnapping, he's looking at a long stretch in jail," Tony confirmed. "It was probably a good thing you gave the title deed to Horvath."

"How so?"

"He'll stick around a while longer, lusting after the diamonds. Give us more of a chance to catch up with him."

Judy wasn't sure if that was good or bad. She was torn between wanting Max brought to justice and wishing he'd leave Diamond Downs for good. But Tony was right. As long as Max thought he could get his hands on the diamonds, he wasn't likely to go far. The thought made her shiver with more than the dampness in the air.

Ryan's arm came around her and she leaned against him, drawing strength from him. She might be handy with a gun when it came to shooting feral pigs, but she had never fired at a human being before and was more shaken than she wanted him to see.

He sensed it anyway. "Can we give our statements later?" he asked Tony.

The officer nodded in understanding. "No reason why not. We need to get these people back to Halls Creek before the storm breaks. I don't want to risk them getting trapped. Cade helped Heather take the other children back earlier, but Tracey wasn't going anywhere without Sunny. The boy's had a rough day and still needs to be seen by a doctor," he added in an undertone.

Judy saw Ryan's eyes flash fire as he digested the officer's implication. "I should go with him.

"If you need me..." He let the statement hang in the air.

"The police are flying his mother and her fiancé down from Lake Argyle," Tracey said. "They should be waiting by the time we get back. Until they get here, I'll stay with him while the police do their job."

At the news, Ryan's grim expression lightened a fraction. "Her fiancé? So Marion is finally doing the deed and giving Sunny his dearest wish, a father of his own."

Ryan sounded as if the announcement wasn't unexpected. Judy hoped he wouldn't feel too left-out of his protégé's new life.

Tracey evidently heard it, too. "He'll still need his favorite mentor," she assured him.

As if to confirm this, Sunny threw himself at Ryan. "Did you hear? My mommy and my new daddy are coming to get me."

Ryan swung the little boy into the air. "How good is that? You'll have lots to tell them, won't you?"

Sunny made a face. "For sure. Only I wish..."

"What, son?"

"I didn't get to write my name on the stone while I was up high."

Ryan shook his head. "It's wrong to write things on stone, or on anything other than writing paper, you know that."

"Then why was there other writing on the stone?"

Judy touched Sunny's small hand. "What kind of other writing?"

"Squiggly, like when you show someone the way somewhere. A m…m…"

"Map?" she supplied.

His face brightened. "That's it. But the writing was all funny."

She exchanged looks with Ryan. "Are you thinking what I'm thinking?"

He inclined his head in agreement. "If the writing was weathered, it could look strange to Sunny."

The child tugged at his arm to reclaim his attention. "I could read a little bit. Like this." Squatting down, he drew a capital J and what looked like a drunken letter L in the dirt with his finger."

Ryan ruffled his hair. "Well done. Your writing is really coming along."

He hugged the child one last time, then handed him into Tracey's care. Goodbyes were said, a handcuffed Coghlan was loaded into the police vehicle and the convoy set off. Judy and Ryan were finally, blissfully, alone.

"Were you sorry not to go with them?" she asked as the dust of departure settled.

"Sunny's in the best hands and will soon have his parents with him as well. I'm not leaving you."

"But…"

He took her chin in his hand. "I'm right where I want to be."

It was unlike her, but she read into the statement and felt a glow steal over her. The approaching storm meant that Cade would probably spend the night with Blake at his place, leaving the homestead to her and Ryan. "Annie Oakley doesn't need looking after," she tried all the same.

"Judy Logan does. It isn't weakness to let someone else take the reins once in a while."

If only he knew how she longed to agree, but resistance ran too deep. Once she allowed herself to need him, she would be vulnerable. And she had to stay strong for her father and Diamond Downs.

Ryan hunkered down beside the letters drawn in the dirt. Taking a twig, he turned the drunken L into a diamond shape. "Jack Logan's mark," she said on a gasp of recognition. "Sunny's writing on the stone must be a map to Great-grandpa's mine. We should check it out."

He straightened. "The map has been there for sixty years. It can wait till tomorrow, if the rain clears. Nightfall and a rising creek will keep Horvath away at least until then," he said, anticipating her objection.

"But we're so close. Not that it matters, now that he has the title deed."

"He doesn't."

She flinched as lightning sheeted across the sky, followed by the roar of thunder almost overhead. "I saw him check the document. You couldn't have made another switch."

"I didn't have to. The deed isn't worth the paper it's written on."

"You're not making sense."

He took her elbow and steered her down the hillside to the plane. "I've been doing some checking. In this state, a law called Adverse Possession means if you occupy and use a piece of land without the owner objecting for a minimum of twelve years, the title to that land passes to you."

"My family has used Cotton Tree Gorge for decades," she said.

He nodded. "If my grandmother's heirs had claimed the gorge within the twelve years, it would have been mine. As things stand, it's still part of Diamond Downs."

Climbing into the plane, she looked back. "You don't mind?"

His look was long and heated. "You know what I want, and it has nothing to do with land or diamonds."

With no answer to this she could live with, she settled at

the controls. By the time she landed the Cessna near the homestead, the rain was sheeting down, making visibility hazardous. Between fighting to stay on course in the buffeting winds and rain, she felt exhaustion creeping up as they ran through the storm to the house.

Pulling down shutters to screen out the weather used her last reserves of energy. She was standing at the kitchen door, watching the rain pelt the thirsty ground, when Ryan began to massage her shoulders. "Mmm, feels wonderful," she said.

"You'll feel even better after you've showered and changed."

"I don't have the energy."

"Then let me help."

She didn't resist when Ryan undressed her and helped her into the shower. "I should be the one taking care of you," she said. "You got clobbered by a rock."

"Fortunately, I have a hard head." He adjusted the water to tepid and held the shower door open for her to step in.

She wasn't embarrassed having him see her naked now. Too tired, she thought. Or perhaps too comfortable in his company. The thought made her push away from his supporting hand. "I can manage."

"Dinner will be ready when you are. Take your time."

Almost dozing off while dressing, she roused herself by putting in a call to Des and Blake at the crocodile farm. Cade had indeed decided to stay the night. He'd already told the others what had happened, saving her having to go into details. Her father required the most reassurance, and she couldn't help worrying. He sounded so ill. But better he heard the story from the family than learned about it from the police tomorrow.

Ryan agreed when she rejoined him in the kitchen. She looked without enthusiasm at the chicken salad he put in front of her. "It looks great, but I'm too tired to eat."

"Just a few bites," he said in the manner of coaxing a child. "Feeding you is the least I can do after you saved my life."

She picked at the chicken, managing to eat some, before putting her fork down. "I've never shot anyone before." To her horror, her voice quavered.

He came around to her side of the table and lifted her to her feet. "Don't fight your feelings. I've seen hardened police officers turn to jelly after their first live-fire incident. You're definitely not hardened."

"No," she agreed, nuzzling closer, absorbing his strength. "Would you keep me company again tonight?"

He rested his chin on the top of her head. "I'll stay as long as you need me."

Afraid to admit how long that might be, she nodded and let him guide her to a chair while he put the salads in the refrigerator and tidied the kitchen. He went around methodically locking the house, sensing her need for security. Then, with an arm around her shoulders, he took her to bed.

Although sex was the last thing she wanted tonight, she'd been prepared to let him make love to her in exchange for the comfort of his presence. But he surprised her in this, too. Setting aside the robe she shrugged off, he dropped a thigh-length cotton nightshirt styled like a man's shirt over her head. He tucked her in and smoothed her hair back. "Give me a minute to shower, and I'll be back to cuddle you to sleep."

She nodded, her tension escalating inexplicably as he went into the bathroom. He was back in record time to ease himself into bed beside her. He wore only a pair of sleep shorts and his heated skin carried the scent of herbal shower gel. Wrapped in his arms, she was pulled against him. Finding herself almost instantly, powerfully aroused, she instinctively tried to turn to him, but he held her tightly. "No demands tonight, my Annie Oakley. You need to sleep."

She needed him, she thought in astonishment, as desire stabbed through her as hot and bright as the lightning forking through the night sky. Knowing she loved him made her want him so much she could hardly stand it. Confusion coiled through her. Moments before, she'd been reluctantly ready to trade sex for comfort. Now what was her excuse?

"You're still too tense," he said, digging his fingers into her shoulders.

She arched like a cat. "This could get to be addictive."

"No reason it shouldn't. You know I'm willing." His hands paused, then continued. "I shouldn't have brought that up. I said no pressure, and I mean it."

But the damage was done. Why couldn't they just enjoy each other without worrying about forever? She didn't need forever. She needed him tonight. Rock-solid, his arms around her to shut out the dreams she feared would come as soon as she closed her eyes. Seeing Horvath about to shoot Ryan was a nightmare she'd relive over and over, along with the kick of the gun as she fired first. How could anyone endure a lifetime of such roller-coaster emotions? The beloved didn't have to be held at gunpoint. How could she stand waiting for him to come home, wondering what might have gone wrong to keep him from her?

How did anyone stand such torment?

Judy couldn't decide what had awakened her. The storm continued its relentless drumming against the roof, and occasional jagged streaks of lightning bathed the room in flickering light. A weight lay across her hip. Ryan's arm. He'd held her all night, soothing her through disturbing dreams that were fading with the dawn. She let them go.

She realized he was awake when his finger traced a lazy circle over her stomach under the nightshirt, making her muscles tighten. "Ryan?"

"Expecting someone else?" he teased.

Energy burned through her. Desire for him was so strong she had to turn over and find his mouth. "No one else."

The kiss lasted a long, long time while he explored the rest of her with slow, deliberate strokes that made her quiver. She felt the surge of his arousal against her, and her own anticipation grew.

His hungry mouth devoured her eyelids, her cheeks, the slim column of her throat and finally, gloriously, her breasts in turn, suckling until she saw stars. Letting her head drop back, she felt her defenses crumble. She had no idea where they would go from here, but he would be part of her life somehow. Not only for this, but for everything else she sensed they could share.

She felt him kick his sleep shorts off. He'd already pushed up her nightshirt. Now she lifted her arms to let him remove it altogether. She wanted no barriers of any kind between them. Not even fear about the past or the future. Now was all that mattered.

Her mouth opened as his mouth became more demanding. His tongue plunged deeper and she drank greedily while her hands roamed where they would over his lean flanks and tumescent sex. His ragged intake of breath proved to her the effect her movements had on him.

His shudders thrilled her. He was hers to command. Was any power more intoxicating than this? To see a lion willingly surrender control to the tamer for no reason other than his own desire?

When he slid his hand down to where she trembled with need and irresistibly began to assuage that need, her mind spun out of control. "Make love to me now," she urged, her tension so tight she couldn't bear it.

"Soon."

Then she was spinning through the stormy sky, whirling and tumbling into a supernova of delight. She had barely drawn breath from the wild ride when he slipped inside her at last and began to take her on a second, even more dizzying ascent to the summit.

Breath rushed through her like a river, catching and releasing as he moved with exquisite slowness, making her want to scream at him that she wasn't fragile. She wouldn't shatter if he went higher, faster, now, now, now.

Who was the tamer and who the tamed? she thought frantically. He had taken control so subtly, taunting her with the promise of pleasure so intense as to be barely endurable. Somehow she did endure it and much more at his behest, until the blood roared in her ears and her heart felt as if it must beat right out of her chest.

The last vestiges of restraint fled and all coherent thought was eclipsed by wave after wave of mind-shattering sensation. Clinging to him, she felt him quake and heard him roar in triumph as the jungle prevailed.

Lying beside him, pleasantly aching and fulfilled, she had to struggle to gather her thoughts. She'd never totally loved before, and never thought she would, so what now? Did she let him go and resume her single life, the life she'd thought she wanted? Was it even possible after this?

If she felt so entangled now, what would marriage to him be like? She had a flash of herself in her mother's shoes, worrying, imagining, sacrificing. Completely ignoring her own needs to give her all to husband and family. When Judy found herself starting to smile at the prospect, thinking it might not be so bad, she knew she was in trouble.

Beside her, Ryan slept deeply, a contented expression on his face. She resisted the urge to kiss him, needing some time to deal with her perturbing feelings. Careful to avoid waking him, she slid out of bed and pulled on a T-shirt, a pair of panties and jeans. The morning air would be cool after the storm. Sliding her feet into sandals, she padded out of the room.

She needed to breathe. Outside the air sparkled, the landscape cleansed by the rain. It would be even better after the wet season really took hold. Some people hated the drumming of rain day after day, isolating the land and forcing thoughts inward. Judy loved the Wet, seeing it as a greening and restoring time for herself, as well as the land.

Wanting to be close to her surroundings, she stepped off the veranda, skirting pools of water, until she stood beside the mended fences of the holding paddock. The dawn chorus of insects and birds giving thanks for the rain rang in her ears. She avoided looking at the destruction of the bunkhouse. It, too, would be restored in time.

Suddenly, bleakness swept over her. What if Horvath's creditors managed to take this place? Her dreaming place. Ryan had ceded his claim to Cotton Tree Gorge and Max was on the run, but his creditors might yet bring them all down. How could she fret over her feelings for Ryan when so much more was at stake?

A sudden noise and a sense that she wasn't alone made her peer into the shadows. Her pulse raced. "Who is it? Who's there?" she demanded before a hand closed over her mouth.

Chapter 15

Panic swept through Judy and she clawed at the hand suffocating her, then felt the icy bite of metal behind her ear. Stop struggling and think, she ordered herself. Her captor could be only one person. Max, holding a gun to her head.

He dragged her backward, her sandals scrabbling for purchase on the muddy ground between the ruins of the bunkhouse and a cleared space used for car parking. Two cars were there, Ryan's and an ancient Jeep kept as a workhorse. Now she recognized another shape.

Instantly, she understood what had awakened her earlier. In spite of the tumult, her pilot's instinct must have registered the distant sound of the helicopter landing not far from the house. Ryan must have heard it, too, but had evidently thought no more about it than Judy had.

The hand on her mouth slackened and she dragged in a tortured breath. Max kept the gun jammed behind her ear as he forced her toward the bubble shape. "This isn't going to work, Max," she protested.

He jabbed her painfully with the gun. "It's already working. I didn't care which of you came with me, but since you conveniently nominated yourself, you can fly this thing. My hand hurt like hell getting here, thanks to you."

"You're crazy, I'm not flying anywhere."

He tugged at her hair and she stifled a cry. "You'd rather I put a bullet through your bedroom window into Sleeping Beauty?"

Her heart threatened to stop as she pictured Ryan lying unsuspecting in the bed they'd shared so recently and recklessly. Max sounded deranged enough to carry out the threat. Her gorge rose at the thought of him playing Peeping Tom.

She didn't let a flicker of expression betray her shock "Why should I care about Smith?" she asked with a deliberately casual lift of her shoulders.

Horvath's mouth thinned. "He's your lover, isn't he?"

The question was oddly reassuring. If he had to ask, he didn't know for sure. Somehow, that was important to her. Bad enough that he must have looked through the window and seen Ryan sleeping in her bedroom. She hated the thought of Max sullying one of the most perfect experiences of her life. "He's *a* lover," she dismissed.

Using his roughly bandaged hand, he prodded her viciously with the gun barrel. "Never mind, we're wasting time. Get in and fly."

Unable to think of an alternative that wouldn't endanger Ryan, she climbed into the pilot's seat of the two-seater Robinson 22. The parking area was hardly big enough for the rotor blades to clear. The R22 was used for mustering cattle because of its maneuverability. Of course, that was in the right hands. She had far fewer hours' flying experience in a helicopter than a fixed-wing craft, but Max was in no mood to listen to reason.

He got in beside her, angling himself to keep the gun

trained on her. When she reached for the safety harness, he snarled, "Forget that. Get going."

Her temper flared. "This thing has no doors. I won't be much use as a pilot if I fall out at five hundred feet."

Her glare daring him to stop her, she snapped the belt and shoulder harness into place. She waited for him to do the same, but he evidently preferred to keep his gun arm unimpeded. Fine. If he chose to risk death, that was his business.

Flipping switches, she saw telltale glows and felt the rotors start to turn. Vibrations jarred her teeth. The turbine temperature gauge told her when the chopper was ready to lift off; then, with a stomach-lurching kick, they were airborne.

"Where to?" she yelled above the throb of the rotors.

"The gorge. I heard what the kid said about a map. We're going to find it."

"You're nuts. The place will be flooded after last night's downpour."

He shook his head. "The kid was up on a ledge. There's an inflatable boat on board. We'll use that in the cavern."

She couldn't take the time to argue. Flying at low level through obstacles required all her concentration. They were at two hundred feet and should really be higher, but Max was urging her to stay low, making his point by jamming the gun into her side.

"You're going the right way for us to end up nose-down in the ground," she roared. Normally they'd use headsets to communicate, but if Max was too impatient for harnesses, he was unlikely to care about other niceties.

At least he pulled the gun barrel away from her side. At this rate, she'd have bruises on her bruises. He was watching for the escarpment above Cotton Tree Gorge, she assumed. She was doing the same. They were cruising at eighty knots. She applied aft cyclic to slow their airspeed for better ground observation. The craft bucked and she decided against increasing power. They had already slowed to just above fifty-three knots, the speed for minimum power in level flight, so she stayed ready to restore their rpms and prevent stalling.

Then a movement on the ground caught her attention. She almost lowered the collective lever in reaction, causing the stall she was so anxious to avoid.

Below them, Ryan was chasing the helicopter in his crazy jalopy, going faster than such a rust heap should be able to. Except it wasn't a rust heap, she remembered, thinking of the turbo-powered Branxton engine he'd installed. He must have heard the chopper take off and decided to follow.

Exhilaration warred with fear. She hadn't been scared for herself, being too furious at Max. Now as she saw him swivel the gun and take aim at Ryan's car, she felt real terror coursing through her.

Without stopping to think, she pushed the helicopter into what was known as the deadman's curve. Life-threatening to those on board and dangerous to the machine, it put them below a hundred feet and down to less than twenty knots airspeed. Experienced pilots used the tactic when mustering cattle amongst trees, but she wasn't that experienced. Her heart rammed into her mouth as she applied enough pedal to slew them to the left and banked at the same time, finding herself hanging from her harness at a forty-five degree angle.

Max wasn't so fortunate. With nothing to grab on to as the machine tilted, he slid sideways, grasping at air as his seat dropped from under him. Man and gun plummeted through the opening and suddenly she had a fight on her hands to stay airborne as he grasped the skid and hung on.

She managed to wrestle the helicopter level again, pulling out of the feared stall. Given enough height, she could have landed the craft on propellers alone, without engine power. Like every pilot, she was trained to handle the critical maneuver called autorotation. But at this low level, she was more likely to plow them straight into the ground.

As it was, keeping the unbalanced craft aloft took every trick she knew and a few she improvised on the spot. They were down to treetop height, Max's dangling legs brushing greenery as he tried to hang on.

Ryan's first thought when he was half-awake and heard the chopper was that some last-minute mustering must be under way before the wet season set in. Only when he reached for Judy on the other side of the bed and found her gone had he come fully alert, putting two and two together.

Plunging into his pants and boots, he'd raced outside in time to glimpse her lifting off at the controls of an R22 with Max beside her brandishing a gun. Never had Ryan felt so helpless, knowing she was up there with a madman while he was on the ground, unable to lift a finger to help.

Think, he'd ordered himself. Max must have overheard Sunny talk about finding a map to the diamond mine and decided to force Judy to act as his guide. There was no way she would have gone willingly. The chopper's heading had suggested Ryan was right.

He'd screamed away from the homestead in his car doing well over a hundred, only slowing down when he reminded himself that he couldn't help Judy if he was dead. In the distance, the helicopter was flying dangerously low and slow. At the thought of her crashing, his heart spiked. If that happened, Horvath had better die with her because his life was over anyway, Ryan resolved. Last night had obliterated any possibility that Judy might not belong with him. They had fitted together like two halves of a whole. All she had to do was accept the fact. Any alternative was unthinkable.

He forced the cold, steely sense of purpose that had served him through countless undercover investigations to take over from hot-blooded anger, making him clear-headed enough to function. Later would be soon enough to plan Horvath's retribution. Right now, Ryan's task was to keep the chopper in sight and be ready to back Judy up when the time came.

The opportunity arose sooner than he expected. Seeing the chopper tilt drunkenly, his hands tightened on the wheel. What the devil was she doing? His question was answered when Horvath slid out the cockpit opening, scrabbling desperately for any handhold. He finally hooked an arm around the skid. A gun dangled from his bandaged hand and his legs pumped air.

Ryan floored the accelerator and closed the distance between them, praying Judy would stay low in spite of the danger. Just a few more minutes, he implored her silently. Then he was under the chopper as it bucked and swayed, unbalanced by Horvath's weight.

The dangling gun was Ryan's target. He jammed the accelerator until he was underneath Horvath. Like a movie stuntman, he swung himself out through the door and put everything he had into a vertical leap, grabbing for the gun. As he'd hoped, the move dislodged Horvath's precarious hold on the skid and the two men plunged into the spinifex grass which cushioned the fall. Ryan heard his car bump up against a tree, the engine snorting steam.

Tucking and rolling, Ryan came up swinging, his doubled fist connecting with Horvath's nose before the other man had regained his feet. Blood spurted and Horvath screamed, but he had the strength of desperation. He rolled away from Ryan, groping for the dropped gun. Unable to find the weapon, he clutched a thick branch of fallen timber. Brandishing the branch like a club, he forced Ryan to duck and weave to stay out of reach.

Even unarmed, Ryan knew he had several advantages. He was fitter and stronger. Max was fighting for a fortune. Ryan was fighting for something infinitely more precious—his future with Judy. Defeat wasn't on his agenda. With a raised forearm, he deflected the branch before it crashed down on him and grabbed the end, pulling Horvath off balance. Then it was Ryan's turn to swing the club and Horvath went down for the count.

Panting, Ryan stood over the prone form; Horvath didn't stir. Pity. Ryan had just started to enjoy repaying him for all the misery he'd caused Judy and her father.

The chopper roared overhead, stirring up leaves and dust as Judy brought it in to land. Crouching to avoid the rotors, she hurried to Ryan, a wrench clutched in one hand. He looked at it wryly. "For me? You shouldn't have."

She looked down at Horvath and shifted the makeshift weapon to her left hand, then touched Ryan's forehead. "What's this?"

He hadn't been aware of the cut above his eye. "It's called blood."

She grimaced. "Will I ever be able to stop patching you up?"

"Only if you stick with me and keep me out of trouble."

Distress flared on her face, quickly masked. "I thought he was going to kill you."

Seeing the look, his heart sang. She wasn't as immune to him as she pretended. "Never occurred to you I might come out on top?"

She grinned, as much with relief as humor. "You did last night."

The throbbing from the cut as he swabbed it with a handkerchief competed with a more elemental throb, making him want to take her in his arms there and then. Hardly good tactics under the circumstances. The wanting didn't lessen. "Was Horvath headed for the gorge?"

"He heard Sunny mention the map and ordered me to help him find it."

Thunderclouds were gathering in the east. "Then maybe we should, while we still have the chance."

Her gaze shifted to the unconscious man. "What about him?"

"I have handcuffs in my working kit. We'll restrain him and leave him here. I'll call Tony Honda to come get him."

She glanced toward the stalled vehicle. "Did you aim for the tree, or was it good luck?"

He gave her a pained look. "I aimed, of course."

The cuffs were old and rusty but did the job of securing Horvath, who hadn't regained consciousness. Ryan bundled the prisoner into the back seat of his car and slammed the door, wishing it were the door to a jail cell. A cursory hunt revealed no sign of the lost gun, and with the storm threatening, Ryan didn't want to take any more time to look. If they were to have any chance of finding the mine, it was now or never.

This time, they were both securely strapped in when she lifted off toward Cotton Tree Gorge. "Max has flipped," Judy said. "He was never that emotionally stable, but he's finally cracked under the pressure."

Ryan set his jaw. "Did he hurt you?"

"He couldn't afford to while he needed my help."

Thinking of the way she'd handled the helicopter, Ryan nodded. "I should have finished him once and for all."

"You don't mean that," she said, afraid that he did. "Handing him over to the police is the right thing to do."

"It's better than he deserves. He took you way from me at gunpoint. I can't forgive that."

The stormy crosswinds demanded concentration, but she glanced at him. "This is why marriage between us won't work. You'd want to wrap me in cotton wool, and I'd be worried sick about you."

"You would?" He sounded almost pleased.

"Speaking hypothetically."

She set them down as close as she safely could to the entrance to the hidden valley. When she pulled out the chopper's first-aid kit and fussed over the cut on his forehead, Ryan fumed with impatience. "We don't have time for this."

"Conditions will be rough in there after last night. You won't be much use if you can't see where you're going."

"I knew it, you do care."

None too gently, she slapped a dressing over the cut. "I don't want the hassle of rescuing you from a flooded river cave."

He grabbed her hand before she pulled it away and pressed his lips to her fingers, sending a jolt of sensation along her arm. "I love it when you fuss. We're made for each other."

She tossed the kit back into the helicopter. "Next time, remind me to let you bleed to death."

The rope ladder was still in place and Ryan led the way down. Following him, Judy was shocked by how high the water had risen during last night's storm. What had been a placid pool at their feet was now a foaming lake almost lapping the bottom of the ladder. The log bridge was still in place but rocked alarmingly as she clambered on to it, steadied by his outstretched hand.

In the main cavern, she noticed how much closer they were to the ancient rock paintings. During the night the trickling creek had swollen with the rain and was now a fast-moving band of brown water filling the cavern floor, forcing them to travel higher up the rocky sides.

At least it wasn't dark. Early morning light angled through the roof of ferns meeting overhead, making it easy to spot the outcrop where Sunny had taken refuge. Reaching it was another matter. At this height, the rock walls were steep and slippery. Twice she almost lost her footing, but both times Ryan's hand closed around her elbow, his strength supporting her. Better not get too dependent on the feeling, she cautioned herself. In spite of his certainty, they were not made for each other. She wouldn't allow it.

The fear that had gripped her when he leaped from his moving car and tackled Max haunted her as they climbed. Marrying Ryan would mean accepting a lifetime of such worry over his safety. Better to walk away now than subject herself to that.

The decision didn't make her feel better. Even the possibility that they were on the verge of finding the legendary mine wasn't as much consolation as it should have been. Focus on the climb, she ordered herself. He couldn't make her marry him. The thought nagged that he might not have to.

Reaching the ledge was another distraction when the limited space forced her to crouch close to Ryan to examine the diagram chiseled in the sandstone. As she fitted herself into the curve of his body, her stomach pressing against his back, she felt the now-familiar flare of need and desire. She pushed it away. "The words don't make any sense."

"That's because they're in Latvian, my grandmother's language."

"Lizina Smith was Latvian?"

He nodded. "Her real name was Sviklies. She changed it to Smith after she emigrated to Australia. My father taught me some of her language as a child after learning it from the relatives who cared for him when his mother died."

"In her turn, Lizina must have taught Jack just enough to make the map." Judy couldn't help smiling. "He made sure whoever found it would have to share the information with her. Even if Max had gotten this far, the map wouldn't have helped him. I can't read it and I'll bet he couldn't either," she said.

"I won't have to, because Smith is going to translate for me."

She jerked around, instinctively clasping Ryan as Max reared up on the ledge. He looked much the worse for wear and his eyes shone with a mad light. But the gun he held on them was too steady to be ignored. With the increasing sunlight to guide him, Max must have found the gun that Judy and Ryan had failed to locate in the darkness.

"How in blazes did you get away?" Ryan demanded.

"When I practiced law in Perth, not all my clients were on the side of good. One in particular taught me a few party tricks, like how to use a belt buckle to jimmy an old-style pair of handcuffs."

"Remind me to update my kit as soon as we get out of here," Ryan said dryly.

"I wouldn't make too many plans yet, although you'll be glad to know your car is still drivable. Faster than it looks, too."

She needed no translation for Ryan's response. It was earthy and crude, but she wholeheartedly agreed, heartily wishing Max would take the advice. Instead he held the gun to her head. "Translate the map, please, Smith."

After everything they'd endured to get this far, she couldn't believe Max was going to win. She opened her mouth to protest, but Ryan shot her a look that told her he was up to something. She subsided into silence, trusting him.

"According to this, there's a fold in the rock a dozen feet to my right," Ryan said, his finger tracing the outlines carved in the rock. "Beyond the fold are two concealed caves. The second leads to the diamonds." He uncoiled from the ledge. "Be my guest."

Horvath gestured with the gun. "You first, then her. I'll follow."

Ryan shrugged. "Your call."

Edging around the fold, she was amazed to find herself in a concealed cleft floored by moss and ferns, the steep sides soaring to a tiny patch of sunlight high overhead where part of the roof had fallen in ages before. A narrow column of calcified rock was all that held up the remaining roof. Two dark half-moons in one wall had to be the cave openings indicated on the map. Below them, the raging river rushed past, the water level higher now than when they had scaled the rope ladder.

Almost at Ryan's feet, a stone the size of a pea glittered and she picked it up. Instantly, Max snatched it out of her hand. "This looks genuine."

"Dear heaven, we've found the mine," she whispered, unable to believe they were really in the place where Jack Logan had discovered a fortune and lost his life. She shivered at the prospect that they might soon join him. Horvath wasn't going to let them go now he'd reached his goal. Whatever Ryan had in mind, he would have to act soon.

Max waved the gun. "Back away, both of you. Judy, up against the column. Smith, arms around her waist."

Horvath pulled out the pair of handcuffs. Judy pressed gingerly against the brittle column. Ryan stood behind her, placing his hands around her on either side of the column. Horvath snapped the cuffs around Ryan's wrists on the far side of the column. Even without restraints on her own wrists, they were both effectively trapped. Any sudden move could shatter the filament of rock and bring the roof down on their heads. She held herself still in Ryan's arms.

"Cozy, a real Romeo and Juliet ending," Horvath sneered. "Too bad your belt buckle is out of reach, Smith." Setting the gun down well away from them, he stooped to enter the second cave.

"You might want to think this over," Ryan suggested, sounding remarkably calm considering the danger.

Horvath looked back. "Because this is the mine, or because it isn't? How about if I try the first opening instead?"

"I wouldn't."

"That's the real mine, isn't it? What's in the other? A hundred-foot drop to my death? Nice try, Smith."

He ducked into the opening and Ryan murmured in her ear, "Whatever happens, don't make any sudden moves or we're both dead."

In spite of his warning, she almost pulled back in shock at

the sound of an anguished scream, then a brief struggle. Only Ryan bracing her kept her from wrenching the column holding up the cave roof. Then Max backed out of the opening performing a bizarre dance. A dance of death, she understood, seeing the huge, golden-tinged head and shining coils enmeshing him. The snake was as thick as her arm and perhaps ten feet long, its fangs embedded in Max's wrist, right on the pulse point.

Like a stone, he toppled backward into the raging river, the King Brown snake, deadliest of its kind, falling with him. The river's roar drowned out the splash, the current washing Max and his killer from sight.

Shuddering, she closed her eyes. "You knew, didn't you?"

His chin rested on top of her head. "Jack's map showed the snake cave. Obviously not the same snake, but it must be a favorite nesting place. I tried to warn Horvath."

"He was too fixated on the diamonds to listen. Do you think a King Brown killed Jack Logan?"

"No. He was too aware the snake was there. I think he became trapped on the outcrop when the cavern flooded. We know his canoe washed up on the floating island just beyond the entrance to this valley, so he would have had no way out. Jack must have known he wouldn't make it, and decided to carve the map for his Lizina to find when the floodwaters receded."

"Horvath's body will probably wash up on the island, too," she said.

"If the crocodiles don't get him first, Tony Honda's people will recover the body." His tone told her he was glad they didn't have that responsibility. "You and I have pressing problems of our own."

Pressing was putting it mildly. Having her so closely aligned with him was taxing his control to the limit, and they didn't need the fit to get any tighter. "Are you getting wet?" he asked on a hunch.

"Can you keep your mind on our problem?"

"I am. Is your shirt getting soaked?"

"Now you mention it, yes. Rainwater's seeping down the column from above."

He'd felt it, too. "Are you slick enough to wriggle out without pulling on the column."

"Just as well nobody else can hear that. You'd get arrested," she said. But she sucked in her breath, held it and began to move carefully. As he'd anticipated, the rain coating the column eased her way.

In a sort of vertical limbo dance, she slid down his body inch by painful inch, her leg and back muscles protesting, until she was low enough to duck under his imprisoned arms without putting any pressure on the cuffs threatening to saw through the column.

When she stood up, she was shaking but free.

He also released the breath he'd been holding. "Keys to the cuffs are in my pocket." His nod indicated which one.

She unlocked the handcuffs, returning the key to him. He pocketed the items then said, "I'm going to check out the second opening." Skirting the delicate column, he ducked low to explore the side cavern. "You might not want to look," he said from inside.

A shiver claimed her. "Is it Jack?"

"It's Jack." Ryan backed out and stood up. In his hand was a pouch made of kangaroo leather. He cupped her hand and spilled the contents into it.

In the light from overhead, the gems sparkled like stars. "Good grief, there must be a fortune here."

"There's an even bigger fortune inside. Jack's remains are lying beside a massive kimberlite pipe. I'm no geologist, but I'd say he enlarged a natural opening and tunneled straight into diamond-bearing rock, what the experts call blue ground. He must have found alluvial diamond deposits in Bowen Creek and backtracked here until he tapped into a fortune."

"All he wanted was to share his find with his beloved Lizina," she said, thinking of the title deed and the map directions in Latvian. Jack's love for Lizina had shone through his every action including deeding the gorge to her, and carving the map in her native language. Yet Jack had died before he could claim his bride.

Life was precarious, nowhere more so than in the outback. Was Judy foolish to deny herself Ryan's love because it would make demands or could be snatched away at any time? The same could be said of any life anywhere. She imagined Lizina Smith turning Jack down on such meaningless grounds. Or her mother refusing Des's love because it might end someday. All life, all love ended. Was that any reason never to let love begin?

The pain she felt at a life without Ryan told Judy more surely than anything else that losing him would be far worse than any demands marriage could impose.

"Yes," she said out loud.

Looking at her intently Ryan raised an eyebrow. "Yes, what?"

She lifted her chin. "Yes, I'll marry you, if you still want me to."

With a groan of frustration, he wrapped his arms around her. "I've always wanted you. You must know by now, I love you, but I was starting to think it might not be enough."

"It's more than enough. I just couldn't see it."

He seemed to be holding his breath. "And now?"

"I've learned from Great-grandpa Jack and his Lizina that it's up to me what I put into a relationship, and what I get out of it. I'm an idiot for being afraid."

"Does it help if I admit to being less than confident myself?" he asked.

Agitation raced through her. "About marrying me?"

He smiled wryly. "Never. More that I might fail at the most important task of my life, being a good husband and father."

Thinking of his prowess as a lover and his gentleness with Sunny, she shook her head. "Have no doubts, you're a worthy heir to Lizina. She'd be as proud of you as I am."

"And Jack of you," Ryan echoed, palming both sides of her face and kissing her with such tenderness that tears welled in her eyes. "I love you and I can't wait for us to marry," he assured her.

Ryan took her by the shoulders. "You know, Jack would approve of both their descendants fulfilling their dream of a future together."

As Judy leaned in to kiss him, she couldn't have agreed more.

Epilogue

Four months later the seasonal rains were finally easing, a symbol of the brighter days ahead for her family, Judy felt. "You look every inch a bride," she said, moving behind Jo Francis to fasten the shawl collar on her prospective sister-in-law's romantic silk shantung dress. The dress emphasized Jo's curvaceous figure, and the matching high-heeled pumps added graceful inches to her five-seven height. Judy brushed her hand down the beaded bodice and lace sleeves, settling them into place. "Has Blake seen your dress yet?"

"You know it's bad luck for the groom to see the bride before the wedding." Jo's vivid blue-green eyes sparkled with happiness. She adjusted the delicately colored wild orchids in her upswept, streaky-blond hair, then extended her hand to admire the princess-cut diamond in the center of her engagement ring. "I can't believe I'm wearing one of your great-grandfather's diamonds on my finger."

Judy's gaze went to the diamond twinkling on her own engagement finger. "If not for him, and you and Blake, this day wouldn't be happening."

Jo smiled. "I can't take credit for falling into the hidden valley by accident. Tom and Shara pointed the way by finding the Uru cave. If anyone's a hero, it's you and Ryan for making the actual discovery." Finding the mine had allowed Des Logan not only to repay the mortgage over Diamond Downs to Max Horvath's estate, but to start restoring the property to prosperity.

Unfortunately, money couldn't repair Des's damaged heart, but less worry and stress and the latest medical treatments were beneficial. Des's need to stay close to medical help was the reason they had chosen to hold the ceremony at Blake's home in the center of his crocodile farm near Halls Creek, where Des was living at present, rather than at Diamond Downs.

"I guess we all contributed," Judy said. "I'm pleased Shara's father arranged for her and Tom to fly back for the occasion. The private jet the king provided is really something. Although I don't understand this ritual engagement thing she and Tom are going through. If they didn't have to wait two hundred days, they could get married today, as well." She shuddered at having to wait two hundred days to marry Ryan.

"As a princess, she doesn't want to buck the system any more than she's already done by falling in love with an Aussie park ranger." Jo hitched up her skirt so she could slide a blue lace garter up her leg before letting the skirt fall back into graceful folds. "Her country has its customs, just as we have ours."

Judy went to answer a knock on the bedroom door, opening it to admit Tracey Blair. The older woman looked stylish in a eucalyptus-green linen jacket and knee-length cream pleated skirt, a tiny gold crucifix around her neck. "Just checking that everything's okay before I start the ceremony," she said. "It's the first time I've been the celebrant at a wedding in a crocodile park. I hope Blake has his pets securely under lock and key."

Jo laughed. "His staff are minding the crocodiles, and the park's closed today so they have nothing else to do."

Judy hugged Tracey. "You're a sweetheart to do this for us."

Tracey blushed with pleasure. "Part of my job. Since I retired from mission work, I don't get many opportunities to keep my hand in." She started for the door, then turned back. "By the way, the best man said to tell you he's here."

Jo and Judy said in unison, "Which one?"

Tracey looked at Judy. "Cade, of course. Tom is already here and holding Blake back from taking off into the bush."

Jo pouted. "Tell Blake he'd better not think about it. He's taught me enough about crocodile hunting these last few weeks for me to track him anywhere." Her loving tone said she wouldn't hesitate.

"I almost forgot. Cade asked me to give you this," Tracey said, closing Judy's hand around a small metal disk. "He said you wanted to wear it for the 'something old.'"

Judy nodded. Ryan had found the medallion made from an antique Latvian gold coin, alongside Jack Logan. They'd recognized it as one worn by Lizina Smith in the old photograph of the two of them with Ryan's father as a little boy. Jack must have carried the medallion with him as a love token, and now Judy planned to wear it at the double wedding she was sharing with Jo. Cade had volunteered to fetch the token for her after it was left behind at Diamond Downs during the rush to get ready.

Jo fastened the medallion in the sweetheart neckline of Judy's short white sequined dress. Instead of a train, Judy had chosen a white taffeta overskirt, longer at the back and split in front, fastened at her waist with a bow.

Jo stepped back to admire the effect. "Unconventional, but very you," she said approvingly. She picked up Judy's satin and pearl headdress and began to arrange it on her short ash-blond hair. "You're going to knock Ryan's socks off."

As Jo fussed with her hair, Judy's mind drifted. Not long ago, she'd been positive this day would never come. After the discovery of the mine, she and Ryan had been lucky to get out before the water became too deep and fast-flowing. Torrential rain had drenched them on the way back to the helicopter and the homestead. Ryan had even been able to retrieve his beloved car before the wet season made the roads impassable.

The following weeks had been taken up with the police investigation into Max Horvath's death; it was finally judged death by misadventure. Then had come the flurry of excitement over the diamond find; early assays were proving that it was richer than anyone had dreamed. The stones in the leather pouch had taken care of Des's immediate financial worries, although he'd insisted on reserving special stones for Blake and Ryan to give to Jo and Judy. Judy's ring held a spectacular pear-shaped diamond set off by two brilliant-cut diamonds in a swirling, contemporary setting. The wedding rings they would exchange with their new husbands each had a row of small diamonds on a wide gold band.

During a break in the wet weather, Jack Logan's remains had been reverently removed from the cavern by boat, and interred in the Logan family plot on Diamond Downs. Ryan was in the process of tracking down Lizina's burial site and arranging for her to be laid to rest alongside Jack. After Jack's determination to ensure the security of the woman he loved, the family had decided they owed the couple this last consideration.

She wasn't sure who first suggested a double wedding, but with Des so ill, one occasion had been deemed stressful enough for him. Now, with Jo to share her excitement, Judy reveled in the romance of the day. "Are you nervous?" she asked Jo now.

"More excited than nervous. I love Blake so much. You?"

"I feel the same about Ryan." She heard the recorded music start and picked up her bouquet, seeing Jo do the same.

Jo's older brother Curt waited to escort her to where Tracey stood with Blake and Ryan under a double archway threaded with flowers from Blake's garden. Tom was Blake's best man, with Cade acting as Ryan's. All four men looked newly minted in white shirts, black pants and shoes that shone. Blake and Tom wore plaited leather bolo ties, while Ryan and Cade had settled on spotted bow ties. Remembering Ryan's muttered curses as he'd wrestled with the tie earlier, Judy smiled. He looked amazing, she thought, having no eyes for anyone but him.

Des was leaning on a cane, looking pale and gaunt but determined to walk his daughter down the aisle. He beamed as he took Judy's arm. "You look gorgeous, sweetheart. Ryan is a lucky man."

She covered her father's hand with her own. "We're lucky to have found each other."

Slowly she started toward Ryan, aware of his loving look and the buzz of pleasure from their guests, including Andy Wandarra and his family, and the other Diamond Downs's workers who'd stayed out of loyalty long after the payroll ran out. Blake's aunt and Jo's boss, Karen Prentiss and her husband, Ron, were there, as well as Jo's other brother, Patrick, some kind of computer genius, Judy gathered. Jo's parents were committed to a medical project in Vanuata, but Jo and Blake would be going there for their honeymoon soon enough.

Ryan's friends Heather and Jeff Wilton had flown in from Lake Argyle, bringing their son Daniel and Sunny and his engaged parents. Most of the people from the region were there, too, and Judy saw café owner, Betty Cline, who'd once been like a mother to Tom, dabbing at her eyes.

By mutual agreement, Tracey focused first on Blake and Jo, reciting the beautiful vows the couple had written between them. She was no more than halfway through when she was interrupted by a loud beeping sound.

Des fumbled at his waist. "It's me, sorry. I forgot to turn the darned thing off."

Judy went hot and cold as realization struck. "Dad, you're not supposed to turn it off. It's the hospital."

Blake squeezed Jo's hand and she nodded in silent agreement. "They have a donor heart for you, don't they?"

"Damned fool time to call," Des muttered. "Ignore it and get on with the ceremony."

"Like hell," Blake muttered. Suddenly the older man was surrounded by four intimidating males and one feisty female, all glowering at him.

Des threw up his hands. "Stand over me all you want, but explain to me how I'm supposed to get to Perth Hospital in time, when there isn't a flight out until tomorrow?"

Princess Shara Najran stepped forward, black-haired, five-seven and delicately built, but with centuries of royal breeding at her command. "I can do that. My father's private jet is fueled and waiting at Halls Creek Airport." Her regal tone dared her prospective father-in-law to argue. "We can radio ahead for emergency clearance to land and arrange to have an ambulance on standby to rush Des straight to the hospital."

Being royal had its advantages, Judy thought. The Branxton 700 executive jet flying the standard of the King of Q'aresh was fast, streamlined and the last word in luxury, Judy knew, having persuaded Shara to give her a tour soon after she and Tom arrived. "Shara, that's the perfect solution. We can continue the weddings when Dad gets back," she said.

"What do you mean, when I get back?" Des groused. "If I have to go, you're all coming with me. We'll do this thing on the way."

Judy sensed his fear that he might not survive the transplant operation and wanted to see them safely married before he went into surgery. Her throat closed with emotion and she forced a smile. "You heard the boss."

A short time later they were airborne, with Tracey reading Blake's and Jo's vows again while steadying herself with a hand on the back of a wide leather seat. Understanding the situation, most of the guests had remained behind at the crocodile park to continue the reception without the key figures.

This time, there were no interruptions when Tracey asked Blake if he took Jo Francis as his wedded wife. Her "I do" rang confidently through the cabin. Then it was the turn of Judy and Ryan to repeat the vows they'd written. "I'm no poet," Ryan had protested, but to Judy the words joining them together as man and wife were the most beautiful she'd ever heard.

"I do," she said firmly, her eyes fixed on Ryan.

He kissed her to the applause of the small group. "I'd expected to be on cloud nine after the ceremony, just not literally," she said when he let her up for air.

An attendant served champagne and canapés, with Des complaining about having to propose a toast with apple juice. Judy didn't care. She and Ryan were husband and wife. All she needed was for her father to be well, and her happiness would be complete.

Seeing Tracey settle into a seat beside Des, Judy raised an eyebrow in Ryan's direction. "What do you think they're saying?"

"How nosy Des's daughter has become now she's a married woman," he said, but so indulgently that she slid her hand into his and tried not to eavesdrop.

"You've been a good friend through all this," Des said to the former missionary. "More than a good friend."

"I care about you, Desmond."

He nodded. "I know. That's become obvious with the time you've spent at the hospital, supporting me through all this medical hooha. I want you to know I appreciate everything you've done. If I had more to offer, I'd be suggesting a third wedding today."

Tracey blushed prettily. "That sounds suspiciously like a proposal, Desmond Logan."

"Call it advance notice. I'll make it formal after we know what today holds." He took her hand. "If I don't make it, I want you to keep an eye on the family for me."

She made a shushing sound. "You'll make it. I've had a private word upstairs. Besides, too many people need you to get well."

He looked around at the happy couples—Blake and Jo, and Ryan and Judy already married, and Tom and Shara preparing for a royal wedding in Q'aresh. Cade had informed Des he'd put in an offer to buy Willundina from Max Horvath's estate, so he'd be settled soon, too. Not married, which troubled Des, but what could he do? The boy—man, he amended inwardly—was attractive enough and enjoyed the company of women. Maybe he just hadn't met the right one yet. "Looks like my work is done," Des said.

"Nonsense, there's always work to be done, For us both."

Looking into Tracey's green eyes, Des smiled. "Maybe I do have something—or someone—extra to live for, after all."

As good as her word, Shara had pulled royal strings and they were cleared to land at a VIP area of Perth airport with minimal delay. An ambulance waited, lights flashing, to whisk Des to the hospital. Cars had also been organized for the rest of the party.

In preparation for this event, Judy had been told there would be a final medical evaluation and laboratory work-up to complete; the actual surgery would take three to four hours. All they could do now was wait. The hours ticked by with infuriating slowness, it seemed to Judy. She looked around and giggled nervously. "It can't be often that a hospital has to contend with two brides, two grooms and their attendants in full regalia in their waiting room."

Ryan squeezed her hand. "We are getting some interesting looks. But none of us is going anywhere until we have news."

Jo had already offered the use of the apartment she still kept in Perth, without any takers. She was sticking around herself, her long train hampering her attempts to pace, Judy noted. The same question hovered on all their lips: how much longer?

A doctor walked into their midst, looking bemused at the activity. The nurses immediately scattered to their duties, recognizing the man's authority, betrayed by his bearing and quiet confidence. He also looked tired, Judy noted. So many people were working to save her father. She couldn't believe Des could be anything but fine.

"Do you have news?" Blake asked for all of them.

The surgeon's face relaxed into a smile. "I'm happy to say there were no complications and Mr. Logan is resting comfortably. He'll need to spend a couple of days in the recovery room, another few days in intensive care and about a week in the transplant unit. Then, with proper monitoring and aftercare, he should be able to look forward to a normal, productive life."

Sighs of relief rippled around the room, and Judy heard Tracey murmur a prayer of thanks. "Amen," she said from the depths of her soul. She blinked away tears instinctively reached for Ryan's hand.

He dabbed at her tears with a snowy handkerchief. "What's this? The doctor said Des is going to be all right."

"They're tears of happiness."

He pulled her head against his shoulder and she let them flow. He had a hard time holding his own emotions in check, and found he wasn't the only one.

In a corner of the room, about halfway to the ceiling, unnoticed by any of the other occupants, a diminutive woman watched in satisfaction. Her hair was rolled up at the front and curled under at the back, and she wore a peplum suit that had been in fashion sixty years before. Beside her, a man in an equally dated single-breasted jacket, white shirt and dark brown pants, gripped her hand as if he never intended to let her go.

"I'm proud of them all," the man said. "They're living examples of the code of the outback. You don't back down, you don't give up, and you stand by your mates."

"What about no mushy stuff?" the woman asked coyly.

"That wasn't in the code when I wrote it," he said.

She regarded him in surprise. "I thought the boys made up the code."

He smiled at her fondly. "Who do you think planted the idea in their heads?"

"I might have known." She linked her arm with his and snuggled against him. "I'm still a bit concerned about Cade."

"No need, he's going to be fine," the man assured her. "Trust me on this. Didn't I tell you the others would all work out?"

"You did and you were right, my *milais,* my darling. *Es tevi milu,* I love you," the woman said. "I think we can safely leave them to enjoy their happiness, don't you?"

The man nodded. Together they turned, walking slowly toward a shaft of sunlight.

Had she really seen what she thought she'd seen? Judy asked herself, looking over Ryan's shoulder. She blinked hard. The corner of the room held nothing but the rays of light from the setting sun spilling from a nearby window. Must have been a trick of the light making her think they were being watched. And some unidentified hospital sound she'd mistaken for the bell-like notes of a woman's laughter. Even as she tried to focus on the sound, it faded like music heard in a dream, then was gone.

* * * * *

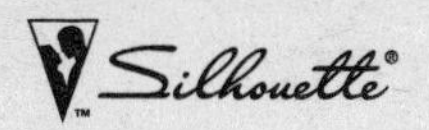

INTIMATE MOMENTS™

presents the next book in
RITA® AWARD-WINNING AUTHOR

Kathleen Creighton's

bestselling miniseries

They'd die for the people they love.
Here's hoping they don't have to....

Undercover Mistress

(Silhouette Intimate Moments #1340, January '05)

When soap opera star Celia Cross found government agent Roy Starr bruised and battered from a mission, she nursed him back to health and helped him crack his case. Celia proved to be quite capable on the job, but now he wanted to turn her into his own personal leading lady....

Available at your favorite retail outlet.

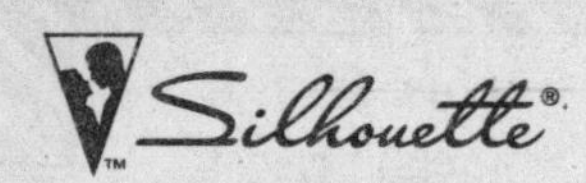

COMING NEXT MONTH

INTIMATE MOMENTS®

#1339 DANGEROUS DISGUISE—Marie Ferrarella
Cavanaugh Justice
Mixing business with pleasure wasn't in detective Jared Cavanaugh's vocabulary—until he saw Maren Minnesota walk into the restaurant where he'd been assigned to work undercover to catch the mob. But when their smoldering attraction for each other threatened his disguise, would he have to risk everything to protect the woman he loved?

#1340 UNDERCOVER MISTRESS—Kathleen Creighton
Starrs of the West
After a hit-and-run accident forced Celia Cross from Hollywood's spotlight, her only refuge was the beach. Then homeland security agent Roy Starr washed ashore, bleeding from an assassin's bullet. Little did she know her mystery man had gotten too close to an international arms dealer. With the killer determined to finish the job and Roy's feelings for his rescuer growing stronger, would this be their beginning—or their end?

#1341 CLOSE TO THE EDGE—Kylie Brant
Private investigator Lucky Boucher knew his attraction to fellow investigator Jacinda Wheeler was a mistake. He was a bayou boy; she was high society. But when a case they were working on turned deadly, keeping his mind off her and on their investigation proved to be an impossible task, because for the first time since he'd met her, their worlds were about to collide.

#1342 CODE NAME: FIANCÉE—Susan Vaughan
Antiterrorist security agent Vanessa Wade felt as false as the rock on her finger. Assigned to impersonate the glamorous fiancée of international businessman Nick Markos, she found herself struggling to remain detached from her "husband-to-be." He was the brother of a traitor—and the man whose kisses made her spin out of control. Could she dare to hope their fake engagement would become a real one?

#1343 RUNNING ON EMPTY—Michelle Celmer
Detective Mitch Thompson was willing to risk his life to uncover the mystery surrounding Jane Doe, the beautiful amnesiac he'd rescued from an unknown assailant. But the more time they spent together trying to unravel the secrets hidden in her memory, the more evident it became that they were falling in love…and that Jane's attacker was determined to stop at nothing to destroy their happiness—not even murder.

#1344 NECESSARY SECRETS—Barbara Phinney
Sylvie Mitchell was living a lie. Pregnant and alone, she'd retreated to her ranch to have the baby in hiding. Then her unborn child's uncle, Jon Cahill, appeared, demanding answers, and she had to lie to the one man she truly loved. She'd lived with the guilt of his brother's death and the government cover-up that had forced her into hiding. When the truth surfaced, would she lose the only man who could keep her—and her baby—safe?

SIMCNM1204